MW00573435

A Brilliant Alliance

THE LOCKWOOD FAMILY

LAURA BEERS

Chapter One

England, 1813

Bennett Lockwood, the Earl of Dunsby, never had an issue with bread… until now. He sat in the pew next to his sister, Elodie, who was happily eating her buttered bread. The chapel was quiet, save for the sound of Elodie's loud, incessant chewing that seemed to echo off the walls.

They were gathered here to celebrate their cousin's wedding to his good friend, Miles. He felt a profound sense of pride that he had brought these two together, knowing the pain they had both endured in their pasts.

Glancing at Elodie, Bennett leaned in and whispered, "Do you mind?"

His sister gave him a look that appeared innocent, but he knew better. "What is wrong?" she asked, matching his tone.

"Why did you bring bread with you to Edwina's wedding?" he asked, trying not to let his annoyance show.

With a slight shrug, Elodie replied, "I was hungry."

Melody, his other sister, chimed in from the pew behind

them. "I tried to convince her not to bring it, but she wouldn't listen."

"Of course not," Bennett muttered under his breath. His sisters were nearly identical, with the same blonde hair and bright blue eyes, but that is where the similarities stopped. Elodie seemed to defy convention, whereas Melody followed the rules, almost to a fault.

Elodie held up the piece of bread towards him. "Would you care for some?"

Bennett ignored her offer as he turned his attention back to the front of the chapel where the short, round vicar had just concluded the service.

With a wide smile, the vicar announced, "And now it is my privilege to officiate the marriage between Lady Edwina Lockwood and Lord Hilgrove. Please come forward."

The happy couple stood from their seats in the back, their beaming smiles radiating pure happiness. The congregation promptly rose as the couple made their way down the aisle, hand in hand. They stood before the vicar, their eyes fixated on each other.

As the vicar began the ceremony, the audience settled into their seats, eagerly awaiting the moment when Edwina and Miles would finally be announced as man and wife.

At the conclusion of the ceremony, Elodie couldn't quite seem to contain her excitement. "This is my favorite part," she whispered to Bennett. "I love it when they kiss."

Bennett lifted his brow. "I do not know why, considering we caught them kissing all the time at Brockhall Manor."

"Yes, but now they are kissing as husband and wife," Elodie replied. "It is completely different."

After a chaste kiss, Edwina and Miles proceeded down the aisle and disappeared through the chapel doors.

Bennett stood up from his seat and adjusted the sleeves on his jacket. "Well, they are officially married now. Shall we return home for the luncheon?"

"But that isn't for another few hours," Elodie protested before taking another bite of bread. "And this dress is starting to itch from the net overlay."

Melody had also risen from her seat. "You could always return home and change into a different gown," she suggested.

With a shake of her head, Elodie said, "Mother would never allow it. She specifically chose our gowns for Edwina's wedding and wouldn't want me to change for any reason."

Bennett placed a comforting hand on Elodie's shoulder. "What a burden you must endure. Whatever shall you do?" he teased.

"You are a man and cannot possibly understand what women must endure in the name of fashion," Elodie responded. "Besides, I fail to see anything wrong with our old gowns."

Melody adopted a tone that sounded very much like Mother's. "They may be suitable for the countryside, but they are much too plain for the upcoming Season," she explained. "We will need to distinguish ourselves from the other debutantes if we hope to secure a brilliant match."

"Do you truly wish to marry your first Season?" Elodie asked. "Because I certainly do not."

Melody tilted her chin defiantly. "It matters not when I marry, but *who* I marry," she declared. "I want a love match."

A small smirk graced Elodie's lips as she quipped, "And I want a unicorn, but we all know that will never happen. Love matches are just as elusive as mythical creatures."

"Unicorns aren't real," Melody said.

"Neither are love matches," Elodie countered with a shrug of her shoulders.

Bennett spoke up, attempting to be the voice of reason. "Let us not forget that we just witnessed our cousin marry for love."

Elodie wiped her gloved hands together, brushing the

crumbs off. "Fine. I will admit it is possible, but we must not get our hopes up. My friend, Diana, thought she had married for love and now she is miserable. She even suspects that her husband has taken a mistress."

"Who is Diana?" Bennett asked, wondering why he had never heard of her until now.

"A friend of mine from our boarding school," Elodie replied.

"You are being quite the naysayer this morning. Perhaps you sniffed too much of the butter on your bread," Melody teased.

Bennett caught the vicar's eye and excused himself from his sisters to approach Mr. Bawden. "Good morning," he greeted. "You did a fine job."

Mr. Bawden tipped his head in acknowledgement, revealing a large bald spot on the back of his head. "Thank you, my lord. I always enjoy marrying couples who are so clearly in love with one another."

He chuckled. "Yes, Edwina and Miles only seemed to have eyes for one another after they got engaged."

"As it should be," Mr. Bawden said, good-naturedly.

Bennett's mother came to stand next to him as she addressed the vicar. "I do hope you intend to join us for the luncheon."

Mr. Bawden grinned. "I will be there, as will my daughter, Mattie."

"Wonderful," his mother exclaimed. "We simply adore Miss Bawden."

The vicar removed a handkerchief and swiped at the beads of sweat that were forming on his brow. "You have always been very kind to her, and for that, I am most appreciative."

His mother smiled. "Your daughter is easy to be kind to," she said. "Furthermore, I have enjoyed watching her grow into a delightful young woman."

"I could not agree with you more, my lady," Mr. Bawden responded.

Turning towards Bennett, his mother asked, "Shall we depart?"

He offered his arm and led her away from the vicar. Once they were outside, he saw his father and sisters were already situated in the coach.

Bennett assisted his mother up the steps of the coach and waited until she was comfortably seated next to her husband. "I will see all of you back at the manor," he said.

His mother gave him a disapproving shake of her head. "I wish you had taken one of the coaches to the chapel," she chided.

"That seems rather silly since I am perfectly content riding my horse," Bennett replied. "Besides, I prefer to be outside over riding in a stuffy coach. The rain has finally stopped, and the sun is peeking through the clouds. It is a perfect day for a quick jaunt through the woodlands."

Elodie removed a fan from her reticule and started fanning her face. "Bennett has chosen wisely. With the arrival of the sun, it is making this coach rather warm and stuffy."

"It is only a short ride back to the manor," his mother reminded them, her tone lacking any sympathy.

"Yes, but not before I look like a bloated catfish," Elodie declared dramatically, puffing out her cheeks to emphasize her point.

Melody poked at her sister's puffy cheeks playfully. "You look rather foolish like that."

Elodie let out a huff of air. "Can we at least open up the windows?" she asked hopefully.

His mother nodded her permission. "There is no need to make everything so dramatic, my dear."

"And with that, I bid you adieu," Bennett said before closing the door.

As he walked towards his horse, Bennett was grateful for

the time to retreat to his own thoughts. He was happy for Miles and Edwina, but a faint sense of envy lingered in his heart. He couldn't help but hope for the kind of love they had found.

He knew that he would need to get married- to produce an heir- but he was not looking forward to the marriage mart. Every young woman would bat her eyelashes at him and offer coy smiles, seeing only his title rather than the man behind it.

Bennett mounted his horse. With a firm grip on the reins, he urged his horse into a gallop, cutting through the open fields and charging towards the woodlands. This uncharted territory was a welcome change from the familiar paths he had explored countless times near his family's manor. The dense canopy provided a comforting shelter from the outside world.

The recent rainfall had transformed the path into a slick and treacherous terrain, but Bennett pushed onwards with reckless abandon. The cool droplets that fell from the trees above were refreshing against his skin and he relished the time alone.

He had every reason to be happy. He was an earl and heir to a marquessate. Their estate was profitable and their relationship with the villagers was stronger than ever. And yet, his heart still felt a longing for something more.

Bennett brought his horse to a sudden stop and looked up at the towering trees. He was almost thirty and his parents had been relentless that he should wed. But he refused to marry for convenience or obligation. He wanted a love match or nothing at all.

Suppressing a chuckle at how much he sounded like his sister, Melody, he turned his horse around to head back in the direction he'd come from. That was when he noticed fresh footprints just off the path. They couldn't have been there long or else the rain would have washed them away.

His curiosity was piqued as he dismounted and moved to

secure his horse, wondering who was wandering on his family's land. He followed the footprints deeper into the woodlands and the terrain became more hazardous. Eventually, he came upon a ravine with a small stream running through it, washing away any trace of footprints.

Disappointed that he'd wasted his time, Bennett was about to turn back when he caught sight of a flash of color further down the ravine. He focused his gaze on it and saw that it was the body of a woman, dressed in a blue gown.

Good gads!

And she was all alone.

Without hesitation, he slid down the side of the ravine and hurried towards the woman's side, unsure of what to expect.

Once he reached her side, he noticed that she was still breathing, her chest rising and falling with each shallow breath. Relief washed over him as he realized she was alive.

Taking only a moment, Bennett perused the length of her, looking for any signs of injuries. Her dark hair fanned out around her, almost like a halo, and her face was an alarming shade of white. She had scratch marks along her skin, evidence of her flight through the trees. One shoe was missing from her foot and dried blood marked her forehead where she must have struck her head.

What terrible misfortune had befallen this young woman? And more importantly, who was she? How had she ended up alone and injured in the woodlands?

He knelt by her side and gently shook her shoulder. "Miss," he said, his voice laced with concern. "Can you hear me?"

No response.

Bennett removed his hand and let out a sigh. He couldn't leave this young woman here. If he didn't get her help, he feared that she would perish. And he couldn't let that weigh heavily on his conscience.

Her gown was exceedingly fine, making him assume her

presence would not be missed for too long. Surely someone was looking for her. But they would never find her here. The woodlands were too dense for riders to happen upon her.

Quite frankly, there was only one choice in his mind. He would take her back to his manor and send for the doctor.

Before he moved her, he shook her once more, hoping for any sign of consciousness. "Miss? If you can hear me, I am going to pick you up now."

Still no response.

With careful movements, Bennett lifted her into his arms, stumbling slightly as he stood. She felt so delicate against him, and he couldn't help but feel a sense of protectiveness towards this unknown woman.

As he made his way back up the ravine, Bennett slipped a few times on the rocky terrain but managed to keep hold of the woman in his arms. He arrived at his horse and carefully placed her on the saddle before taking a seat behind her. He wrapped his arms around her as they rode off, aware of how it might look to anyone who saw them.

But above all else, Bennett was a gentleman.

He urged his horse forward, mindful of not jostling the injured woman too much. The manor wasn't far, and he knew they needed to reach it quickly for her sake.

Delphine awoke with a pounding headache, her eyes reluctant to open. As she blinked her vision into focus, she found herself lying in a luxurious bed with an unfamiliar canopy draped above her.

Where was she?

Confusion set in as she tried to piece together where she was. She turned her head to one side and saw lavender-papered walls, heavy drapes framing two tall windows, and a writing desk in the corner. Sunlight streamed through the windows, casting a warm glow over the room.

A soft clinking sound caught her attention and she slowly turned her head to see a petite blonde maid tidying up at the dressing table.

With a raspy voice, Delphine managed to croak out, "Where am I?"

The maid's eyes widened. "You are awake." Her words were more of a statement than a question. "The doctor will want to speak with you immediately."

In one quick motion, the maid scurried out of the room, leaving Delphine alone. She noticed a glass of water on the bedside table and realized how dry her throat felt. With great effort, she reached for the glass and took a small sip, enjoying the cool water on her lips.

Delphine returned the glass to the table and propped herself up against the plush pillows behind her. Though her head still throbbed with pain, she needed to understand what had happened to her. As she absentmindedly touched the bandage wrapped around her head, she searched her memory for any clues.

What had happened to her?

As she tried to recall her memories, the door opened, revealing a tall, distinguished man with silvered hair and rounded spectacles perched on his nose.

The man approached the bed and Delphine instinctively reached for the soft silk blanket to cover herself.

When he smiled at her, all her defenses melted away. "Hello, I am Doctor Anderson," he said, introducing himself in a soothing voice. "I am pleased to see that you are awake."

Befuddlement clouded Delphine's mind as she tried to piece together where she was. "Where am I?" she asked.

The doctor pulled a chair closer to the bed and sat down. "You are at the country home of Lord and Lady Dallington," he informed her gently.

That would explain her opulent surroundings, but those names did not sound familiar. Furrowing her brow, she asked, "Am I acquainted with them?"

"It appears not," Doctor Anderson replied. "Their son, Lord Dunsby, found you in the woodlands on their property. Do you remember how you ended up there?"

She gave him a blank stare, unable to recall anything. "No, I do not." Why couldn't she remember?

The doctor gave her a reassuring look. "That is all right. Perhaps we should start at the beginning," he suggested. "What is your name?"

That was an easy question. "My name is Delphine…" Her words trailed off as she struggled to remember more about herself.

"It is nice to meet you, Miss Delphine," the doctor said. "Can you recall your surname or where you are from?"

Delphine racked her brain to try to remember but her mind was blank. She couldn't remember anything, other than her given name. How was that possible? It didn't help that her head was pounding, robbing her of the ability to think clearly.

The doctor's comforting voice broke through her musings. "It is all right. These things can happen after a head injury."

"I had a head injury?" Delphine asked. Why did this all seem so preposterous?

"Yes, you had a nasty bump on your head when Lord Dunsby found you. You have been asleep for two days now," Doctor Anderson revealed.

Two days?!

She couldn't believe it. But as she tried to recall anything about her past, she was met with a frustrating blankness. How could this have happened?

The doctor continued. "Now that you are awake, we will figure all this out," he replied. "You just need to be patient with yourself."

She brought a hand to her head and winced at the bump

on top of her head, just as the doctor had informed her of. "My head hurts," she confessed. "And my neck is rather sore. It is difficult to move."

"That is not unexpected," the doctor replied sympathetically. "Your body just needs time to recover."

"None of this makes sense," Delphine said, feeling a sense of panic rising within her. Why couldn't she even remember her name?

"It will, in time," the doctor assured her. "But for now, we will just provide you with a calm environment for your memory to return."

Delphine glanced down and realized that she was in a wrapper. "Was I wandering in the woodlands dressed like this?"

"No, you were discovered in a ravine, unconscious and bleeding from your forehead. I'm afraid that the gown you were found in was terribly soiled and ripped," Doctor Anderson responded. "The maids bathed you and dressed you in more comfortable attire."

"None of this makes sense," Delphine declared, repeating herself. "If I was on Lord Dallington's land, he must know who I am. He has to. I do not think I am one to trespass on others' lands."

"I'm afraid not. You are a stranger to him."

Delphine lowered her gaze, feeling like a stranger to herself as well. She needed to remember so she could go home. Wherever that was. A thought occurred to her. "Surely someone has come looking for me."

The doctor shook his head. "I am sure they will, but as for now, you just need to rest. Your memory should come back in time."

"Should?" she repeated with trepidation in her voice.

"Brain injuries are unpredictable," Doctor Anderson said. "But you need not worry about that. Everything will be fine."

Delphine closed her eyes, feeling overwhelmed and beaten.

What would happen to her if her memories never came back to her? The thought was terrifying. What was worse was that she felt the doctor was just trying to pacify her. What wasn't he telling her?

A knock sounded at the door before it was pushed open. A tall, elegant woman with blonde hair and kind eyes stepped into the room, clad in a blue muslin gown.

"Good morning," she greeted with a warm smile. "It is good to see you awake, young lady. I am Lady Dallington and you are most welcome here."

Delphine offered her a weak but grateful smile. "Thank you, my lady."

The doctor rose from his seat and turned his attention towards Lady Dallington. "This is Miss Delphine, but I'm afraid she remembers little else. We must be patient, and her memories should return with time."

Lady Dallington nodded in understanding. "Then we shall make Miss Delphine as comfortable as possible for the time being."

Feeling overwhelmed by her gratitude for these complete strangers, Delphine spoke up again. "Thank you. I hope to repay your kindness one day."

"Do not concern yourself with such things," Lady Dallington responded. "You should focus on getting better."

Delphine did have a question. "What became of the gown that I arrived in?"

Lady Dallington waved her hand in front of her. "We disposed of it. It was in terrible shape and no amount of washing and mending would have repaired it."

"What am I to wear then?" Delphine asked anxiously.

"You and my twin daughters are of a similar size," Lady Dallington replied. "They will have no objections to allowing you to borrow some of their gowns."

Delphine felt a pang of guilt at imposing herself on these strangers. "I couldn't possibly…"

"Nonsense," Lady Dallington insisted, speaking over her. "Besides, my daughters are starting to receive their new gowns for the upcoming Season and will have little use for their old ones."

Unsure of what else she could say, she murmured, "Thank you."

Lady Dallington clasped her hands together. "You must be famished."

As if on cue, Delphine's stomach rumbled loudly. "I am," she admitted.

"I shall send a tray up from the kitchen," Lady Dallington said. "Do you have a preference for breakfast?"

"A boiled egg and two pieces of toast, please," Delphine responded without the slightest hint of hesitation.

Lady Dallington turned towards the maid who stood quietly in the corner and ordered, "Will you inform the cook of Miss Delphine's request?"

With a knitted brow, Delphine went to address the doctor. "How is it that I can remember what I eat for breakfast but I can't recall my own surname?"

Doctor Anderson's eyes held understanding. "That is not entirely unexpected. The brain is complex and sometimes there is no rhyme or reason why we can recall certain information after a trauma such as yours."

Delphine felt discouraged. She closed her eyes tightly, trying to force any memories to the surface. But all she was met with was a void- no names, no faces, no places.

Lady Dallington must have sensed her frustration because she moved closer to the bed. "Try to think of this as an adventure," she encouraged.

Her eyes opened. "An adventure?" It was evident that she and Lady Dallington had two different definitions of what an adventure was.

"Yes, we have some clues as to who you are," Lady Dallington replied. "Your muslin gown was the height of fashion and you had a coral necklace around your neck, indicating to me that you are a woman of means."

"If that is the case, why has no one come looking for me?" Delphine asked.

Lady Dallington gave her a pointed look. "Who says they are not?" she asked. "My son informed me that he found you in a ravine after searching through the woodlands for some time. You were even missing a shoe."

While grateful for Lady Dallington's optimism, Delphine couldn't help but feel anxious at the thought of being lost and alone with no memory of who she was or where she belonged. Did she have a family? A home?

The doctor spoke up, breaking the tense silence. "We should let Miss Delphine rest. We do not wish to overwhelm her."

"I understand," Lady Dallington responded. "Do you like to read? We have a well-stocked library that you are welcome to use."

Delphine scrunched her nose. "I think so."

"Perhaps I shall select a few books for you and have them sent up," Lady Dallington suggested.

"I would appreciate that, but I do not think I could read right now. My head hurts," she admitted.

Lady Dallington acknowledged her words with a smile. "When you are up to it, you are welcome to leave your bedchamber and venture around our home. A change of scenery might do you some good."

Delphine returned her smile. "Thank you, my lady," she said. "I do hope to thank Lord Dunsby for saving me and bringing me here."

"In due time, you will. For now, focus on resting and recovering," Lady Dallington encouraged.

Doctor Anderson gestured towards the door and addressed Lady Dallington. "May I speak to you privately in the corridor?"

Lady Dallington tipped her head. "Of course, Doctor."

Left alone in the room, Delphine's gaze drifted up towards the intricately woven canopy above her. She let out a frustrated sigh, feeling overwhelmed by her situation. She yearned for her memories to return, to bring some sense of familiarity back into her life. Did this mean she wasn't a patient person?

A wave of sadness washed over her. She hated the idea of relying on Lady Dallington and her family's generosity, but she had no other options. She was trapped here, with no clear direction or purpose.

Tears welled up in Delphine's eyes and she didn't bother to fight them. In this moment, she allowed herself to feel scared and uncertain about what the future held. At least until breakfast arrived, she would allow herself this moment of weakness before putting on a brave face once again.

Chapter Two

Bennett stepped into the dining room and saw his sisters sitting at the long, rectangular table, their heads hunched over the newssheets.

Knowing no good could come out of this, he inquired, "What has caught your attention so intently?"

Elodie neatly folded the newssheets and placed them onto the table. "Nothing in particular. How was your ride this morning?" she asked innocently. Too innocently. His sisters were up to something. But what?

Bennett approached the table and extended his hand out. "May I see?"

With a flourish, Elodie handed him the newssheets. "You are making a big ado out of nothing."

"Is that so?" Bennett scanned the pages for any hint of what had captured his sisters' interest. "Perhaps you could save us a considerable amount of time and tell me what had you two so engrossed?"

Melody sipped her cup of chocolate as she informed him, "If you must know, it is the first article on the Society page."

Bennett flipped to the back of the newssheets and perused

the article. When he lowered it, he asked, "Why do either of you care about Lord Willowbrook and his latest exploits?"

"Well, he is quite handsome," Melody said wistfully.

"But he is also a rake of the highest order, and you would be wise to avoid him this Season," Bennett advised in the sternest voice he could muster up. He didn't want his sisters anywhere near Lord Willowbrook- or any rake- when they arrived in London.

Melody smiled. "Very well, Brother," she said quickly. He could tell that she was just appeasing him. Which infuriated him even more.

Bennett set the newssheets down with a heavy thud. "I am serious, Melody. Just being associated with Lord Willowbrook could ruin your reputation."

And once again, a rapid reply followed. "I understand." Melody even had the nerve to smile at him. As if he were the one acting irrational.

"No, you clearly do not understand," Bennett pressed, his frustration mounting. "You must stay away from him at all costs."

Melody tipped her head. "I will."

Bennett didn't know what it would take to get through to his sister. Melody may be the more rational twin, but she still had a stubborn streak to her.

His mother glided into the room with Doctor Anderson by her side. "I am calling a family meeting," she declared.

"Should we not send for Winston?" Bennett asked. "Or Father, for that matter?"

She waved her hand in front of her. "There is no need. Winston is no doubt holed up in his room working, and Father is at meetings in the village. I shall speak to them later."

Bennett leaned back against the long, rectangular dining table. "Then why call it a family meeting at all?"

"Because it is my right as a mother to call meetings whenever I so desire," his mother remarked. "But on a serious note, the young lady Bennett rescued from the woodlands just awoke."

Elodie gasped. "That is wonderful news. Did she say why she was wandering in the woodlands?"

"Well… no," his mother said. "She is having a hard time recalling who she is and why she was in the woodlands."

Bennett lifted his brow skeptically. "That is rather odd, is it not?"

The doctor stepped forward and spoke up. "If I may," he started, "brain injuries are complex, and no one is the same. But once the swelling has gone down, I do believe this young woman's memories will come back."

"How long will that take?" Melody asked.

The doctor shrugged. "It could be hours or days, but it is imperative that you give her a calm space for her memories to return."

Bennett didn't want to be the naysayer, but he had to ask the question. "What if her memories do not come back?"

"Let us not focus on the negative, but rather on the positive," the doctor said, skirting around his question. "She remembers her given name is Delphine."

His mother smiled. "Miss Delphine seems like a lovely young lady and is a guest in our home while she recovers. We must shower her with kindness and hope her memories will return quickly."

"But do not attempt to force them," the doctor advised. "Allow them to return naturally."

Clasping her hands in front of her, his mother informed Bennett, "Miss Delphine has expressed a desire to thank you for saving her life."

With a smirk on his lips, Bennett turned towards his sister. "That does not surprise me. I was her hero, after all. A hero to one, a hero to all."

Elodie shook her head. "You are trying too hard, Brother,"

she said good-naturedly. "True heroes don't brag about their accomplishments."

"Well, I did save Miss Delphine's life, which is more than you have done," Bennett responded, puffing out his chest. "Do you suppose someone will write a book about my heroic actions?"

Melody giggled. "If they did, no one would read it."

Bennett put a hand to his chest, feigning outrage. "I disagree. People will one day make up folk songs about me and future generations will sing my praises. Perhaps I will even be in the Society pages that you two so love to read."

"How dull," Elodie quipped.

His mother cleared her throat, drawing back their attention. "You three digress, as usual," she remarked. "Can we return to the matter at hand, please?"

Doctor Anderson shifted his leather satchel in his hand. "It has been my experience from the war that people with head injuries are scared, not being able to access their memories. Miss Delphine is in a fragile state and should be treated with care."

"May we visit with Miss Delphine?" Elodie asked.

"I think that is a fine idea, assuming you speak softly to her," the doctor encouraged. "You do not want to upset her more than she already is."

Bennett crossed his arms over his chest as he asked, "Should we send riders out to look for anyone that may be searching for Miss Delphine?"

"I think that might be a waste of time, considering there are many roads that cross near that section of woodlands," his mother responded.

Elodie reached for her teacup and said, "I will go visit Miss Delphine after breakfast."

Bennett winced, wondering if that was the best idea. "Perhaps I shall go speak to her first."

"Why?" Elodie asked. "I am a delight. Many people have told me so."

"Yes, but you also say outlandish things that might frighten the poor girl," Bennett remarked.

After Elodie returned the teacup to her saucer, she suggested, "Maybe if we all shout at Miss Delphine at the precise same time, it will jar her memories."

Bennett looked heavenward. "Do you even hear yourself speak?"

"I do, and I think my plan is ingenious," Elodie replied with a smirk. "Being startled every so often keeps one alert."

His mother gave Elodie a pointed look. "No one is going to shout at Miss Delphine," she said firmly. "We must strive to be patient."

Doctor Anderson turned towards Bennett's mother. "I will return tomorrow to look in on Miss Delphine, but until then, I will be visiting a few of my patients in the next village over."

"Thank you, Doctor," she responded.

Once the doctor departed from the dining room, Elodie asked, "Has anyone considered that Miss Delphine is lying about losing her memories?"

Bennett uncrossed his arms, wondering what outlandish thing his sister was going to say next. "Why, pray tell, would she do that?"

Elodie's eyes held amusement as she asked, "What if she is hiding out from an evil stepmother that is intent on marrying her off to a prince in a faraway land?"

"You have been reading far too many fairy tales, Sister," Bennett declared as he straightened up from the chair. "And to prove it to you, I will go speak to Miss Delphine now."

"But you haven't had breakfast yet," Elodie said.

Bennett reached for a piece of toast on Elodie's plate. "Now I have," he said before taking a bite.

Elodie held up a fork. "Next time, I shall defend my plate with the necessary force."

Melody picked up a piece of toast off her plate and placed it on Elodie's plate. "You can have my toast."

"Thank you, but I was rather fond of the toast that Bennett is eating. It was buttered precisely the way I like it," Elodie joked, lowering the fork to the table.

Bennett chuckled. "You should have eaten faster."

"Why should I?" Elodie asked. "No one else has dared to steal food off my plate before."

"Consider it a tithe," Bennett said.

His mother went to sit at the head of the table. "I would be remiss if I did not inform you that stealing food off another's plate is considered uncouth."

Bennett took a step back. "And on that note, I shall go speak to Miss Delphine."

With a stern look, his mother advised, "Be mindful to have maids present when you visit Miss Delphine since it is rather inappropriate to visit a young woman in her bedchamber. If not for the unusual circumstances, I would never permit such a thing."

"I am not completely uncivilized, Mother," Bennett said. "I do know the rules of Polite Society."

His mother didn't look convinced. "Very well, but do not upset Miss Delphine. She has been through enough."

Bennett brought a hand to his chest in a dramatic fashion. "Why would you even suggest such a thing? I am above all else a gentleman."

"A gentleman does not steal food off plates," Elodie interjected.

"Well, I promise I will not steal food off Miss Delphine's plate," Bennett said. "Now, if you will excuse me, I am off to charm yet another lady."

After Bennett departed from the dining room, he ascended the grand staircase that led to the bedchambers on the second level. It wasn't long before he arrived at the guest bedchamber that Miss Delphine was residing in.

He rapped on the door and it was promptly opened by a maid.

"Is Miss Delphine awake?" Bennett asked.

The maid tipped her head in affirmation and opened the door wide for him to enter. "Yes, my lord," she replied with a curtsy. "Please, do come in."

Bennett stepped into the room and saw that Miss Delphine was sitting up in bed with a tray of food in front of her. His gaze immediately went to her forehead, where a thick bandage was wrapped around it. However, he was pleased to see that her complexion had returned to its natural color and the scratches that had marred her face when he first found her had faded. Even under these circumstances, he could tell she was beautiful with high cheekbones and a delicately pointed nose.

Miss Delphine met his gaze with curiosity and asked, "Are you another doctor?"

"I am not," he replied. "I am Lord Dunsby."

Her eyes widened in surprise. "My lord, I cannot thank you enough for what you did," she rushed out. "From what I have been told, you saved my life. I owe you a great debt."

Bennett offered her a smile, hoping to set her at ease. "You owe me nothing. It is not often that I am able to save a woman in distress." He gestured towards the chair by her bedside. "May I?"

Miss Delphine nodded, granting him permission to sit down.

As he settled into the seat, he said, "I understand that we are to call you Miss Delphine for now."

Tears welled up in her eyes, then spilled over, a silent testament to the emotions that must be swelling inside of her. "Why cannot I remember who I am?" she asked with a tremble in her voice.

He could hear the fear in her voice and the surge of protection that he felt when he had held her in his arms earlier returned. He couldn't deny the feeling of responsibility that washed over him. He would do whatever it took to help this young woman regain her memories.

Delphine could feel the tears start to stream down her face and she ducked her head, embarrassed by the show of her emotions. She may not remember much, but she knew that this was not how a lady acted.

"I am sorry, my lord," she said in a shaky voice. "I fear that I am not quite myself at the moment."

"You have nothing to apologize for," Lord Dunsby reassured her. The way he spoke his words, she believed him.

"I just wish I could remember."

Lord Dunsby reached into his jacket pocket and removed a white handkerchief, extending it towards her. "Just as we have questions about you, you must have questions about me and my family. Would it help if I told you a bit about myself? It might help jog your memory."

She accepted the handkerchief and wiped her eyes. "I suppose it couldn't hurt." Which was the truth. Her situation couldn't get much worse.

"Very good," Lord Dunsby said, settling back in his chair. "I was born on a crisp morning in the spring, and I have been told that I was the handsomest of babies. Which is good. I have seen some rather unfortunate babies in my day." He shuddered dramatically to emphasize his point.

Delphine could hear the amusement in his tone, and she felt herself begin to relax. Bringing her gaze up, she asked, "Are not all babies a blessing?"

"They are, regardless of their attractiveness," Lord Dunsby said with a smile. "Furthermore, I was, and still am, the most important person in my parents' lives. They only had my brother and sisters to be my playmates. They are to entertain me."

"Are your siblings aware of that fact?"

His smile only seemed to grow. "How could they not be? Besides, my mother calls me her favorite all the time."

"I do not think a mother has a favorite child."

"You would think, but I would like to think I gave my parents the most important gift of all." He paused. "The gift of being *my* parents."

A laugh escaped Delphine's lips and she brought her hand up to cover her mouth. "How generous of you, my lord."

"I thought so, as well," Lord Dunsby said. "Now, here I am, nearing thirty years old and I have still managed to avoid the parson's mouse trap. Which is for the best. If I took a wife, how would my family manage without my constant presence?"

"I would imagine they would continue on as they have been," Delphine replied.

With a glance over his shoulder, Lord Dunsby lowered his voice and said in a conspiratorial tone, "I am, by far, the most interesting person in my family."

Finding herself amused by his antics, she asked, "If that is the case, why are you whispering?"

He shrugged. "Sometimes the truth hurts."

"And you speak the truth?"

Bringing a hand to his chest, Lord Dunsby replied, "Always."

Delphine took a brief moment to study the handsome Lord Dunsby. His sharp jawline was accentuated by faint stubble. His dark hair was brushed forward and fell slightly longer than was considered fashionable. But she found it suited him, giving him an air of ruggedness and mystery. His piercing blue eyes danced with mirth, and she couldn't help but be charmed by him.

Knowing that she must look a fright to him, Delphine brought a hand to the bandage around her head.

Lord Dunsby leaned forward in his seat, the concern etched on his face. "Are you in pain? Is this conversation too taxing for you?" His voice was gentle yet strong, making her feel seen and cared for.

"No, the pounding in my head has finally started to subside," Delphine admitted with a sigh of relief.

"That is good," Lord Dunsby said. "Now where were we? Would you like to know what sports I excel in? I assure you that the list is extensive and it could take quite some time."

Delphine lowered her hand to the covers. "As intriguing as that sounds, perhaps you can tell me more about your family."

Lord Dunsby bobbed his head. "I have a younger brother named Winston. He is a prominent barrister in London and he is much more serious than me. But I urge you to never get into a debate with him. He can be rather persistent."

"Understood. I will not debate with Lord Winston."

"After Winston, I have twin sisters named Elodie and Melody. Elodie says- and does- the most outlandish things and Melody is much more reserved, albeit quite stubborn," Lord Dunsby shared. "They all adore me. Relentlessly, in fact."

Delphine could feel the weight of her burdens seem much more tolerable as she listened to Lord Dunsby. He had a way of making her feel at ease and she felt comfortable around him. It was as if she had known him for years.

"What of your parents?" she asked.

Lord Dunsby put his hands out to his sides. "My father is a stickler for propriety, but he does have a good heart. And my mother is one of the most generous people you will ever meet. She has a knack for making you feel accepted, no matter the situation."

Delphine felt herself nod in agreement. "Lady Dallington was very kind to me when I met her earlier. I am most grateful for her hospitality."

"You are welcome here," Lord Dunsby said. "No doubt my sisters appreciate it since it will take my mother's attention away from them for a few days. My mother is preparing them for the Season and has been rather relentless. I found Elodie hiding in a closet to get away from my mother a few days ago."

"That seems rather drastic."

Lord Dunsby chuckled. "Not for Elodie," he said. "On her trip home from boarding school, the driver grew ill so she stepped in and drove the coach."

Delphine's brow shot up. "How did she even know to do such a thing?"

"I never said that she did it well, just that she did it," Lord Dunsby replied. "My father was outraged when he found out, but my sisters insisted it was the only way."

With a wave of her hand, Delphine said, "That sounds so much like my friend, Charlotte. She hasn't driven a coach but she wouldn't hesitate…" Her words came to an abrupt stop and her eyes grew wide. "I have a friend!"

Lord Dunsby's eyes crinkled around the edges. "I did not doubt that for a second. Most people have at least one friend. I have many, in fact. Too many to count."

"You don't understand. I can remember Charlotte. She is tall, blonde, thin- but not too thin- and she has an infectious laugh," Delphine said.

"Well, I am glad you clarified her 'thinness.' If she was too thin, I doubt you could be friends with her," Lord Dunsby teased.

Delphine bit her lower lip. "She lives in…" Her voice trailed off as she willed herself to remember. It was on the tip of her tongue. Where did Charlotte live?

Lord Dunsby's calming voice interrupted her thoughts. "Do not try to force it," he advised. "It will come. Just be patient."

She heard his words of advice but she wanted to do this.

She *needed* to do this. As she forced herself to remember, her mind suddenly cleared and she knew the answer. "Skidbrooke," Delphine shouted triumphantly. "Charlotte lives in Skidbrooke and so do I. That is where my country estate is."

"Your country estate?" Lord Dunsby asked. "What else do you remember?"

Delphine let out a sigh of relief as her memories came flooding back to her. "I remember everything," she admitted. "My father was an earl and I am a countess." She felt her face light up at that realization.

Lord Dunsby eyed her with disbelief. "You are married, then?"

"No, I am a countess in my own right. Suo Jure Countess of Dunrobin. It is an old Scottish title that is allowed to be passed to the 'heir general,'" Delphine explained. "I also have a country home in Scotland and a townhouse in London."

"I am afraid I am not acquainted with your father, Lord Dunrobin."

"That does not surprise me since he detested going to London, or being social, for that matter. My father was many years older than my mother when they wed. It was an arranged marriage so he could get a male heir," Delphine said. "Unfortunately, he got me. A woman. An utter disgrace."

Lord Dunsby frowned. "Your father called you that?"

"He called me a lot worse, I am afraid," Delphine replied as she attempted to keep the hurt out of her voice. "I was told that he refused to even look at me until I was nearly a hundred days old."

"That was awful of him."

Delphine couldn't quite believe that she had been so vulnerable with Lord Dunsby. A man that was practically a stranger to her. They hadn't even been properly introduced. Although, he had saved her from death and he would have held her in his arms, causing her face to burn with embarrassment. That realization was mortifying. She had never been so familiar with a gentleman before.

But she felt safe around Lord Dunsby.

What an odd reaction to a man that she hardly knew.

Lord Dunsby gave her an encouraging look. "If you remember everything, how did you end up here in the woodlands?"

The excitement she had just felt diminished as she furrowed her brow in thought. "I don't recall," she shared. "The last thing I remember was sitting in my drawing room, working on my needlework, and speaking to Charlotte. We were discussing the latest fashions for the upcoming Season and I had an appointment with the dressmaker."

"Am I to assume this is to be your first Season?"

"It is, but I delayed it by three years due to my mother," Delphine replied. "She was not up to traveling to London due to her fragile health, and I did not wish to leave her to have a Season."

Lord Dunsby's eyes held compassion as he asked, "May I ask when she passed?"

"Almost a year ago," Delphine said, her voice growing soft. "That is one memory that I wish I could forget."

"Pardon me for saying so, but I think it is a good thing that you can remember every moment with your mother."

"The doctor said she had cancer of the stomach. I have been told that it was a painful way to die, but my mother never let on that she was in pain," Delphine said. "But I could see it in her eyes even when she tried to pretend all was well."

Delphine blinked back the tears that were forming in her eyes, knowing she couldn't keep crying around Lord Dunsby. What he must think of her show of emotions. But then she stopped herself. Why did it matter what he thought of her? She remembered who she was and where she was from. She could go home now.

She sat straight up in bed. "Now that I know who I am, I

can go home," she said. "If you are not opposed, I could make use of your coach and…"

Lord Dunsby held his hand up, stilling her words. "Slow down, my lady," he encouraged. "You are still recovering from a brain injury. I do not think you should be so quick to leave."

"I am perfectly fine now," Delphine said. "My head no longer hurts and I have all my memories back."

"Except why you entered the woodlands in the first place wearing only one shoe," Lord Dunsby pointed out.

Delphine reluctantly admitted that Lord Dunsby did have a point, albeit weakly. She didn't wish to impose on his family any longer than necessary, but she doubted she could travel in her condition.

"Why don't we start with you joining us for dinner this evening?" Lord Dunsby suggested.

"I suppose that is wise," Delphine agreed reluctantly.

"Good, we are in agreement, then," he responded. "And tomorrow, when the doctor comes to visit, we can discuss when you can travel home."

Delphine leaned back against the plush pillows. "Very well," she conceded.

There was a gentle rap at the door before a maid stepped into the room, holding two books in her hand. "Hello. I am Marie, Lady Dallington's lady's maid. She thought you might like me to read to you," she said.

Lord Dunsby rose and turned towards Marie. "Which books did my mother select from the library?"

Marie read off the titles. "*Colonel Jack* and *Tales of Fashionable Life*."

His blue eyes gleamed with curiosity as he inquired, "Do either of those titles suit your fancy?"

Delphine considered the options before her. "I have yet to read *Colonel Jack*," she admitted.

A look of approval crossed Lord Dunsby's face. "Ah, a wise choice. That particular book was written by Daniel Defoe and I think it rivals his other books. It does a decent job of tackling the subjects of money and crime."

"You make it sound rather intriguing," Delphine said.

His expression softened as he gazed at her. "You are in good hands, my lady. I hope to see you this evening for dinner."

"I hope to be there, assuming I have something more suitable to wear," Delphine responded as she glanced down at her white wrapper.

With a graceful bow, Lord Dunsby assured her, "That should not be an issue. I shall go speak to my mother at once."

As he made his way towards the door, Delphine wasn't quite ready to say goodbye. "Lord Dunsby," she called out.

He stopped and turned back around to face her. "Yes, my lady?"

Her heart fluttered nervously as she searched for the right words. "Thank you. For everything," she managed to say, hoping that her gratitude shone through. If it wasn't for him, she wasn't sure if she would still be alive. Which was a morbid and terrifying thought.

A warm smile spread across his face. "You are welcome."

And with those parting words, he left the room, leaving Delphine with the sudden urge to follow him.

Chapter Three

As Bennett made his way down to the drawing room, he realized that he was smiling. He rather enjoyed conversing with Lady Dunrobin, and not just because he helped her regain her memories, but because she had been vulnerable with him. Unlike many women he knew, who hid behind carefully constructed facades, she had shown him glimpses of her true self. It was a refreshing change from the tiresome game of pretense he had grown weary of.

In his youth, he had relished playing the game. It was fun. Exciting, even. Until it wasn't. He had lost the game when he had fallen for a young woman that didn't return his affection. Now, he harbored a deep aversion to the charade.

Entering the drawing room, he found his mother and sisters sitting on the settees, engaging in conversation.

His mother acknowledged him as he walked further into the room. "How did your visit with Miss Delphine go?" she asked, lowering her needlework to her lap.

"It went well," he admitted, a hint of pride evident as he straightened in his posture. "I, Bennett Lockwood, the Earl of Dunsby, helped her regain most of her memories."

"You did?" his mother asked. "How did you accomplish such a feat?"

"I suppose I charmed her into remembering," Bennett replied with a cocky grin.

Elodie rolled her eyes. "Oh, dear. You are delusional, Brother."

"Then how else can you explain what happened?" Bennett inquired.

"Maybe your conversation was so dull that her mind wandered, bringing her memories back with it," Elodie proposed.

Bennett's grin widened. "No lady has ever complained about my conversational skills before."

"Or are they too busy trying to snag an earl?" Elodie retorted.

Leaning forward, his mother looked less than amused as she placed her needlework onto the table. "Can we focus on what is truly important here?" she asked.

"Yes, Mother," Bennett and Elodie said in unison.

His mother gave him an expectant look. "What can you tell us about this mysterious Miss Delphine?"

Bennett sat on a chair before revealing, "She is actually a countess in her own right, the Countess of Dunrobin."

"That is rare," his mother remarked.

"It is an old Scottish title, but it sounded as if she spent most of her time in Skidbrooke where her country estate is," Bennett revealed.

Melody spoke up. "Did Lady Dunrobin say why she was in the woodlands?"

Bennett shook his head. "I'm afraid those memories have not returned," he said. "Despite this, she has an immense desire to go home."

His mother didn't look surprised by what he had revealed. "I do not fault her for that, but it is much too soon for her to travel. She needs time to recover," she insisted.

"I agree wholeheartedly," Bennett said. "I invited her to dine with us this evening, assuming she can borrow a gown."

Elodie jumped up from her seat. "She can borrow one of mine. I will take it to her now," she said eagerly.

Bennett eyed his sister with curiosity, knowing she was not one to do things out of the goodness of her heart. "Why are you so eager to see Lady Dunrobin?"

Placing a hand on her hip, Elodie replied, "She is a countess in her own right. I have never met someone like her before. I bet she is intriguing."

"She is in a rather vulnerable position, and you need to be compassionate about her plight," Bennett stated.

Elodie dropped her hand to her side, looking put out. "I can behave like a lady when I choose to," she defended.

Melody nodded in agreement. "It is a rare sighting, but it is true. I have seen it on an occasion or two." She rose. "Perhaps I will accompany Elodie to visit Lady Dunrobin."

Bennett went to object, but his mother spoke first. "That is a fine idea," she said. "I think Lady Dunrobin would look especially lovely in Elodie's pink gown with the flowers. Off you go, girls."

Turning a questioning glance to his mother, he waited until his sisters left the room before asking, "Why are you so eager for them to visit with Lady Dunrobin?"

His mother reached forward and grabbed her needlework. "I would imagine that Lady Dunrobin would enjoy the company, seeing as she is cooped up in her bedchamber."

"It isn't as if she is alone, considering you sent your lady's maid to read to her," Bennett pointed out.

"Yes, but it would be beneficial for Elodie and Melody to be associated with Lady Dunrobin when we arrive for the Season," his mother said. "I have no doubt that Lady Dunrobin will create quite a stir amongst the other debutantes."

Bennett settled back into his seat. "As will Elodie and

Melody," he remarked. "I am not sure if the *ton* is ready for them."

"They will rise to the occasion."

With a glance over his shoulder, Bennett said, "I did discover something rather disconcerting this morning." He paused. "Melody was reading an article about Lord Willowbrook in the newssheets and mentioned he was handsome."

His mother gave him a blank stare. "And?"

"There is nothing else, but is that not sufficient?" Bennett asked. "I don't want Melody anywhere near rakes or fortune hunters."

"You have nothing to worry about. Melody is smart enough to stay away from rakes. Besides, you cannot go a day without reading something in the newssheets about Lord Willowbrook. The *ton* seems to adore him."

"I just do not like it."

With an understanding look, his mother said, "Your sisters are growing up. They are going to forge their own paths, and we must give them the room to do so."

"I do not intend to let them out of my sight in London," Bennett stated firmly.

"Nor I, but we can't very well keep them prisoners in our townhouse."

Bennett shrugged. "I could keep Elodie on a very long leash."

His mother looked displeased at his attempt at humor. "That is awful of you to even say."

"We both know that if anyone will cause trouble it will be Elodie," Bennett argued. "She is a hoyden of the highest order."

"She is still young," his mother defended.

Leaning forward in his seat, he snatched a biscuit off the tray. "Why can't Elodie be more like Melody?"

"Melody may not be as loud as Elodie, but she has a quiet strength about her."

"She is much more agreeable."

His mother smiled. "Do not mistake her agreeableness for obedience. Melody has a voice, but unlike Elodie, she holds it in."

Bennett took a bite of his biscuit before saying, "As long as Melody stays away from rakes, I will be pleased."

"What of Lord Byron?"

He shot up in his seat, outraged by the mere insinuation of such a thing. "Absolutely not!" he shouted. "I do not want her to associate with him either. He may be a celebrated poet, but if the rumors are to be believed, he is a scoundrel that seduces young girls."

His mother did not appear the least bit concerned by his admission. "My point being that there are worse people that you should be concerned with."

"You would be all right with Melody marrying a rake?" Bennett asked in disbelief.

"No, I would not, and do not mistake that," his mother quickly replied. "I just propose we let Melody come to the same conclusion that we have on her own."

Bennett didn't quite like that idea. He wished that his sisters would do as they were told. It would be much simpler. "I am not looking forward to this Season," he muttered.

"I do hope that you will take advantage of this Season-more so than in the past," his mother remarked.

"What are you implying?"

His mother grew solemn. "I know that I have joked about it, but it is time for you to take a wife. You are nearing thirty and are an earl. You should have no issues with selecting a bride," she said.

He sighed, knowing that he should have seen this conversation coming. Again. If his mother wasn't talking about him getting married, it was his father. It seemed that they both had little else to talk to him about.

Bennett rose, having an immense desire to leave and end this conversation. "Do we have to talk about this now?"

"When would you care to talk about it?"

He tossed his hands up in the air. "I don't know. Maybe never."

"Do be serious."

"I am," he replied. "Why is me taking a wife so important to you?"

Rising, his mother eyed him with a look that could only be construed as sympathy. "I want you to be happy."

"I am happy."

"Are you?"

Bennett gave her a resolute nod. "I am," he said firmly, hoping to end this line of questioning. He was happy. So why couldn't he convince his mother otherwise?

His mother considered him for a long moment before putting her hands up in surrender. "All right. I shall drop it… for now."

"Thank you," he said. "I think I shall go on a ride now."

"Enjoy your ride, Dear."

Turning on his heel, he departed from the study and headed towards the stables. He probably should have been more patient with his mother since he knew she just wanted him to be happy. But a wife would not guarantee his happiness.

As he opened the door to the stables, he stepped inside and saw his late uncle's black stallion in the back stall. Hercules was an ornery thing, refusing to let anyone ride him, despite his many attempts at doing so.

Bennett reached for an apple in the bucket and held it up to the horse. "How are you, Hercules?"

The horse refused the offering and moved away from him.

He chuckled. "Not quite in the mood to talk, are we?"

The groom approached him and asked, "Do you want to have another go at riding Hercules?"

"No, Jack," Bennett replied. "I think I have learned my lesson. Perhaps it is time that we sold him."

Jack looked displeased. "Your uncle loved this horse. He would be mighty sad if you got rid of him."

"I know, but what choice do we have?" Bennett asked. "Hercules barely seems to tolerate any of us."

"Just give him more time, my lord," Jack attempted.

Bennett nodded. "I am not sure if time is what is needed, but I am not in a rush to get rid of Hercules."

Jack gestured towards his stallion in the stall over. "Would you care for me to saddle your horse?"

"No, I will do it," he replied.

As he went about saddling his horse, Bennett knew this was a menial task, far below what an earl should do, but he enjoyed doing some things for himself. It was a refreshing change of pace.

Delphine sat propped up in her bed as the lady's maid read from a book. She should be listening, but she found her mind was wandering. Now that she had her memories back, she was anxious to return home.

It had been such an unnerving experience to forget who she was, even for a short period of time. Her past, her memories, were what made her who she was. But the events of the last few days still eluded her, despite trying her best to remember. Why had she left the safety of her country home to go traipsing through the woodlands many miles away?

It would come back to her. She was sure of that.

A knock came at the door before it was pushed open, revealing two identical blonde-haired young women.

The lady's maid stopped reading and rose. "My ladies," she said with a brief curtsy before exiting the room.

The young women approached the bed with smiles on their faces.

"Good morning," the first one greeted. "My name is Lady Melody."

The other one spoke up. "And I am Lady Elodie." She held up a pink dress that was draped over her arm. "We brought you a gown to wear tonight for dinner."

Delphine returned their smiles, finding their kindness to be infectious. "That is kind of you. Thank you."

A maid stepped forward to retrieve the dress from Elodie and she relinquished her hold on it.

"We came to see how you are faring," Melody said.

"I am as well as can be expected," Delphine remarked. "I want to leave my bed but the maids have discouraged me from doing so. At least, for now."

Melody gave her an understanding look. "I am sure that they are just following the doctor's orders."

Delphine nodded her agreement. "Now that my memories have returned, I remember that patience is not one of my virtues," she admitted.

Elodie giggled. "Mine either," she said. "I am often getting in trouble because I want to do things for myself."

"It is true," Melody agreed.

Taking a step back, Elodie gestured towards the window and addressed Delphine. "Why don't you try walking to the window and back?"

Melody looked unsure. "Are you sure that is a good idea?"

Elodie shrugged. "If Lady Dunrobin wishes to dine with us, then she will need to walk to the dining room this evening on the main floor. That is much further than the window in her bedchamber."

Delphine had to admit that Elodie did have a point. "You are right," she said as she moved to sit on the edge of the bed. She put her feet onto the ground and stood. At first, she wobbled on them as she tried to gain her footing, taking a long moment before she stood upright.

She took a deep breath before she slowly began to walk towards the window with Elodie remaining close by her side.

Once she arrived, she placed her hand on the windowsill and smiled triumphantly. "I did it," she said in between breaths. It had been harder than she had anticipated but the most important thing was that she had accomplished what she had set out to do.

Elodie gestured towards the bed and encouraged, "Do you want to walk back?"

With a glance at the settee, she replied, "I think I would rather sit for a moment before returning to the bed."

"Very well," Elodie acknowledged.

Delphine moved towards the settee and sat down, feeling her heart race in her chest. Why did the simplest movements cause her such trouble?

Elodie came to sit down next to her. "You did well," she praised.

"You are much too kind. I just walked to the window and back and now I am out of breath," Delphine said, feeling slightly discouraged. If she could hardly walk to the window, how was she going to make her way to the dining room?

"The only thing that matters is that you took the first step," Elodie declared.

Turning her attention towards Melody, Delphine asked, "Is your sister always so optimistic?"

Melody gave her an amused look. "This is out of character for her. Normally, she is quite the naysayer."

"There is no shame in speaking one's mind," Elodie defended. "If you two aren't nice, I will start speaking in Russian."

"You speak Russian?" Delphine asked incredulously.

"Я немного говорю по-русски," Elodie responded.

Delphine lifted her brow. "What did you just say?"

"I merely said that I speak a little Russian," Elodie shared. "One of the maids at our boarding school was born in Russia and she helped me learn some of the words. I even acquired a few books for her and she would read them to me."

Delphine sat back in the settee as she started to feel much better. "I speak French, Italian and Latin, but I never learned Russian."

"Most genteel women don't, but I dabbled in learning Russian as well. It is the most fascinating language," Melody said, coming closer to the settee.

"You both speak Russian?" Delphine asked. For some reason, that seemed rather extraordinary to her.

Elodie bobbed her head in agreement. "I simply adore Russian literature. I especially enjoyed *Nal and Damayanti* by Gavriil Derzhavin. It has such lyrical beauty and emotional depth." She offered a sheepish smile. "At least the parts I understood, which was very little."

"You better not let Father hear you say that. He is insistent that we always behave like proper ladies," Melody remarked. "He would not be impressed that we learned some Russian."

With a sigh, Elodie said, "Do not remind me. Ever since Father inherited his title, he has become a stickler for propriety."

"He just wants what is best for us," Melody stated.

"Or what is best for him," Elodie muttered. "I just miss when Father was quick to smile and not quick to criticize."

Melody shifted her gaze to Delphine to explain. "My father became the Marquess of Dallington a little over four months ago when my uncle passed away. He is still adjusting to the pressures that are associated with his title."

"I understand," Delphine said. "I inherited my title when I was four and ten years old, forcing me to grow up faster than I would have liked."

Elodie reached for a pillow and placed it behind

Delphine's back. "What is it like being a countess in your own right?"

"I suppose I don't know any differently," Delphine replied. "I have been given a great responsibility and I hope I prove myself worthy in time."

With a curious look, Elodie asked, "If you are from Scotland, why do you not speak with a Scottish brogue?"

Delphine found the question to be fair. "My father was Scottish, but my mother was not, and she ensured I was educated by an English governess after my father died. But I sound plenty Scottish when Ah'm at oor country estate there."

"Do you live in a castle?" Elodie pressed.

"I do, at least when I am in Scotland," Delphine replied. "It was built in the late sixteenth century but underwent significant renovations before I was born."

Elodie let out a wistful sigh. "I want to live in a castle and be a countess without a husband telling me what to do."

Melody shook her head. "You must pardon my sister. She has seemingly developed an aversion to marriage."

"I do not want a man controlling me," Elodie said with a slight lift of her chin.

"Father doesn't do that to Mother," Melody contended. "And Uncle Richard loved his wife so much that he never even so much as looked at another woman."

Elodie met Delphine's gaze. "What are your thoughts on marriage?"

Delphine considered her next words carefully. "I have no intention of marrying, at least right now. Though I understand the necessity of securing an heir in due course, I see no urgency in hastening such matters."

"I do not fault you for that," Melody responded.

As she played with the strings of her dressing gown, Delphine shared, "I have had many gentlemen that have tried to woo me over the years, but I am not interested. I have too much at stake to throw it all away for a chance at love."

"And if you fall in love?" Melody asked.

"My mother always told me that there is no room for love in marriage," Delphine replied. "Marriage is a simple transaction between two people and emotions would just complicate that."

Melody exchanged a look with her sister before saying, "I take it that there was no love lost between your mother and father."

Delphine shook her head. "No. My father married my mother for the sole purpose of producing a male heir. And she failed. Instead of a boy, she conceived me and my father never let her live that down."

"I'm sorry," Elodie murmured.

"There is no reason to be sorry," Delphine said. "My father was cantankerous and only seemed to get worse as he got older. I fully understood the reality of my situation. I was born a disappointment to my father, and nothing could change that."

Elodie turned towards her sister. "Father does not look so bad anymore," she said lightly, no doubt in an attempt to lighten the mood.

Delphine offered them a weak smile. "It is my turn to apologize. I do not wish to turn anyone away from marriage. To most women, it is of vital importance."

"My cousin just married for love so I know it is possible to acquire a love match," Melody shared.

"Yes, Edwina and Lord Hilgrove are madly in love," Elodie confirmed. "I thought my brother, Winston, was going to escort them himself to Gretna Green to get married. He got tired of the blatant affection between them."

There was a firm knock at the door, followed by the graceful entrance of Lady Dallington into the room. Her eyes grew wide at the sight of Delphine sitting on the settee. "What is Lady Dunrobin doing out of bed?" she asked. "She shouldn't be walking about just yet."

Elodie rose from her seat. "It was my idea. I thought a walk to the windows would do her some good."

Delphine wasn't about to let Elodie take the blame for her actions. "Elodie may have suggested such a thing, but I made the decision to do so."

Lady Dallington's eyes softened. "I understand that you intend to join us for dinner," she said. "Are you sure you are up to it?"

"Oh, yes!" Delphine exclaimed. "I need to experience life out of these four walls. I daresay that I might go mad if I remain cooped up in here."

"Very well, but we should let you rest so you can regain your strength," Lady Dallington responded.

Delphine tipped her head. "Thank you, my lady."

Lady Dallington gestured towards the door. "Girls, shall we?" she asked. "The dressmaker is coming for the final fitting of your ballgowns."

Elodie groaned in response. "How many fittings does Mrs. Harper need to do?"

"As many as it takes," Lady Dallington said.

Melody went to stand by her mother and explained, "You must excuse Elodie. She refuses to stand still and gets poked by the needles."

"I think Mrs. Harper does it on purpose," Elodie muttered.

Lady Dallington laughed. "Poor child. What a burden you must endure," she joked.

As Delphine listened to them banter back and forth, she felt a smile on her lips. It had been some time since she had been around a family that so clearly loved one another. She felt a twinge of jealousy at that thought. Her parents had hardly spoken to one another, and when they did so, it had just been in passing.

Growing up was a lonely existence since her father was

insistent that she learn of his ways. It wasn't until he died that she was able to spend time with her mother.

"Dear?" Lady Dallington asked, her expression filled with concern. "Are you all right?"

Delphine straightened in her seat, embarrassed she had been caught woolgathering. "I am well. Just lost in my own thoughts."

Lady Dallington hesitated. "If the thought of dinner is too taxing for you, we can send a tray up. No one would blame you for that."

"No, I want to join you for dinner," Delphine assured her. "I will be fine."

"If you are sure," Lady Dallington said before departing from the bedchamber.

After Melody followed her mother out, Elodie turned back to face Delphine. "For what it is worth, I think you are quite brave."

"Thank you," Delphine said. "I don't feel brave." Which was the truth. She felt like a burden to this kind family that had taken her in.

Elodie gave her an encouraging smile. "Be patient. You will be home in your magnificent castle in no time."

As Elodie left, closing the door behind her, Delphine settled back into her seat. What a wonderful twist of fate that she was found by a handsome earl who brought her home to a loving family.

Perhaps someone should write a book about that. It would be far more interesting than *Colonel Jack*.

Chapter Four

The sound of the dinner bell could be heard echoing throughout the main level as Bennett stepped into the drawing room. His brother, Winston, stood by the mantel, his expression distant as he cradled a drink in his hand.

Approaching Winston, Bennett ventured, "Dare I ask as to what's occupying your thoughts?"

Winston met his gaze, a crease of concern etched upon his brow. "I'm afraid there's much weighing on my mind."

"Is it related to the case you're currently working on?" Bennett inquired.

"That, and other matters," Winston admitted with a hint of discomfort. "I find myself grappling with a sense of uncertainty about my future."

Bennett's brow furrowed in confusion. "I don't understand. Are you not established as a barrister?"

"I am, but the process is slow, far slower than I would like to admit," Winston shared. "I have only been working as a barrister for a year now and my cases are far and few between. I have a winning record but what does that even mean when I have so few cases?"

"You must be patient with yourself," Bennett encouraged.

"I know, but it is hard when I am working so hard to get out of Father's shadow," Winston said, bringing the glass up to his lips. "It was much easier when he wasn't a marquess."

Bennett leaned against the mantel, a flicker of surprise causing his brows to raise as he registered his brother's hidden struggles. He had assumed all was well with Winston, having read about his cases in the newssheets.

"It will get easier with time," Bennett offered, attempting to provide reassurance.

"Says the earl who is the heir to a marquessate," Winston grumbled. "I am just the second son, the spare."

"You are so much more than that," Bennett pressed.

Winston placed his glass onto the mantel and sighed. "I know, but what if I can't prove myself? Will I be forced to return home to help with the estate?"

"There is no shame in coming home. You must know that, especially since we could always use your help," Bennett said. "Father has only just started letting me help with the accounts and there is much work that needs to be done."

"No, thank you. I have no desire to help build *your* legacy and not mine," Winston responded. "I need to do this on my own."

Bennett offered a firm nod, his confidence in his brother's abilities unwavering. While Winston might not see it himself, Bennett had full faith in his potential. "And you will," he reassured his brother, understanding how one's worries could overshadow their own capabilities.

Winston raised an eyebrow. "When did you get so blasted optimistic?" he asked.

"One of us has to be," Bennett replied.

Casting a brief glance towards the door, Winston lowered his voice, his demeanor growing solemn. "We do have a problem, though," he admitted.

Sensing the gravity of Winston's words, Bennett straightened up. "What is it?" he inquired, his tone reflecting concern.

"Father asked me to look into the situation with our aunt, Sarah, and her son," Winston started. "There is no chance that Parliament will grant a divorce in her case so I hired a Bow Street Runner to keep an eye on her abusive husband. However, I just received word that Isaac managed to elude the Runner."

"How competent is this Bow Street Runner if he was eluded so easily?" Bennett asked skeptically.

"I assure you he is very competent," Winston replied. "I have used Jasper on a few of my cases and he has never let me down before."

Concern welled up inside of him as he crossed his arms over his chest, worried for his aunt's wellbeing. Though he had never met Isaac, he had heard unsettling rumors about his violent tendencies towards his wife and son.

"Do you suppose Isaac has discovered that Sarah is here?" Bennett asked, his voice laced with apprehension.

"That is my fear. So I asked Jasper to come keep a watchful eye on Sarah, at least from a distance," Winston explained.

Bennett paused to reflect on his aunt's plight. She had only mustered the courage to flee when her husband's abuse extended to their son. Now, she remained hidden in a cottage near their village, her safety paramount. To minimize the risk, they had maintained minimal contact with her.

As Bennett dwelled on his aunt, he noticed his mother leading Lady Dunrobin into the room. He had to look twice to confirm it was truly her. Gone was the white bandage that once adorned her head. Instead, she wore a pink gown, her dark hair elegantly styled atop her head. Tendrils framed her face, accentuating her beauty to a degree that left him enchanted. Her beauty stole his breath and he wasn't sure if he wanted it back.

Winston leaned closer to him and whispered, "You are staring, Brother." His words held amusement.

Bennett blinked and shifted his gaze towards his mother. "Good evening, Mother," he greeted.

His mother smiled. "Good evening, Bennett." She turned towards Lady Dunrobin. "Does Lady Dunrobin not look lovely this evening?"

No.

She didn't just look lovely, but rather her beauty seemed to make the room brighter somehow.

But he couldn't say that. Instead, he bowed. "Yes, she does," he replied.

Lady Dunrobin went to drop into a curtsy, but his mother reached out and stopped her. "We do not stand on formalities here and I think it would be best if you avoided curtsying for now, given your condition."

"You may be right," Lady Dunrobin said.

Bennett chuckled. "You need to be careful saying those words around my mother, my lady. She tends to think she is right about most things."

Lady Dunrobin seemed to visibly relax, which had been his intention. "I shall keep that in mind," she said. "Since your family does not stand on formalities here, I would prefer to be called Delphine. I feel that it is only proper considering how kind everyone has been to me."

"You are easy to be kind to," Bennett remarked, holding her gaze. Why had he admitted such a thing?

Delphine ducked her head, but not before he saw a blush stain her cheeks. "That is kind of you to say so, my lord."

"Bennett," he corrected. "If I am to call you by your given name, it is only fair if you call me by mine as well."

Bringing her gaze back up, Delphine said, "I would like that."

As they held each other's gaze, something passed between them. Something he didn't quite understand. They were two strangers, yet in her eyes, he saw himself. In her future.

That was impossible.

He broke his gaze and turned away, embarrassed by his own thoughts. Delphine was a guest in their home, and she would leave as soon as she was able. So why was he acting like a love-craved fool? He had been around beautiful women before but none of them had ever affected him like Delphine had.

He needed a drink.

Bennett walked over to the drink cart and poured himself a drink. He took a sip and hoped to calm his wandering thoughts. For that is just what they were. His thoughts. He had no intention of acting on them.

But his mother had other ideas.

"Dear," his mother said, addressing Bennett, "would you mind showing Delphine the library after dinner?"

Botheration.

He wanted to say no, but propriety won out.

Bennett mustered up a smile to his face. "I would be honored," he said, hoping his words sounded genuine enough.

Delphine smiled, and he had to force himself to look away, as if he had encountered that smile before in his dreams. What was wrong with him?

Fortunately, before he could delve much deeper into that question, his sisters stepped into the room.

Elodie gasped when her eyes landed on Delphine. "You look radiant," she announced.

Melody nodded her agreement. "I must agree with Elodie, and that pink dress suits you rather nicely."

Delphine held out the folds of her gown. "I do appreciate Elodie letting me borrow one of her gowns. It is nice not being in my wrapper."

"I shall have my lady's maid bring more gowns to your bedchamber," Elodie said. "It is the least we could do."

"That is most kind of you, but I am hoping to leave tomorrow once I speak to the doctor," Delphine responded.

Lady Dallington interjected, "Let's not get ahead of

ourselves. You are still recovering from a brain injury, and we do not want you to be jostled about in the coach on your journey home."

Delphine reached up and touched her bruised forehead. "With every moment, every step, I feel my strength returning to me."

"That is good, but before we make any plans, let us confer with the doctor," his mother advised.

Winston stepped forward and bowed in Delphine's direction. "Forgive my family's manners, my lady, but they have failed to introduce us. I am Winston, the younger son, the spare." He paused, a mischievous grin spreading across his lips. "Or, as some would say, the more handsome son."

Delphine went to drop into a curtsy but stopped herself. "It is a pleasure to meet you," she said. "I understand that you are a barrister."

"I am," Winston responded.

"Bennett told me a bit about your family when I first woke up and was trying to remember my memories," Delphine shared.

A faint smirk played at the corners of Winston's lips. "I shudder to think what Bennett told you about us."

Delphine returned his smile with one of her own. "It was all good… well, mostly good," she joked.

Bennett did not like the way that Winston was watching Delphine. An unfamiliar, and unwelcome, pang of jealousy surged through him. Clearing his throat, he redirected everyone's attention. "Is Father joining us for dinner?" He already knew the answer to that question, but he asked it anyways.

"He is," his mother confirmed. "He is in the study, finishing up working on the accounts."

"Perhaps Winston should go inform him that dinner is ready," Bennett suggested. "After all, he might not have heard the dinner bell."

Elodie chimed in, "Everyone in the whole manor can hear the dinner bell. White makes sure of that."

Bennett returned his attention to his drink, knowing how foolish he sounded. Why did he care that his brother was acting like a fool by smiling at Delphine like that? He shouldn't. Winston could flirt with whomever he pleased. Delphine wasn't his to claim, and he had already decided he had no intention of pursuing her.

Fortunately, his father entered the room and announced, "I apologize for being late but I assure you that it couldn't be helped."

"Of course not, my love," his mother responded, exchanging a look of love with her husband. "But now that you are here, I can introduce you to our guest, Lady Dunrobin."

His father's eyes shifted towards Delphine and his eyes crinkled around the edges. "So you are the countess that I have been hearing about," he said in a kind voice. "You are most welcome here."

Delphine dropped down into a curtsy and wobbled on her feet, causing Bennett to hurry forward to steady her.

"My apologies," Delphine said with an apologetic look. "Perhaps I am not as sure-footed as I led myself to believe."

Bennett released his hold on her arm but remained close. "You must remember to be patient with yourself. Everyone recovers at their own pace."

His father spoke up. "Bennett is right- for once."

"Et tu, Father?" Bennett asked dramatically, placing a hand over his chest. "I will have you know that I am right most of the time."

With a chuckle, his father replied, "I do have to get a jab in a time or two to keep you humble."

"I assure you that I am humble enough," Bennett said.

Melody giggled. "Says the man that can't pass by a mirror without sneaking a glance at himself."

"That is emphatically not true," Bennett declared. "But if it were, would you blame me? Mirrors love me."

Reaching out, his father offered an arm to his mother. "And on that note, we should go eat dinner before it gets cold."

Bennett offered his arm to Delphine. "May I escort you into dinner?" he asked.

"Thank you, my lord," she replied as she placed her hand atop his sleeve. Despite her wearing gloves, he swore he felt the warmth of her hand, leaving an imprint.

Botheration.

He needed to collect his wits before he made a complete and utter fool of himself around Delphine.

Delphine settled into the chair that Bennett had courteously pulled out for her. Adjusting herself, she reached for a white linen napkin and draped it across her lap.

Bennett took a seat beside her on the left, while Winston occupied the spot to her right. Across from her sat Elodie and Melody, with Lord and Lady Dallington positioned at the ends of the long, rectangular table.

As the footmen served bowls of soup, Delphine delicately picked up her spoon and began to eat, aiming to remain a silent observer for the time being. However, luck seemed to be against her.

Lord Dallington directed his attention towards her. "I had the privilege of meeting your father once," he remarked. "He was just starting up his company and had sought the advice of my brother. I had no idea he would become such a successful goat cheese maker."

"It was his passion," Delphine shared, hoping to keep the bitterness out of her tone. Her father spent more time with the goats than he did with his own daughter. But then again, did she even want to spend time with him?

Winston leaned towards her and said, "What an interesting profession for an earl."

"It was, but I do not think he intended it to grow as big as it did," Delphine responded. "My hope is to expand it even further."

Lord Dallington furrowed his brow. "I do hope you have a good man of business to help you since your interests no doubt lie elsewhere."

Delphine felt her back grow rigid at that archaic remark. But it wasn't anything she hadn't heard before. "My *interests* are in ensuring that my company and estate are profitable," she asserted.

"Yes, but you are…" Lord Dallington started, waving his fork in the air.

"A woman?" Delphine asked as she finished his thought.

Lord Dallington looked at her thoughtfully. "Yes, a woman," he replied. "Surely you want to get married and have children. Not tend to goats."

Delphine shifted in her chair to face Lord Dallington. "What a keen observation, my lord. But, as a woman, I do not need a man to take care of me. I have my own funds available to me and my own title."

He chuckled, as if the mere thought was amusing. "Women are lonely creatures and require companionship."

Lady Dallington cleared her throat. "Lionel…" Her words carried a warning.

Putting his hand up, Lord Dallington said, "I apologize if what I said offended Lady Dunrobin, but it is no different than what any member of high Society would think."

Elodie spoke up. "Then the problem is with high Society and not Delphine. What would it benefit her if she were to wed?"

"She would have a husband to help her with the more serious matters," Lord Dallington stated plainly.

What an absurd thing to say, Delphine thought. But she needed to be careful and not insult her host. "I assure you that I am of a more serious nature," she settled on. "Marriage is not something that would benefit me at this time. I am content on my own, considering I spend all my time ensuring that my estate and business are thriving."

Bennett reached for his glass and interrupted. "Perhaps we could talk about something else and not interrogate our guest."

"I am not interrogating her," Lord Dallington defended.

Lady Dallington bobbed her head. "You are, my dear," she stated. "We could always go around the table and share one interesting fact that we have learned recently."

Melody let out a slight groan. "I hate this game. I never know what to say."

Shifting her gaze to Lord Dallington, his wife asked, "What tidbit do you wish to share with us?"

Lord Dallington considered her for a moment before saying, "I have recently discovered that if we invest in new farm equipment our profits could go up as much as ten percent."

"Well, that was not at all interesting," Lady Dallington remarked.

"I disagree," Lord Dallington stated.

Lady Dallington shifted her gaze towards Winston and gave him an expectant look. "Do try to do better than your father," she said lightly.

Winston placed his spoon down and shared, "If you see a sheep on its back then you should gently roll it back to its feet."

"How did you learn of this?" Elodie asked.

"I recently bought a sheep farm with some of my inheritance," Winston announced.

The clatter of Lord Dallington's dropped spoon echoed through the room. "You did what?" he exclaimed.

"Must I repeat myself?" Winston responded calmly, unperturbed by his father's outburst.

"But you are a barrister," Lord Dallington protested.

Winston remained composed, responding to his father's reaction with great poise. "I am. But being a barrister is not as lucrative as I would like. I thought I would branch out and try my hand at business."

Lord Dallington frowned. "Do you know anything about sheep?"

"Apparently, he knows enough to not let them sleep on their backs," Elodie quipped.

Delphine resisted the urge to laugh at Elodie's remark, despite wanting to very much. But it was neither the time nor the place to do so.

As Lord Dallington opened his mouth to no doubt continue the conversation, Lady Dallington spoke up. "Let's move on, shall we?" She met Delphine's gaze. "What say you?"

"I suppose an interesting fact would be that goat cheese has a tangy flavor and may turn slightly yellow as it ages," Delphine said. "Is that sufficient?"

Lady Dallington nodded in approval before moving on to Bennett. "Son?"

Bennett grinned. "I do not have anything as interesting as facts about goat cheese, but pigs are excellent swimmers."

"But they are so enormous," Melody said.

"I can't explain it, but my friend at Eton claims that he was saved from drowning by a pig," Bennett responded.

Delphine smiled at the thought of a pig swimming. "Now I almost want to toss a pig into a lake to see it swim. Although, I truly doubt I could even pick one up."

"What if that particular pig could not swim?" Elodie questioned. "You would have to jump in after it to save it."

"That is all right. My mother taught me how to swim in the lake at our country estate," Delphine said.

Elodie cast a frustrated glance towards her parents. "I was not allowed to learn how to swim. My parents said it wasn't a skill that a genteel lady should possess."

"What if you are in a boat and it capsizes?" Delphine asked.

"I suppose I will sink to the bottom and die," Elodie responded in a dramatic voice. "It is a good thing that I am a twin so my parents will still have at least one daughter."

Lady Dallington shook her head. "What nonsense are you spewing?"

"Delphine is a countess and she can swim," Elodie said. "Maybe I can learn to walk along the bottom of a lake like a hippopotamus." Her face lit up. "That is my interesting anecdote."

"There we go," Lady Dallington said. "I knew that Elodie would eventually get there. Melody?"

Melody put her spoon down and made a face. "I hate this game. I never have anything interesting to say."

"Everything you say is interesting, Sister," Bennett joked.

Delphine brought her fingers up to her lips to hide her smile at Bennett's remark. Why did she find him so amusing?

"I was recently learning about the language of the fan and if you drop the fan in front of a gentleman it means you two are meant to be friends," Melody said.

Winston yawned. "That was rather boring."

"At least mine was practical," Melody remarked. "When am I ever going to see a sheep sleeping on its back?"

"Sheep don't sleep on their backs. That is how they suffocate to death," Winston responded.

Bennett turned towards his mother. "It is Mother's turn now. Although, another fun fact is that four of them have been about animals."

"Mine is not about an animal, but rather a book," Lady

Dallington said. "The title of *Sense and Sensibility* was originally *Elinor and Marianne* but it was changed before being published."

Delphine reached for her glass before saying, "I did enjoy reading *Sense and Sensibility*. I loved the contrast between the two sisters and their different approaches to life and love."

"It is a shame that it was written by A Lady," Lord Dallington said.

Bennett looked heavenward, as if anticipating that his father's words would undoubtedly provoke a reaction from the women at the table. "Why, Father?" he sighed.

In response, Lord Dallington's lips curled slightly, making it appear that he knew precisely what he was doing.

"Some of the greatest books written have been by women," Delphine declared. "Eliza Haywood, Mary Wortley Montagu and Mary Astell- just to name a few."

"Yes, but there are more books written by men than women," Lord Dallington argued.

Delphine sucked in a breath, knowing it was not the time or place to release her sharp tongue. She was a guest in Lord Dallington's home, and although his opinions were offensive to her, they were not unfounded.

Lady Dallington gave her husband a pointed look. "Perhaps we should not say things that might offend our guest."

"I am merely stating a fact," Lord Dallington stated before turning his attention towards Delphine. "I am sorry if the truth offends you."

Bennett groaned. "That was hardly an apology, Father. People tend to be remorseful when they apologize."

"Why should I be remorseful?" Lord Dallington asked, his voice tinged with amusement, suggesting he was rather enjoying the debate. "Is it not true that more men have written books than women over the course of time?"

As Elodie leaned to the side to allow a footman to collect her bowl, she addressed her father. "You are being utterly ridiculous. Everyone knows why there are fewer women authors than men."

"Be that as it may, I cannot rewrite history," Lord Dallington said.

Lady Dallington caught everyone's attention by tapping her fork against her glass. "As Delphine is our guest, why don't we take this opportunity to learn more about her?" she suggested.

Bennett nodded in agreement. "Mother is right. I, for one, would like to learn more about Delphine."

A footman placed a plate of food in front of her as Delphine modestly protested, "I assure you that I am not that interesting."

"I beg to differ," Bennett responded. "I find you to be utterly captivating."

Meeting Bennett's gaze briefly, Delphine responded, "That is kind of you to say." She struggled to keep the blush from rising in her cheeks. Why did his words have such an effect on her?

Winston turned towards her. "I also find you to be quite fascinating. Probably even more so than my brother."

"Boys, please," Lady Dallington said. "I think we can all agree that Delphine is a remarkable young woman. Now perhaps we should eat before our food gets cold."

Delphine picked up her fork and knife to begin eating the mutton on her plate. As she took a bite, she was grateful for the silence so she could collect her thoughts.

But it didn't last long.

Elodie placed her fork down and asked, "Do you play pall-mall, Delphine?"

"I do," she confirmed.

"Wonderful, we shall have to play once you are feeling better," Elodie responded. "Although, our numbers are odd so we will have to ask Miss Bawden to play with us."

Winston dropped his fork onto his plate and let out a sigh. "Must you bring up that infuriating woman?"

Elodie gave him an innocent look. "Do you take issue with Miss Bawden, Brother?"

"I do not take issue with her, but I assure you that she takes issue with me," Winston grumbled.

"Regardless, who else do you propose should come play with us?" Elodie asked.

"Miss Bawden is the obvious choice," Melody expressed. "She has been playing with us for years."

"Fine, invite Miss Bawden," Winston remarked.

Elodie smiled victoriously. "There is nothing more enjoyable than watching Winston and Miss Bawden battle it out on the lawn."

Delphine saw that Winston's jaw was clenched and he was taking deep breaths, no doubt in an attempt to calm himself. What was it about Miss Bawden that evoked such a reaction in Winston?

Bennett must have sensed her curiosity and leaned closer to her. "Miss Bawden and Winston have been at odds with one another since we used to visit Brockhall Manor as children."

"Dare I ask why?" Delphine asked.

"The story is too long and convoluted, I'm afraid," Bennett replied as he straightened in his chair.

Lady Dallington smiled brightly, as if she knew a secret that no one else was privy to. "I think Miss Bawden is a lovely young woman and she is always welcome here."

Winston reached for his napkin and tossed it onto his plate. "If you will excuse me, I have lost my appetite."

"Dear…" Lady Dallington started.

He put his hand up, stilling her words. "I have work that I must see to," he said, pushing back his chair. "Excuse me."

After Winston departed from the dining room, Lady

Dallington cast a disapproving look at Elodie. "I do not know why you insist on antagonizing him."

Elodie's lips twitched. "I have a theory that those two secretly love one another and are both too stubborn to admit it."

Lady Dallington gave her a pointed look. "Do keep your opinions to yourself, Child."

"All right, then I won't say that this mutton is a little dry," Elodie said as she pushed the meat around her plate.

Shifting her gaze towards her husband, Lady Dallington declared, "I have failed as a mother."

Bennett smirked. "Or did Elodie fail *you* as a daughter?"

Delphine couldn't suppress a laugh at the unexpected remark, but to her dismay, a snort escaped her. She quickly brought her hand to her mouth, hoping to conceal the embarrassing sound.

Unfortunately, luck was not on her side.

"Did you just snort?" Bennett teased, a playful glint in his eyes.

Feeling mortified, Delphine pressed her lips together as she tried to maintain her composure. "A true gentleman would not comment on such a thing."

"I have been known to snort a time or two, so you are in good company," Bennett remarked.

Delphine offered him a grateful look. "Thank you, but it is not something that I do on purpose."

"That is a shame," he said with a wink.

And with that simple gesture, she felt her face growing warm, finding it entirely unfair for a man to be as devilishly handsome as Bennett was.

Chapter Five

As Bennett and Delphine strolled down the lengthy corridors of Brockhall Manor, he couldn't help but notice the tension in her jaw and the unsteadiness in her steps.

With genuine concern, he said, "If this is too taxing for you, I can always show you the library tomorrow."

"No, it is fine," she replied hastily, but her demeanor suggested otherwise. Her shoulders seemed to droop slightly, betraying her true feelings.

He wondered why she was being so stubborn about this.

Up ahead, he saw two chairs that were situated against the wall and he had an idea. He glanced over at her. "Would you mind if we took a break?"

"I told you that I can handle it," she replied with a stubborn tilt of her chin.

He smiled, hoping to disarm her. "I know, but I ate a lot of mutton and I just need a moment to rest."

Bennett could see the indecisiveness in Delphine's eyes and he wondered if his plan would work. After a moment, she sighed. "I suppose we could sit down for a moment. But only because you requested it, not me."

"Thank you, my lady," he said as he gestured towards the chair.

He waited until she sat down before he did the same. He could see the visible relief in her features as she leaned back against the chair. Now he just needed to find a way to distract her so she could get some rest that she so clearly needed.

"Besides the occasional snorting, is there anything else I should know about you?" he teased.

She pursed her lips, annoyance visible on her face. "I wish you wouldn't tease me about that. It is not something that I do on purpose."

He nudged his shoulder against hers. "I think it is endearing."

Delphine did not look convinced. "I think not," she huffed.

"In a world where conformity is expected, it is nice to see someone who dares to stand out," Bennett stated.

"You are kind, but I know what you are trying to do," she said. "You are trying to distract me so we can sit here longer."

He feigned innocence. "I am doing no such thing!" he declared.

Her face softened, and a laugh escaped her lips. "I think it is sweet. I do not know why I can't admit that I need help."

"Most people can't," he said.

"My father always said that it was a sign of weakness," Delphine said, her smile dimming. "I often wonder if I had been born a boy if my father would have been happy. He always seemed so miserable, especially when he was around me."

Hearing the heartache in her voice, Bennett shifted in his seat to face her. "I do not think that would have made a difference. Happiness comes from within."

Delphine's gaze turned downcast. "I do not know why I insist on sharing such things with you. It is in the past and that is where it will remain."

Bennett found he was curious about one thing. "You speak of your father's desire of having a boy, but what of your mother?"

"My mother's only duty was to produce my father a son, and she failed," Delphine said. "When I was about five years old, my father had his mistress move into the country estate. With us. My mother tried to make it work for my sake. But after many difficult years of all living together under the same roof, she decided it was best to live apart, leaving me alone with them."

Bennett winced. "I'm sorry," he said, knowing his words were wholly inadequate.

Delphine started fidgeting with her hands in her lap. "After my father died, I was sent to live with my mother. She was kind to me, but I could see the disappointment in her eyes. Her whole life would have been better if I had just been born a boy."

"You don't know that," Bennett attempted.

"Perhaps not, but I was a grand disappointment the moment I was born and now I have to fight to prove myself," Delphine said.

"You have nothing to prove."

Delphine stared at him in astonishment, as if he had sprouted a second head. "How naïve you are if you truly think that," she said. "I have to work twice as hard to prove I am somewhat competent. Sometimes I am utterly exhausted by it all. But every day, I have to wake up and do it all over again, knowing that people are just waiting for me to fail."

"Are you one of those people?" Bennett asked.

She hesitated before continuing. "I am," she replied. "I feel the need to prove to myself that I am just as capable, if not more so, than my father. And I must do it on my own."

Bennett seemed to consider her words before saying, "It sounds as if you could stand to have some fun."

With a wistful sigh, she responded, "Maybe someday. But for now, I have far too much to do."

"How about now?" Bennett asked. "We could play 'who is snooping on us'."

Delphine eyed him curiously. "I am not familiar with that game."

Bennett pointed down the hall where he could see his sister's head peeking out from the parlor.

Delphine followed his gaze and asked, "How did you know?"

"Elodie thinks she is sneaky, but she is not very light on her feet," Bennett replied. "I worry about her making her debut in high Society. She is young and doesn't seem to desire to ever get married."

"She will rise to the challenge," Delphine stated.

Bennett wasn't entirely convinced. Elodie was a hoyden, but she possessed a good heart, one that he feared might be taken advantage of.

Delphine must have sensed his apprehension because she said, "Sometimes, the people we least expect will surprise us in ways we never thought possible."

"If someone is going to surprise me, it would be Elodie," Bennett joked.

A wistful look came into Delphine's eye. "I wish I had a brother such as you," she said. "I can tell by the way you and your family interact with one another that you truly love each other."

"We do, no matter how much we try to deny it," Bennett remarked with a boyish grin. "But I am the bond that keeps this family together. Me, and only me."

Delphine gave him an amused look. "What a burden you must endure, my lord," she teased.

Bennett brought a hand over his heart. "Thank you. It is good to feel seen."

Delphine yawned and her hand flew up to cover her

mouth. "My apologies," she rushed out. "I must be more tired than I have led myself to believe."

"Why must you feel the need to constantly apologize?" Bennett asked. "You have had a long day and I do not fault you for that."

"But I spent most of the time in bed," Delphine argued.

"Your body is still recovering, and it needs rest." He rose and extended his hand. "Come. Allow me to walk you back to your bedchamber."

Delphine's expression betrayed her inner conflict as she inquired, "What about the tour of the library?"

Bennett smirked. "Rest assured, it will still be there tomorrow. I will make sure of it," he declared with confidence.

His words elicited the intended response, prompting Delphine to place her gloved hand in his and accept his assistance in standing up. "Thank you," she said gratefully.

Keeping hold of her hand, Bennett moved it into the crook of his arm. "I know you will insist that you can do it on your own, but I would feel much better if you allowed me to escort you."

Rather than argue with him, she conceded. "Very well, but only because I am too tired to fight you."

"I shall take that as a win," Bennett said.

As they made their way towards the grand staircase, Delphine asked, "You mentioned you are worried about Elodie, but what of Melody?"

"I am worried about both of my sisters," he admitted. "The *ton* can be cruel and uninviting to debutantes- or anyone that they perceive doesn't belong."

Delphine nodded. "That is what my mother told me as well, but Charlotte convinced me to attend the Season."

"Now is Charlotte truly your only friend?" he teased.

She laughed, just as he intended. "I do have others, but I have known Charlotte for a long time. She is the granddaughter of a viscount and is hoping for a brilliant match this Season."

"Most women are," Bennett remarked.

There was the slightest sway in Delphine's steps as they made their way down the corridor and she had a firm grip on his arm. Her gaze remained fixed ahead, determination gleaming in her eyes, undeterred by any distractions.

Bennett couldn't help but wonder why she was so adamant to do this on her own when he was willing to help her.

With a glance at him, Delphine asked, "And what of your story? Why are you not wed with hordes of children running about?" Her tone was light and teasing.

He chuckled. "I suppose I haven't found the right one."

"You desire a love match?" she asked, the surprise evident in her voice.

"I do," he said.

Delphine regarded him with a hint of skepticism in her gaze. "I daresay that love matches are rare and elusive. But I commend your aspiration for one," she remarked. "I, however, am too pragmatic to think love has any place in marriage."

"That is a sad way to look at marriage," Bennett countered.

"In my honest opinion, it is best if hearts are not involved when negotiating the terms of the marriage contract," Delphine responded firmly.

Bennett felt a pang of sadness for Delphine, knowing that her perspective arose from her experiences. He considered himself fortunate to have witnessed something different. "Despite his flaws, my father loves my mother dearly, and I aspire to have what they share."

A wistful look came to Delphine's expression. "It must have been wonderful to be raised in a home full of love," she murmured.

"It was." Bennett was aware of his privileged upbringing and the warmth of familial love that surrounded him. He understood that not everyone was as fortunate, particularly among the members of high Society.

"I know I must marry for the sake of an heir, but I won't do it anytime soon. I have far too many things I need to do before I take a husband and lose some of the privileges that have been afforded to me," Delphine said. "I have even compiled a list of the attributes that I expect my husband to have."

"Dare I ask what is on that list?"

Delphine pressed her lips together. "Honorable, hard-working, honest- just to name a few," she replied. "I know you must think I am foolish, but to me, a marriage is a business transaction. And I am far too young to even consider marrying."

"Have you not reached your majority?"

"I have, but I need to prove to myself that I don't need a husband, but rather, I *want* a husband. There is a difference between the two, and I do not wish to tie myself to anyone right now," Delphine said, her tone resolute. "I have too much to accomplish."

Bennett eyed her with compassion. "Are you not lonely?"

"I am well acquainted with loneliness," she sighed. "Quite frankly, I wouldn't even desire taking a husband if I didn't require an heir. I just refuse to let my cousin inherit, not after everything he has done."

Before he could respond, Delphine came to an abrupt stop and brought a hand up to her head. Her breathing grew labored, and her complexion visibly paled.

"What is wrong?" he asked, concern evident in his voice.

"I am just feeling rather lightheaded," she replied weakly.

Without asking for permission, he scooped her up in his arms and reassured her, "I have you."

Delphine remained rigid in his arms for a moment before gradually relaxing against him. She slipped her arm around his neck and rested her head against his chest.

"Thank you," she murmured in such a soft voice that he almost missed it.

As he walked down the corridor with a purposeful stride, Elodie stepped out into the corridor and asked, "Is Delphine all right?"

"She will be," Bennett replied. "She just needs to rest."

Elodie looked unsure. "We could send someone to fetch the doctor."

"At this hour?" he asked. "No, she will be fine until Doctor Anderson arrives tomorrow."

"I am going to find Mother. She will know what to do," Elodie asserted before she headed down the corridor at a clipped pace.

Delphine looked up at him, her face still far too pale for his liking. "I do not wish to be a burden," she said.

"Too late," he remarked with a smile. "Everyone will fuss over you now. It is too late to stop what has already been set into motion."

"I'm sorry."

Bennett tightened his hold on her as he started up the stairs. "You have nothing to be sorry for. If anything, it is I that should be apologizing to you. I should have insisted you rest after dinner rather than tour the library."

"But I wanted to see the library," Delphine said.

"It is nothing special," Bennett responded. "It is a room full of books and two long windows along the back wall."

Delphine gave him the briefest of smiles. "You would make a terrible tour guide," she murmured.

"Indeed. I think I will stick with being an earl, considering the benefits are much better," he joked.

As he approached the guest bedchamber that Delphine was residing in, his mother caught up with him, matching his stride.

"Allow me," she said as she went to open the door.

Bennett stepped into the room and gently placed Delphine

down onto the bed. "Rest, my dear," he encouraged before taking a step back.

His mother moved closer to Delphine, and with concern in her voice, said, "I will take it from here, Bennett. You may go."

With a parting glance at Delphine, he knew she was going to be all right. His mother would see to that. So why was he so worried about her?

He had no quick answer, but knew he was worried...

Desperately so.

As the morning sun streamed through the window of Delphine's bedchamber, she sat propped up on her bed, finishing her breakfast. She wished she could claim she had a restless night's sleep, but that would be a lie. All she dreamed about was being held in Bennett's arms.

She knew she had to leave this place, and quickly. Staying here would only lead to developing feelings for a man she had no right to. He sought a love match, but she doubted she was capable of such vulnerability. Trusting a man with her heart seemed reckless.

So why did the mere thought of leaving Brockhall Manor leave her with a profound sense of sadness?

She should feel mortification that Bennett had cradled her in his arms the night before when she had grown light-headed. But instead, she felt like she had found a home in his arms, a place that she never wanted to leave. Which was absurd. She hardly knew the man. Surely this must be because she'd hit her head and she had lost all rational sense.

A knock echoed throughout the room before the door was pushed open, revealing Doctor Anderson. He smiled warmly.

"Good morning, my lady," he greeted. "I understand that some of your memories have returned."

"Most have, except for how I ended up in the woodlands," Delphine replied.

Doctor Anderson approached the bed and came to a stop next to her. "That is not entirely unexpected, and you mustn't try to force these memories to return. But I should warn you that they might never be recovered."

"I need to know why I was in those woodlands," Delphine said. "It wasn't as if I could have walked from my country estate there. I must have been traveling in a carriage with someone."

The doctor reached for a chair and positioned it next to the bed. "I do not doubt something traumatic happened, but you are safe now. It is important that you know that."

Delphine did feel safe, safer than she had ever before. But that didn't mean she wanted to give up hope she would recover these memories.

"You are young, and in good health, but the brain works in complex ways," the doctor said. "Just try to rest up and recover your strength."

She perked up. "May I go home?"

Doctor Anderson shook his head. "I'm afraid not. I would like you to remain at Brockhall Manor for at least another three days while you recuperate."

"Three days?" she asked. A part of her wanted to return home, but another part of her wanted to stay. And it was that part of her that scared her. She needed to return home to her estate, her tenants and her business.

"I know this must be hard for you, but I do not feel it is safe for you to travel," the doctor explained. "I spoke to Lady Dallington about this and she is in agreement."

"So I am to impose on their hospitality even longer?" Delphine asked.

The doctor offered her a kind look. "I do not believe they

feel like it is an imposition," he said. "Lady Dallington seemed rather excited at the prospect that you will be staying longer."

Delphine leaned her head back against the wall and stared up at the canopy above her bed. She didn't wish to defy the doctor, but could she remain here for another three days, lounging in bed, knowing there was so much work to be done back at home?

A maid stepped closer to the bed and removed the breakfast tray. "Will there be anything else, my lady?" she asked in a soft voice.

"Not at this time," Delphine replied.

As the maid left the room, the doctor leaned forward in his seat and studied her. "Your color looks much better, but it is what I can't see that concerns me. I have seen a person's whole demeanor change after an accident such as yours."

"I assure you that I am fine," she asserted.

"You say that, but one more hit to the head could be dire," the doctor informed her.

Delphine shuddered at that thought. "I will be careful."

The doctor looked as if he wanted to say more, but instead he sat back in his seat, giving her a concerned look. "I will not continue to lecture you, but I cannot stress enough the importance of listening to your body."

"My body is telling me that I might go mad if I stay in this bed for another moment," Delphine said, softening her words with a smile.

He chuckled. "Go explore the gardens, but do not overly tax yourself," he advised her.

As he uttered his words, Lady Dallington entered the room with a bright smile on her face. "Isn't it wonderful, Dear?" she asked. "You will be staying with us longer."

Delphine could hear the genuineness in the woman's voice and she appreciated it. It made her feel less of a burden. "I do not wish to be an imposition…"

Lady Dallington waved her hand dismissively in front of

her. "Nonsense," she declared. "It is our pleasure to have you here. We adore having house guests."

"You are most kind and I hope to one day return the favor," Delphine said.

Approaching the bed, Lady Dallington responded, "Having you in our home has been a privilege. There is no favor to return."

Delphine appreciated Lady Dallington even more. She was taking this difficult situation for her and making it seem as if she was doing them a favor.

Doctor Anderson rose from his seat. "For now, I do not want Lady Dunrobin to venture anywhere farther than your gardens. I fear too much exertion would be detrimental in her delicate condition."

"Understood, Doctor," Lady Dallington said with a bob of her head.

"If you need me for any reason, please send word at once," he responded with a bow.

Doctor Anderson turned to leave but Delphine spoke up, stopping him. "Thank you, Doctor."

He turned back towards the bed. "You should know how lucky you truly are. If Lord Dunsby hadn't found you when he did, you would have succumbed to your injuries. You have been given a second chance at life. I hope you do not waste it."

Delphine considered the doctor's words as he turned to leave, knowing they would remain with her for quite some time. She had come so close to death, but she had survived. Now she didn't want to squander this opportunity.

Once the doctor departed from her bedchamber, Lady Dallington clasped her hands together. "What would you like to do today?" she asked.

"I want to get out of this bed," Delphine replied.

"Good," Lady Dallington said. "Bennett is rather eager to show you the library this morning."

Delphine eyed her curiously. "Did Bennett say such a thing?"

"No, but a mother knows these types of things," Lady Dallington replied. "I will send in a maid so she can assist you in dressing. I have even pulled a few gowns from Elodie and Melody's wardrobes. I do believe these gowns will suit you nicely."

"That is most generous of you," Delphine stated. "And are you sure that they do not mind me borrowing their gowns?"

"Not in the least. Melody is practically counting down the moments until her Society gowns arrive."

Delphine fingered the strings of her dressing gown as she shared, "I do wish I shared Melody's enthusiasm about the Season. I find that I am dreading it."

"You'll change your mind," Lady Dallington encouraged as she came to sit down on the chair. "Before my Lionel inherited his title, I worried for my daughters' prospects. Our station did not allow me to hope for a titled gentleman for my daughters. But now…" She paused. "Now they could marry a prince if they so desired."

"That sounds terrifying."

Lady Dallington laughed. "I do not aspire for them to marry a prince either, but as a daughter of a marquess, it is not out of the realm of possibility for them. Or for you, for that matter."

Delphine made a face. "Me, marry a prince? I think not. I would rather shoot myself in the foot," she said. "I tend to avoid social events whenever possible. I am much happier at my country estate, ensuring it is profitable."

"But don't you get lonely?"

Delphine sighed. "I have been lonely for as long as I can remember," she admitted. "But my dear friend, Charlotte, makes it tolerable."

"I am glad that you have a friend in this girl, but what of

marriage? Children? Surely, you want those?" Lady Dallington prodded.

"Eventually, I will need to take a husband, but it is not something that I will do on a whim," Delphine said. "I will give it serious consideration, knowing I will lose some of the freedoms that have been afforded to me."

Lady Dallington gave her an understanding look. "And what of love?"

"What of it?" she asked. "Love is not a contract. One can break their vows of love without just cause, leaving the other to be devastated by their actions. And as a woman, there is nothing I could do to stop it."

Lady Dallington leaned forward and patted her hand. "Life has a way of unraveling our carefully constructed plans."

"Not mine," Delphine insisted. "I know what I want out of life, and I know precisely what I need to do to achieve it."

A smile came to Lady Dallington's lips. "My point being is that Bennett found you in the woodlands. Had he not done such a thing then our paths might not have crossed until we were in London for the Season."

A soft knock came at the door before a maid stepped into the room with a jonquil dress draped over her arm. "I was told to come help Lady Dunrobin get dressed for the day," she said.

Lady Dallington rose from her chair. "Thank you," she replied. "I shall leave you to it, but I will go and inform Bennett you will be available to tour the library soon."

"I do not wish to be a bother," Delphine remarked.

Coming to a stop near the door, Lady Dallington just smiled. "You are no bother, Dear. I daresay that you have brought hope to our doorstep."

Unsure of what Lady Dallington was referring to, Delphine went to ask her but she departed the room before she could speak up.

The maid approached the bed. "Shall we dress you, my lady?"

"If you don't mind," Delphine replied, placing her feet over the side of the bed. "Do you know what Lady Dallington was referring to about 'bringing hope to their doorstep'?"

She shook her head. "I do not."

Delphine retreated to her own thoughts as she got dressed. What an odd thing for Lady Dallington to say to her. It didn't appear that anyone was lacking hope at Brockhall Manor. Everyone seemed rather content with their lots in life. Well, everyone but Elodie. She didn't seem entirely happy, but that could just come from the expectations that had been placed on her to find a love match.

It was a short time later that she found herself dressed and her hair was pulled back into a loose chignon. She exited her bedchamber and saw Bennett was leaning his shoulder against the opposite wall.

He straightened when he saw her. "Delphine," he greeted with a slight bow. "I have come to escort you to the library."

"Have you been waiting for long?"

"Not long," Bennett replied. "But I would wait until the end of time to be able to escort such a lovely lady to the library."

She arched an eyebrow. "Please say that line has not worked before."

"I don't know. I have never tried it on a young woman before," Bennett said with a cocky grin.

"I would retire that phrase," she encouraged.

"Duly noted, my lady," Bennett said as he offered his arm. "Just so you know, most women are flattered when offered such praises."

Delphine placed her hand on his arm and replied, "But I am not like most women. I prefer when a man is genuine in his affection."

"Who says I wasn't genuine?" Bennett asked with a wink.

She laughed. "Are you ever serious?"

Bennett's face grew solemn. "I can be," he said in a deep voice. "I am serious Bennett now. I will only respond in a tone that proves how serious I can be."

"You are a fool," she joked.

His hand flew up to his chest, feigning outrage. "I am no fool and I find great insult in your accusing me of such. I am an earl and I demand respect."

"My apologies, my lord," she responded. "I meant no disrespect calling you a fool."

"Good, because serious men- such as myself- do not like being teased," Bennett said. "We prefer stimulating conversations about how clever and important we are."

Delphine couldn't help but smile at this ridiculous conversation. Why could Bennett make her smile like no one else ever could? It was nearly impossible to not be in a pleasant mood when speaking to him.

And in that moment, she realized something she hadn't anticipated: she had developed the tiniest of feelings for this man.

Chapter Six

As Bennett led Delphine into the library, she let out a slight gasp as she beheld the grandeur of the room. Bookshelves lined the walls, and sunlight streamed in through two large windows, casting a gentle glow across the room.

Delphine came to a stop in the center of the room, her hands stretched out wide. "There are so many books here," she said. "I do not think I have ever seen such an enormous library before."

"I daresay that you are easy to impress," Bennett teased, secretly pleased with her reaction. He had always loved this room and spent every opportunity that he could in it.

Walking over to one of the bookshelves, Delphine ran her hand along the spines and asked, "What book shall I select?"

"Any one that strikes your fancy, I suppose."

A mischievous glint came into Delphine's eyes. "Are there any books written by ladies in here?"

Bennett nodded. "Despite my father's objections on women writers, his collection does boast many of them."

"What about the ones that were written by 'A Lady'?"

"I doubt those two books are in here," Bennett replied. "More than likely they are in my sisters' bedchambers."

Delphine turned her attention back towards the books. "This library puts mine to shame," she said.

"It isn't a contest," he joked.

"Perhaps not, but there are so many first editions in here," Delphine said as she pulled out a book and inspected it.

Bennett stepped closer to her but was mindful to maintain a proper distance. "My grandmother was an avid reader. She felt reading a book a day led to her longevity."

Delphine looked at him in disbelief. "A book a day? Surely, you jest."

"She did little else but read," Bennett admitted. "I have never seen a woman devour so many books."

A wistful look came into Delphine's eyes. "I wish I had the time to read as much as your grandmother. I feel as if I am in constant meetings with my man of business, stewards, land agents, and tenants."

"I am sure you can delegate some of those meetings to others," Bennett encouraged.

Delphine shook her head. "I am fanatical when it comes to knowing the minute details of my business since I am ultimately responsible for my successes or failures."

Bennett found himself nodding in agreement with Delphine's philosophy, understanding the consequences of becoming too complacent with one's business.

Leaning his shoulder against the bookshelf, he confided, "Recently, we discovered that our man of business was stealing from us. He was taking the money meant for the upkeep of the village and squandering it on gambling and other bad business deals." He paused. "If it wasn't for my cousin who discovered his deceit, he could have ruined us."

"That is one of my fears, to place trust in the wrong person," Delphine shared.

Without hesitation, he declared, "You can trust me."

Delphine smiled and it spilled over into her eyes. "I do,"

she said. "Perhaps it has something to do with you saving my life."

Bennett couldn't resist puffing out his chest slightly. "I don't often get to save a damsel in distress, but when I do, I do it well."

"Well, the doctor told me how close I came to dying so I do believe I owe you my life," Delphine said.

"As I have said before, you owe me nothing," Bennett insisted. "I am so grateful that I was there to help you."

"I think it goes without saying but so am I," Delphine responded.

Bennett brought up his hand and rubbed his chin thoughtfully. "By saving your life, do I get three wishes?"

Delphine's laughter filled the room, a joyous sound that warmed his heart. "That is only if you save a genie," she said.

"My mistake," Bennett responded, dropping his hand. "But I do have something I want you to do for me."

"What is it?"

Bennett glanced at the open door. "I think I would like to play a joke on Elodie, assuming you have no objections."

Delphine turned to face him. "What do you have in mind?"

In a low voice, Bennett replied, "You have certain traditions in Scotland, do you not?"

"We do," Delphine replied. "My father was insistent that I grew up knowing our heritage."

"What if we played into those traditions?" Bennett asked.

A line between Delphine's brow appeared. "Meaning?"

Bennett leaned forward and replied, "What if I brought in a bagpiper to regale us with music every morning? Perhaps just outside of Elodie's window- say at dawn?"

Delphine looked unsure. "Would she not get angry with us?"

"Not if we said it was to help you recover your memories," Bennett replied. "Besides, Elodie has been relentless in following us around. She is even outside in the corridor as we speak."

Shifting her gaze towards the door, Delphine asked, "How do you know?"

"I saw her peeking in just a moment ago," Bennett replied. "I think it is time to teach her a lesson."

"I do not wish to upset Elodie since she has been so kind to me," Delphine said.

"Trust me. My sister is many things, but she does have an excellent sense of humor. Like me. I am constantly being told how amusing I am."

Delphine grinned. "Who are these people?" she asked. "I only wonder because it sounds as if they are imaginary."

Bennett chuckled. "I do not have imaginary friends. At least, not anymore."

"But you had them?"

"Not exactly, but I wanted one," Bennett replied. "My nursemaid once told me a story about how our ancestors roamed the halls of our home, and I was adamant about wanting to see them. I set up a fort in the corridor where all the family's portraits are hung and waited for one of them to appear. But they never came. Night after night went by and I didn't see one ghost."

"I take it that you gave up."

"Only because my parents refused to let me keep the fort in the corridor and gave my nursemaid a stern reprimand," Bennett said. "I was disappointed, though. I have never seen a ghost, but I do believe they exist."

Delphine shuddered. "I have no desire to see a ghost."

"Not even if it was a family member?" Bennett asked. "What of your mother?"

She grew silent. "It would be nice to see my mother again."

Bennett's lips twitched. "What if we built a fort and wait to see if your mother appears?" he suggested.

"Why would she appear at your country estate?"

"Why not?" Bennett asked. "She might want to meet me."

Delphine gave him an amused look. "If ghosts are real- and I'm not saying they are- why would my mother want to meet you when she could meet anyone from the beginning of time?"

Bennett smirked. "Because, my dear, I saved your life. And that makes me the most important person in your life."

"You are far too cocky, my lord," Delphine remarked.

"Am I?" Bennett asked. "I think I am the right amount of cockiness for an earl, especially one that is as handsome as me."

Delphine rolled her eyes. "Now you have passed the cockiness threshold. I would curtail it a bit."

Bennett held her gaze. "But you didn't deny that I was handsome."

"You are… adequate," Delphine replied.

"Merely adequate?" Bennett asked. "I did save your life. Should that not count for something?"

Delphine pressed her lips together before saying, "Fine, my lord. Some might consider you handsome enough to tempt them."

"Are you one of those people?"

An adorable blush came to Delphine's cheeks as she ducked her head. "I would prefer if we spoke about books since we are in the library."

Bennett decided to take pity on Delphine, even though he very much hoped that she found him attractive. For she had beguiled him by her beauty. But it wasn't just her beauty that tempted him. No, it was much more than that. It was her kindness, her determination, and the way she made everything that much more enjoyable.

Remaining close, Bennett reached for a book and held it up. "What of this book?"

Delphine brought her gaze back up and studied it. "I do not think I should read a book on religion."

"Whyever not?"

"Women are supposed to avoid certain topics…"

Bennett spoke over her. "Do you intend to obey all of the rules of high Society?"

"Well, no, but…"

"Read the book, Delphine," Bennett urged. "Who cares what Society says is appropriate to read? The more you read, the more questions arise, encouraging you to seek out the truth."

Delphine accepted the book with a thoughtful look. "Do you promise not to tell?"

"Who would I tell, Delphie?"

Her eyes widened. "My mother used to call me that," she said softly.

"I could use another nickname," Bennett suggested. "Lina, Phin, Delly, Fifi…"

Delphine put a hand on his sleeve, stilling his words. "I would prefer if you called me Delphie," she said. "Besides, those other nicknames are awful, especially Fifi."

"I know. I was trying too hard," Bennett said.

"What of you?" Delphine asked. "Do you have a nickname?"

Bennett shrugged. "You could call me Ben, Bennie, or En."

Delphine studied him for a moment as she removed her hand. "I think I shall keep calling you Bennett. It suits you."

Letting out a sigh of relief, Bennett said, "Good, because all of my suggestions of nicknames were awful."

"Why did you suggest them then?"

"For fun," Bennett replied with a smile. "You could always call me your hero. Or Lord of Handsomeness."

Delphine let out a huff. "You are relentless, my lord."

"Relentlessly handsome?" Bennett asked.

"Good heavens, you must be drunk." Delphine tsked. "And at such an early hour, my lord."

"Only drunk on you," Bennett bantered with a flirtatious smile.

Delphine made a face. "That was awful. Truly awful," she declared. "I think I would rather tour the library on my own."

Bennett straightened and took a step back. "Very well," he said. "But I need to set our plans in motion."

"What plans?"

"You are about to be transported back into Scotland," Bennett said with an exaggerated bow. "And I assure you that it will be spectacular."

Delphine held her hand up. "Wait," she said. "What if we start small? Perhaps invite a bagpiper to join us over dinner first."

Bennett bobbed his head. "Good idea. I will see what I can do."

As Bennett departed from the library, he wasn't quite sure what ideas he wanted to implement but he hoped his plan would goad Elodie. He could see her peeking out of a closet at him, and he didn't bother to acknowledge her.

The sun streamed in through the windows of the library as Delphine read her book on the religions of the world. It was fascinating to learn about other people's beliefs.

Elodie entered the room and Delphine promptly closed the book, finding herself feeling embarrassed at being caught reading such a book.

With a curious look, Elodie asked, "Dare I ask what you were reading?"

"Nothing of note," Delphine replied hastily.

Elodie approached her, looking unconcerned. "If you were reading a naughty book, I promise I won't tell."

"What is a 'naughty book'?" Delphine asked.

As she sat down on a chair, Elodie lowered her voice and replied, "Anything where kissing or other things are discussed."

Delphine lifted her brow. "What do you know about 'other things'?"

"Not much, considering no one speaks about such things, but I have read a book or two on anatomy," Elodie replied. "I do believe I got the gist of it."

"I'm afraid I know nothing about such things," Delphine admitted.

Elodie glanced down at the book in her hand. "Then, pray tell, what were you reading that caused you to act so squeamish?"

Delphine decided to just tell her the truth and be done with it. She held up the book. "It is a book on the various religions of the world."

"Is that all?" Elodie asked. "I have read that book before and it is not the least bit scandalous."

"Your father lets you read these books?"

Elodie grinned. "No, but my father doesn't always know what I am up to."

Delphine turned her head towards the bookshelves that were filled with books. "I find that I am rather envious of all the books that your family has acquired over the years. I daresay that my library is lacking at home."

"Why have you not acquired more books?"

"I suppose it hasn't been a priority since I have been so busy tending to my other tasks," Delphine admitted.

"Is there anything more important than reading?" Elodie asked. "It transports me to another place, another time, where I am not so odd."

Delphine could hear the sadness in her voice, prompting her to say, "You are not odd."

"I am, but thank you for saying so," Elodie said. "It is hard being the way I am when Melody is so perfect."

"No one is perfect."

Elodie sighed. "Melody and I may look alike but that is where the similarities stop. Melody acts the part of a proper lady and I do not. There are too many things that I want to do with my life to give it all up by getting married."

"I understand that feeling all too well," Delphine said.

"I know you do, which is why I feel comfortable telling you such things," Elodie remarked. "When we go to Town for the Season, I will be dressed up and paraded around as if I am merely on display."

Delphine offered her an encouraging smile. "Do not fret. I will be there as well."

"Yes, but you are a countess with your own fortune," Elodie said. "If I do not marry- and well- I am nothing."

Moving to the edge of her seat, Delphine held Elodie's gaze. "That is rubbish. You are more than just a debutante seeking a groom. You have so much to offer the world. You just have to discover what that is."

Elodie gave her a weak smile. "Thank you, but you are the lucky one. You don't have to marry to have a future."

"Some people do find happiness within the bounds of marriage," Delphine said. "Don't discount what you do not know."

"I would rather be ridiculously wealthy and not have to answer to anyone."

Delphine laughed. "Wouldn't that be nice? But everyone answers to someone; even our king does."

A knock came at the door, interrupting their conversation.

Bennett stepped into the room and bowed. "Pardon the interruption but pall-mall has been set up on the lawn."

Elodie jumped up from her seat. "What fun! I haven't played pall-mall in ages."

Rising, Delphine asked, "Do you think that is wise if I play?"

"I do," Bennett replied. "But just as a precaution, I asked the servants to place extra chairs around the lawn so you may sit at any point."

"That is most thoughtful of you," Delphine acknowledged.

Bennett approached her and offered his arm. "May I escort you to the lawn, my lady?" he asked.

Delphine moved to put the book onto the table before placing a hand on his sleeve. "You may."

In a low voice, Bennett asked in a teasing voice, "How did you enjoy reading such a scandalous book?"

"It was rather informative," Delphine admitted.

Elodie spoke up. "I need to go retrieve a bonnet from my bedchamber. I will meet you on the lawn," she said before hurrying out of the room.

As Bennett led them into the corridor, Delphine said, "Elodie is an intriguing person."

"That is one word for it," Bennett quipped.

"No, I am serious," Delphine remarked. "I do believe she is trying her best, and you should try to support her."

Bennett glanced over at her. "Where is this coming from?"

Delphine didn't want to betray Elodie's confidences, so she was careful to skirt around the truth. "We had a conversation, and I am beginning to see her for who she truly is."

"She is a hoyden, but she does have a good heart," Bennett said.

"That she does and I hope you don't put too much pressure on her to wed," Delphine stated.

Bennett came to a stop in the corridor and turned to face her. "I do not care if Elodie weds."

"You don't?" Delphine asked.

He shook his head. "I only care that my sister is happy. If she chooses to be a spinster, I shall support her decision."

Delphine stared deep into Bennett's eyes and saw that he was in earnest. "I believe you," she said. "You are a good brother and so different than the other men of the *ton*."

"I am flattered that you think so," he responded.

While they descended the stairs, Delphine shared, "My cousin, Vincent, is truly awful. He has been trying to contest my title for as long as I can remember, and before that, it was his father. He smiles to my face but would gladly put a dagger in my back if given the chance."

"On what grounds does Vincent contest your position as heir?"

Delphine blew out a puff of air. "It is simply because I am a woman. No one has given them much heed, but they keep trying, nevertheless."

"Well, if you require a barrister, I can highly recommend my brother," Bennett said.

"It has not come to that… yet. But the future is uncertain."

Bennett regarded her with a pensive expression. "Would it help if you secured an heir?"

Delphine's lips formed a slight frown as she replied, "It would help, but I am not quite ready to marry. I have so much that I want to do with my life first. A husband, or child, would be an imposition at this point. Quite frankly, I am content on my own, at least for now."

In a reflective tone, Bennett said, "I used to think that way- and still do, at times. But I do find myself feeling lonely on occasion. It would be nice to truly trust someone, to let them in, and be utterly devoted to one another."

"I do not wish to offend you but that sounds like a fairy tale," Delphine stated. "Love is easily corruptible."

Bennett chuckled. "You are quite the naysayer."

"No, I am a pragmatist."

As he led her out the main door that was being held open by a footman, Bennett leaned closer and joked, "Perhaps you should write a book and use that line as the title."

Delphine felt her lips curl into a smile. "I know you believe in the mystical force called love, but it is just that- 'mystical.'"

"Love is real," Bennett said firmly. "You just haven't met the one you can't live without."

"I could not disagree with you more," Delphine argued. "I have only seen unhappy marriages, including my parents'. The mere thought of love matches is utterly preposterous."

Bennett seemed to consider her words thoughtfully before responding, "I want to marry my best friend. A woman who makes me want to be a better man. Someone who I can talk about my day and laugh with. An equal in every way." He paused, his gaze piercing. "If you did have a chance at love, would you fight for it?"

Delphine was taken aback by the raw emotion that Bennett displayed, and she hoped that he would find someone who shared his passion and ideals about love. But it couldn't be her. She didn't believe in love- or at least that is what she kept telling herself.

Feeling a need to lighten the conversation, she patted Bennett's sleeve gently. "Perhaps it is you that should write a book. I must say that your take on love would be much more appealing than mine."

Bennett let out a heavy sigh. "If I did write a book, it would be extremely popular and I am not sure if I am ready for that type of notoriety."

"Of course not, my lord," Delphine said as her eyes scanned over the expansive lawn. True to Bennett's word, there were chairs spread throughout the lawn, including one next to each arch that had been set up.

"Will that be enough chairs?" Bennett asked.

Delphine slipped her hand off his arm as she turned to face him. "It might be too many chairs."

"One can never be too prepared," Bennett said.

She couldn't help but notice a red-haired young woman standing next to Elodie and Melody and she was stretching with a mallet in her hand.

Bennett followed her gaze. "That is Miss Bawden. She is the eldest daughter of our dear vicar."

"What is she doing?"

"I would think it is fairly obvious," Bennett replied. "She is stretching."

Delphine pressed her lips together. "But, why?"

Bennett shrugged. "I don't rightly know, but she has been doing so since we were little. I should warn you that she is very competitive."

"That is not the least bit surprising since she is stretching for a game of pall-mall," Delphine remarked.

Turning his head towards the manor, Bennett said, "But you need to prepare yourself when my brother arrives. A game with Miss Bawden and my brother never ends well."

"Then why did you arrange this game?"

A boyish grin came to Bennett's lips. "Oh, I assure you that it is quite entertaining for the rest of us."

"You are awful," Delphine murmured.

"Trust me, you are in for a fun-filled afternoon." Bennett gestured towards a chair. "Would you care to sit while I select a mallet for you?"

Delphine was about to refuse but she had to admit that she was rather tired. Rather than fight Bennett on this, she decided to graciously accept his offer. "Thank you, Benny."

"Benny?" he repeated. "It almost sounds as if you are calling me a bunny. I thought we decided that we would stick with my given name."

"We did, but I was just trying something out," Delphine said.

Bennett's eyes held amusement as he replied, "I do enjoy how much you are trying, but you must let it come naturally."

"Like you do?"

"Precisely," Bennett replied. "Now, do you have a specific color of mallet that you would prefer?"

"I do not," she replied.

Bennett held her gaze a moment longer than would be considered proper, but she didn't mind. She rather enjoyed admiring his blue eyes. They held a warmth to them that made her want to linger there.

"Delphine!" Elodie shouted.

Turning her head, she watched as Elodie, Melody and Miss Bawden approached them. They came to a stop in front of her and Elodie gestured towards Miss Bawden. "Lady Dunrobin, may I introduce Miss Bawden, our dear friend."

Miss Bawden dropped into a curtsy. "My lady."

Delphine tipped her head in response. "It is a pleasure to meet you," she said. "I have heard that you are rather competitive in pall-mall."

"It is true, but my lucky blue mallet let me down a few weeks ago," Miss Bawden shared, holding up the mallet. "Lord Dunsby and I lost to Lord Hilgrove and Edwina by one point."

"You have a lucky mallet?" Delphine inquired.

Miss Bawden bobbed her head. "I do, but I do not think it is magical anymore."

Delphine shifted her gaze to Elodie and Melody since she was not quite sure what to make of Miss Bawden. Was she in earnest?

Melody gave her an understanding look. "I assure you that Miss Bawden is not mad, but she is rather serious about pall-mall."

Before she could respond, Miss Bawden let out a groan. "You didn't tell me that Lord Winston was playing today."

Elodie gave her a look filled with innocence. "Didn't I?" she asked. "That must have slipped my mind."

Delphine turned her head to see Winston approaching, and by the look on his face, he didn't seem pleased to see Miss Bawden either.

Chapter Seven

Standing on the front lawn where the pall-mall course was set up, Bennett addressed the assembled group with grandiosity. "The game to end all games shall commence forthwith!"

Elodie did not look the least bit amused. "Aren't you being a tad bit overdramatic? It is a game of pall-mall, not an innovative scientific discovery."

"Only a tad bit?" Winston muttered under his breath.

Bennett smiled. "We need to prove to Delphine that we are a fun family."

"If you have to try to convince her of such a thing, then perhaps we aren't truly a 'fun family,'" Melody remarked. "We might just be an 'adequately fun' family."

From her seated position, Delphine's lips curled into a smile. "I think your family is delightful."

"Just delightful?" Bennett asked, feigning disappointment.

"Is that not enough?" Delphine inquired.

Bennett held her gaze and brought his hand up to cover the side of his mouth. In a hushed voice, he asked, "It is because of Winston, isn't it? He is far too serious and lacks the ability to have fun."

Winston looked heavenward. "I can hear you, Brother."

"Good! At least we know your hearing is impeccable," Bennett quipped. "But you will need to work on being more fun."

"I can be fun," Winston declared.

Bennett put his hand up in surrender. "I believe you. Although, I haven't seen a lot of fun out of you since you started working as a barrister."

Winston selected a mallet and asked, "Can we please play pall-mall and end this ridiculous conversation?"

"Of course," Bennett replied. "I thought it would be best if we played in pairs. I will partner with Delphine, assuming that is all right with her."

"It is," Delphine said as her eyes lit up. Or had he just imagined that? He hoped not. He found that he greatly wanted to partner with her for this game.

Bennett nodded in approval. "Good. Now who else—"

Elodie cut him off and announced, "I will partner with Melody!"

Turning his attention towards Miss Bawden and Winston, Bennett said, "That just leaves you two."

Miss Bawden exchanged a look of disdain with Winston before saying, "As much as I would love to partner with Lord Winston, I think it might be best if we partner with someone else."

Winston cleared his throat. "I must agree with Miss Bawden. We have tried being partners before and it did not end well."

"No, it did not," Miss Bawden admitted. "I do believe the game ended when my mallet 'accidentally' hit Lord Winston."

Winston rubbed his arm. "Yes, I remember that day rather clearly, and I do not recall it being an accident."

"In my defense, I wasn't aiming at you," Miss Bawden said.

"That is your defense?" Winston asked incredulously. "Why were you throwing a mallet in the first place?"

Miss Bawden tilted her chin stubbornly. "You could have moved out of the way, my lord," she said dryly.

Bennett was about to interrupt their spat when Melody spoke first. "I will partner with Miss Bawden."

A look of relief came to Miss Bawden's face. "Thank you, Lady Melody," she murmured.

Winston moved to stand by Elodie, nudging her with his right arm. "Which means we are partners. I do hope you won't throw a mallet at me."

"The day is still young," Elodie said, her lips curled up into a smile. "But I am playing to win, Brother."

"As am I," Winston assured her.

Elodie didn't quite look convinced but she didn't press the issue. "Shall we begin?"

Bennett clasped his hands together and declared, "Let the game begin!" He hurried over to Delphine and offered his arm to assist her in rising.

"Thank you," she murmured.

Leaning closer, Bennett said, "I hope you are prepared for this."

Delphine offered him a baffled look. "Whatever do you mean?"

"Our games of pall-mall can get rather intense," Bennett warned. "They are not for the faint of heart."

"But it is just a game," Delphine attempted.

Bennett huffed. "Just a game?" he repeated. "Dear heavens, you are not ready for this. Perhaps you should go inside and work on your needlework over a cup of tea."

Delphine's eyes grew determined. "I assure you that I can handle a game of pall-mall with your family."

"So say you," Bennett said.

Elodie's voice broke through their conversation. "Are you two quite finished conversing? We have a game that we must play and it is Delphine's turn."

Bennett hoped the look he gave Delphine conveyed that he told her so. "Run, Delphine. Run," he teased.

Holding up her mallet, Delphine brushed past him to where the first arch was set. She positioned herself near the ball and brought the mallet back. In a smooth motion, she hit the ball and it soared right past the arch.

Delphine winced. "I'm sorry, Bennett. That wasn't my finest shot."

"No need to apologize," Bennett said as he came closer to her. "I anticipated this and I am prepared to play like I have never played before."

Elodie lifted her brow. "What words are you mincing? Are you drunk?"

Delphine giggled. "I asked him the same thing earlier."

"Will you just hit your ball so Winston and I can beat you two already?" Elodie asked.

Bennett approached his ball and asked, "What is your hurry?"

"I do not wish to lollygag on the lawn all afternoon when I have very important things to do later," Elodie said.

"Dare I ask what those things are?" Winston asked.

Elodie didn't look the least bit ashamed as she revealed, "A nap."

"That is your important thing to do today?" Winston inquired.

With a slight shrug, Elodie said, "Naps are very important. I am a much happier person with a daily nap."

Winston shuddered. "I would hate to see you without a nap then."

Bennett made a few practice swings with the mallet before he stepped forward and lined the ball up with the arch. With practiced ease, he hit the ball and it sailed through the arch. He held up his mallet in triumph.

"Calm down, Brother," Melody teased, "you hit the ball

through the arch. It wasn't as if you defeated Napoleon single-handedly."

"It was an impressive shot," Bennett declared.

Delphine clapped her hands together. "It was a fine shot."

Bennett saw that Delphine was standing and he gestured towards a footman to bring her a chair.

A footman rushed to do his bidding and moved a chair next to Delphine. She murmured her gratitude before she sat down. Another footman stepped forward with a parasol to shade her from the sun.

Melody approached Bennett and asked in a low voice, "Why are there so many chairs on the lawn?"

"For Delphine, of course," Bennett replied.

"Yes, but the sheer number of chairs on the lawn is almost comical," Melody remarked.

Bennett shifted his gaze towards Delphine and saw that she was watching the game of pall-mall unfold. A small smile was on her lips and he found himself transfixed. He loved nothing more than seeing Delphine smile.

"Brother," Melody said, her voice breaking through his thoughts. "Did you hear me?"

Tearing his gaze away from Delphine, he replied, "I did not."

Melody glanced at Delphine, a knowing look gracing her expression. "I asked if I could sit on one of the chairs. Or are they all reserved for Delphine?"

"They are for everyone to enjoy," Bennett said.

"Thank you," Melody remarked before she went to hit her ball.

Bennett walked over to where Delphine sat and crouched down next to her. "Are you comfortable?"

"I am," Delphine replied. "Thank you for seeing to all of this. Although, truth be told, it seems rather extravagant."

"It is no less than you deserve," Bennett said.

Delphine glanced at the footman that was holding the

parasol. "You are much too kind, considering I could have done with a lot less."

"Indeed, but I couldn't risk you nearly fainting again," Bennett said. "Unless that was your nefarious plan to get me to carry you to your room."

"You found me out, my lord," Delphine said with a grin.

Bennett leaned closer and studied her face, looking for any sign of discomfort. "Are you thirsty? Hungry?" he asked.

"If I am, you do not need to trouble yourself. I know where the refreshment table is," Delphine replied.

"Very well, but you must promise me that you will not overtax yourself," Bennett said.

Delphine nodded. "I shall be careful."

Rising, Bennett was about to walk away when Delphine continued. "Thank you, Bennett. I can't remember the last time that someone showed me such care."

Bennett bowed. "It is my pleasure, my lady."

As he held her gaze, he couldn't help but admire the brown flecks in her eyes, feeling as if her soul was staring deep into his. Somehow, she could hold him there, just with her gaze, mesmerizing him. She was so beautiful to him. And he couldn't help but wonder what it would be like to court her.

But he had no intention of doing so.

Delphine had no desire to marry for the time being, and neither did he.

So why couldn't he stop staring at her?

Winston cleared his throat, drawing his attention. "It is Delphine's turn," he revealed. "If we wish to finish before Elodie's nap time, we must hurry this along."

Delphine rose from her seat and picked up her mallet. She walked over to her ball and hit it towards the nearest arch, but it stopped short of it.

"That was awful," Bennett declared.

"As I told you- multiple times- I have not played this game

in ages," Delphine said, not showing a hint of embarrassment for her poorly aligned shot.

Melody offered Delphine an encouraging look. "Do not get discouraged. This game is meant to be fun."

"Fun?" Bennett asked. "No, this game is a serious competition meant to weed out the weaklings."

"Then why are you playing?" Winston quipped. "I heard you lost your last match to Miles and Edwina."

"I did, but that was intentional. I wanted Miles to win so he would dance the first set with Edwina," Bennett revealed.

Winston arched an eyebrow. "You- deliberately losing a game?" he asked. "That doesn't sound like you."

"Well, my plan worked brilliantly since Edwina and Miles are happily married now," Bennett said.

Elodie yawned. "If you do not take your turn this instant, I shall pull two chairs together and take a nap."

Bennett moved to take his next shot, knowing his sister would not hesitate to do such a thing.

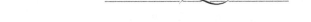

The maid had just finished styling Delphine's hair when the dinner bell rang, beckoning everyone to the drawing room.

Rising, Delphine murmured her thanks as she reached for her gloves. She put them on and took a moment to admire herself in the mirror. She was mindful to take extra time with her appearance this evening, but it had nothing to do with Bennett. At least, that is what she kept telling herself. But even she knew that she couldn't fathom that lie.

Her feelings were starting to deepen for Bennett and becoming deucedly inconvenient. How could she not care for such a man? He had shown her nothing but kindness, wanting nothing in return. He was patient, compassionate and had opened his home to her. He was a rarity amongst the other gentlemen she was acquainted with.

But once she recovered from her injuries, she would return home until the Season. At least she could see him in Town. Not that anything would come from that. The hard part was that she would be forced to watch the women fall all over themselves when they saw Bennett. She had no doubt that he would be one of the Season's most eligible bachelors.

The maid took a step back and asked, "Will there be anything else, my lady?"

Delphine offered her a weak smile. "Not at this time. Thank you," she replied as she walked towards the door.

As she opened the door, she saw Bennett leaning against the opposite wall as he adjusted his black jacket sleeve. He stood up straight when he saw her.

"Delphie," he greeted with a slight bow.

She smiled. "Bennett," she said. "What a pleasant surprise. I must assume you are here to escort me down to the drawing room."

"I am." His eyes perused the length of her, and in them, she saw approval. Never had she felt more beautiful. Never had she wanted to look so beautiful. "You look lovely," he said.

Delphine could feel her cheeks grow warm at his praise, but she worked hard to appear unaffected. "Thank you," she murmured.

Bennett stepped forward and offered his arm. "I do think there should be a law against you looking this beautiful."

After she took a moment to compose herself, she replied, "Flattery, my lord?" She was pleased that her voice sounded so steady, unlike the beating of her heart.

"It is merely the truth," he said. "I have no doubt that your mere presence will cause quite the stir amongst the *ton*."

Delphine placed her hand on his sleeve. "I will only be there for my friend, Charlotte."

"You say that now, but the gentlemen will be lined up to dance with you, including me," Bennett said.

"You wish to dance with me?"

"Why wouldn't I?" he asked. "I would never complain about having such a beautiful woman in my arms."

Delphine eyed him curiously. "You are far too complimentary this evening. What do you want, my lord?"

Bennett brought his arm to his chest, feigning innocence. "Can a gentleman not compliment you without wanting something else in return?"

"In my experience, no. People always want something from me," Delphine admitted. "I suppose it is the same for you."

His expression grew reflective. "It is. That is the burden of being in our positions."

Delphine kept her gaze straight ahead as she said, "That is why it has been so nice to be around your family. You understand the burdens that I must bear alone."

"You don't have to bear those burdens alone," Bennett said. "I would be more than happy to assist you in any way I can."

"But you have your own problems to deal with."

Bennett came to a stop and gently turned her to face him. "I consider you a friend, Delphie. And friends help one another."

Friends.

Why did her heart stutter at that word? That is what she wanted. So why did it sound so wrong?

Knowing he was still waiting for a response, she said, "I feel the same about you." There. That was at least true. She wanted him in her life, and she was willing to take him as a friend.

He leaned closer as he held her gaze. "I find that I do want something from you."

"You do?" She wasn't sure if she should feel disappointment or not.

Bennett's lips quirked. "I feel it is my duty to tell you that your pall-mall skills could use some work. You should practice more."

A laugh escaped her lips. "Is that all?" she asked. "I thought you were going to ask for something more pertinent."

"From you, no. All I want is for you to be happy."

"Why?"

A line between his brow appeared. "Why would I want you to be happy?" he ventured. "Is this one of those impossible questions that women ask? The ones that have no right answer? My mother warned me about those."

Delphine placed a hand on his sleeve. "What I am attempting to say, but failing miserably, is that you have been so kind to me. And you have wanted nothing in return. Why is that?"

Understanding dawned on his features. "I hope in this home that you have had a reprieve from your burdens- even for a moment."

"I have," she replied. "I hope you know how truly blessed you are to have such a loving family as yours."

"You say that now, but Elodie and Winston will no doubt be more irritating this evening after their win," Bennett said.

Bennett was so close that Delphine could smell his orange shaving soap, but she had no objections. She rather liked him this close. It seemed familiar.

But he must not have felt the same because he took her hand and placed it into the crook of his arm. "Shall we join my family before they come looking for us?"

"I think that is a wise idea," she replied.

As Bennett led her down the stairs, he glanced over at her. "Do you have any fond childhood memories?"

Delphine considered his question before sharing, "When I was younger, I used to beg for a dog. I wanted to hold it in my arms and take it everywhere with me. My parents didn't think I was old enough for the responsibility of a puppy, but I was relentless."

"I take it that you got a dog," he said knowingly.

"Yes, but it only took me a few hours before I realized I couldn't keep the dog. My eyes turned red and I couldn't stop sneezing whenever I was around it," Delphine shared. "It was awful, and I was so disappointed."

Bennett offered her an apologetic smile. "That must have been difficult for you."

"My father- in a rare showing of emotion- brought me a baby goat that had been rejected by her mother," Delphine said. "He showed me how to feed it and care for it. We became the best of friends and Luna would follow me everywhere I would go."

"You named the goat 'Luna'?"

She shrugged. "What else would you name a goat?"

"I suppose I haven't given it much thought, but I doubt I would name it after the moon," Bennett replied.

"Luna will still run to the fence to see me, despite making new friends when we reintroduced her to the other goats," Delphine said.

Bennett chuckled as they stepped into the drawing room. "Besides Charlotte and Luna, do you have any other friends?"

"Is that not sufficient?" Delphine asked. "Besides, now I can count you as a friend as well."

"Yes, you can."

Delphine glanced around the room and saw that they were the first ones there. "How is it that we are the first to arrive?"

As she finished saying her words, the butler stepped into the room and held up a paper. He cleared his throat. "May I announce the arrival of the winners of the pall-mall game this afternoon," he started. "Lord Winston, the brave, and the very talented, and equally witty, Lady Elodie."

"Oh, brother," Bennett muttered.

Elodie swept into the room on Winston's arm, her head held high. "I do believe that was a fitting tribute to our accomplishment this afternoon."

"You won one game, Sister," Bennett remarked dryly. "You might want to calm down on the high-handedness."

"I do believe that is one more game than you have won," Elodie quipped.

Bennett turned to Delphine and whispered, "I did warn you."

Elodie's eyes roamed over the room and disappointment flickered in her eyes. "I knew we should have waited," she said. "Perhaps we should make our entrance when everyone else arrives."

Winston shook his head. "I am not going to do that again, considering I didn't want to do it the first time."

"You are no fun," Elodie teased.

Melody and Lady Dallington stepped into the room, both wearing bright smiles on their faces. "I do hope you haven't waited for long. Melody and I were discussing the food for the soiree that we are hosting in three days' time."

"What soiree?" Elodie asked.

Lady Dallington waved a hand towards Delphine. "The one for Delphine, of course," she said. "We couldn't very well have her leave us without a soiree to honor her."

"That is not necessary—" Delphine started.

Speaking over her, Lady Dallington asserted, "It is entirely necessary, and the invitations have already been sent out."

Bennett frowned. "Do you think that is wise, considering Delphine is still recovering from her injuries?"

"Every day, Delphine is growing stronger, and it isn't as if she has to dance the night away," Lady Dallington replied. "She can remain seated and have the guests flock to her."

Delphine had no desire to attend a soiree in her honor, but she didn't dare be rude to Lady Dallington. No, she couldn't do that, especially since she looked rather pleased with herself.

Bennett crossed his arms over his chest. "I wish you would have at least asked Delphine if she wanted this."

Lady Dallington gave him a blank look, as if she couldn't quite make sense of what he was saying. "Who wouldn't wish to have a party in their honor? There will be dancing, conversation, and food. Loads of food."

Delphine smiled. "I consider it a great honor, my lady. Thank you." She hoped her words sounded somewhat convincing.

Lord Dallington entered the room and kissed his wife on her cheek. "Good evening, Dearest," he said. "I am famished. Is dinner ready?"

"It is," Lady Dallington confirmed.

As they started to file out of the room, Bennett offered his arm to Delphine. "You are a terrible liar," he said in a hushed voice. "You no more want this soiree than a rock in your boot."

Delphine wondered how Bennett had been able to see right through her. "Was it so obvious?"

"It was to me, but I do not fault you for it," he said. "My mother loves any reason to throw a party. One time, she threw a party because the flowers bloomed early in the season."

"I dislike social events. Yet I attend far too many of them for my liking," Delphine shared. "It is the curse of our positions in Society."

Their conversation came to a halt when they stepped into the dining room. Bennett dropped his arm and pulled out her chair. Once she was situated, he claimed the seat next to her and reached for his napkin.

Winston sat on the other side of her and leaned towards her. "You played magnificently at pall-mall today."

"You are much too kind, my lord," Delphine said. "But I did manage to finish the game without fainting."

Melody spoke up from across the table. "That is because you had an ample number of places to sit down."

"It is true," Delphine agreed. "Bennett ensured I was well taken care of."

"He is rather thoughtful," Melody agreed.

Lady Dallington spoke up from one of the ends of the table as she addressed Delphine. "I took the liberty of sending a rider to your country estate to inform them that you are safe and being well taken care of for now. I must imagine that they are beside themselves with worry."

"Thank you, my lady," Delphine said, touched by her thoughtfulness.

The footmen began to place bowls of soup in front of them and Delphine reached for a spoon. The conversation started around her and she felt herself smile. How she loved being around the Lockwood family- even if just for a moment.

Chapter Eight

It was time. The game was afoot. Bennett leaned towards Delphine and whispered, "Are you ready?"

"For what?" she asked.

Bennett smirked. "For anything."

The footmen came to collect their empty soup bowls and Bennett tipped his head at White, informing him that he was ready for his surprise.

As White went to do his bidding, Bennett's eyes roamed over the table as he said, "As you all know, Delphine's memories of why she was in the woodlands have not returned."

His mother interjected, "There is no shame in that."

"No, there isn't," Bennett agreed. "But I spoke to Doctor Anderson and he suggested that we try to keep things as normal as possible for Delphine. Which is why I have taken the liberty of ensuring Delphine feels at home."

"That was kind of you, Brother," Elodie acknowledged.

Bennett nodded. "I am glad that you approve, considering I took the liberty of inviting Mr. Campbell to serenade us with music."

The stocky Mr. Campbell entered the room with a set of bagpipes in his hands and went to stand in the corner. He was dressed in a kilt, knee-high socks, and a jacket adorned with buttons.

Melody offered him a curious look. "A bagpiper?"

"Yes, I was most fortunate to find one from our village," Bennett replied. "Mr. Campbell has agreed to play for us while we eat a traditional Scottish meal."

"Dare I ask what that meal will be?" Elodie asked.

"Haggis," Bennett declared.

As if on cue, Elodie groaned as the footmen placed the plates of food in front of everyone.

Bennett continued, amused by Elodie's reaction. "Haggis is a savory pudding made from a blend of minced sheep's heart, liver and lungs and mixed with oatmeal, suet, onions, spices and seasonings," he shared.

With a glance at Delphine, his father asked, "You enjoy this food- this haggis?"

Delphine smiled. "I do," she replied. "It was my father's favorite meal. Many people would argue that it is our national dish."

Elodie frowned as she looked down at her plate. "I cannot eat this."

"I know it is not what you are accustomed to, but when prepared correctly, it can be quite delicious," Delphine said.

"It looks inedible," Elodie stated.

Delphine reached for her fork and took a bite of the haggis. After she swallowed, she announced, "I assure you it is quite edible."

Elodie turned towards her mother. "Could we eat something else? Anything else, really?"

His mother looked hesitant. "Bennett went through all this trouble for Delphine. We should at least try to eat the haggis."

"And once we are done, we are having Tipsy Laird for dessert," Bennett announced.

Elodie picked up her fork and started poking at the haggis. "I have had nightmares that have started very much like this."

Melody laughed. "Just try it," she encouraged. "It isn't as awful as it looks."

"You tried it?" Elodie asked.

"Yes, while you were complaining, I tried some of the meat and potatoes," Melody replied. "It is similar to some meals our cook prepared at our boarding school."

Elodie placed her fork down and reached for a piece of bread in the center of the table. "I am just fine with bread this evening."

"You will need more in your stomach if you want some Tipsy Laird," Bennett said. "The sponge cake is soaked in sherry."

Elodie winced. "I think I will pass."

Winston, who had been quiet for most of the meal, interjected, "I will eat your haggis. I rather enjoy the unique texture that is both crumbly and moist."

"You are welcome to it," Elodie said, pushing her plate away.

Bennett couldn't help but tease his sister. "You should try new things," he said. "I assure you that haggis won't kill you."

Elodie didn't quite look convinced. "I'm afraid I had my fill of sheep's liver today."

"Very well, but you must at least enjoy the soulful music of the bagpipes," Bennett said as he directed Mr. Campbell to begin.

As the music from the bagpipes filled the room, Bennett glanced at Delphine and noticed her lips slightly moving as she sang along to the song. How was it that with each passing day she grew more beautiful to him?

Bennett turned his attention to the haggis on his plate and he had to admit that Elodie was right. It did not look very appealing, but he had to try it. He picked up his fork and hoped his reluctance did not show.

He took a bite and slowly chewed the nutty and grainy texture. It wasn't as awful as he thought it would be, but he knew he would have a hard time finishing all of the food on his plate.

Delphine did not seem to have the same problem. She had started eating her haggis as her eyes remained on the bagpiper.

Once the song came to a close, Delphine clapped her hands together and announced, "That was lovely. I haven't heard *Amazing Grace* played on the bagpipes since I was little."

"Thank you, my lady," Mr. Campbell said. "I will now play a folk song."

Before Mr. Campbell could start playing again, Elodie asked, "Is it difficult to play the bagpipes?"

"It can be rather challenging for beginners, but I have been playing since I was young," Mr. Campbell replied.

Elodie perked up. "May I try?"

Mr. Campbell looked hesitant. "Women don't play the bagpipes, at least not in public, my lady."

Turning her head towards her mother, Elodie asked, "Can I learn how to play the bagpipes?"

"Absolutely not!" her father shouted, tossing down his napkin. "Did you not hear the man? A lady does not play the bagpipes."

Appearing unperturbed by her father's outburst, Elodie said, "I am proficient in the pianoforte, violin, and guitar. Why not the bagpipes?"

Delphine gave Elodie an amused look. "Bagpipes require a lot of physical energy to play. Furthermore, you would have to find someone to instruct you, which might be difficult outside of Scotland."

"Mr. Campbell can instruct me," Elodie attempted.

The bagpiper put his hand up. "I am no instructor," he replied. "My father taught me, just as he learned from his."

Her father shook his head. "You are not learning how to play the bagpipes, Elodie, and that is final."

Bennett could see the disappointment in Elodie's expression, but he had to agree with his father. A lady did not play the bagpipes, especially the daughter of a marquess.

"I assure you that playing the bagpipes is much harder than it looks," Delphine said as she addressed Elodie. "It took me quite some time to learn."

Elodie lifted her brow. "You know how to play the bagpipes?"

"I do," Delphine replied. "My grandmother taught me, but I have only ever played it in the privacy of our music room."

Bennett shifted in his chair to face Delphine. "What other talents are you hiding from us?" he asked with playful curiosity, though his question held a hint of sincerity.

Delphine shot him an amused glance. "I assure you that I am not hiding anything from you or your family."

"Does eating haggis and hearing the bagpipes help recall any of your forgotten memories?" his mother asked.

"I'm afraid not," Delphine replied. "Although, they do bring back pleasant memories for me. I haven't thought of my grandmother in quite some time."

"Then this dinner has been a success, at least in my opinion," Bennett said.

Delphine reached out and placed a hand on his sleeve. "Thank you, Bennett," she murmured. "I wish I could do something to repay your kindness."

Bennett placed his hand over hers. "Just you being here with me…" He cleared his throat, wondering where that slip of the tongue had even come from. "I mean with us, is enough for me."

"Well, I shall think of something," Delphine said.

As she withdrew her hand from under his, Bennett found that he already missed the loss of contact. What was wrong with him? She was just a friend. So why was he already thinking of other ways to make her smile?

Winston placed his fork and knife onto his plate, indicating he was done. "That was delicious."

"I am glad that you enjoyed haggis," Delphine said.

"There is a Scottish pub near my office in London that serves haggis and I eat there quite frequently," Winston admitted.

Delphine reached for her glass as she asked, "How do you enjoy being a barrister?"

"It is quite different than what I thought it would be," Winston admitted in a solemn voice.

White approached Winston with a silver tray in his hand. "A note was delivered for you, my lord."

Winston reached up and accepted it. He unfolded it and read the contents before crumpling the paper in his hand. "A word, Father."

"Right at this very moment?" his father asked.

Pushing back his chair, Winston replied, "Yes, it is of the utmost importance."

"Very well," his father replied. "We shall discuss whatever this important matter is over a glass of port."

Winston gave Bennett a pointed look. "It might be best if you joined us."

In a swift motion, Bennett rose and followed the other men out of the room. None of them spoke as they headed towards the study in the rear of the manor.

Once they stepped into the study, Winston closed the door behind him. "That note was from Jasper, the Bow Street Runner I hired to keep an eye on Isaac."

His father walked over to the drink cart and picked up the decanter. "Can this Jasper be trusted to be discreet?"

"Yes, I have used him on a few of my cases," Winston replied. "Jasper suspects that Isaac has learned of Aunt Sarah's location and is on his way to our village."

"But we have been so careful, especially of late," his father said, his hand stilling with the decanter.

"That may be true, but we need to be extra vigilant for the time being," Winston remarked. "Which is why I asked Jasper to come to the village and keep watch on Aunt Sarah."

His father poured three drinks before placing the decanter down on the tray. "I want Isaac nowhere near Sarah."

"That will be hard, considering Isaac is her husband. He has every right to take her away," Bennett acknowledged.

Picking up a glass, his father brought it to his lips while saying, "Isaac is a blackguard."

"I won't disagree with you, but you will need to keep your distance from Aunt Sarah and her son until we are sure it is safe," Bennett said.

Winston bobbed his head in agreement. "I explained Aunt Sarah's circumstances and he suggested we move her to another residence for now. I will know more once Jasper arrives tomorrow."

His father tossed back his drink and slammed the glass onto the tray. "I do not like this. Not one bit. What if I paid Isaac off to leave Sarah alone?"

"If you did such a thing, you could put Aunt Sarah at greater risk," Winston responded. "Just trust me. I will ensure your sister and son remain safe."

Bennett saw the reluctant nod of his father's head before Lord Dallington departed from the room without another word.

Winston sighed. "Father doesn't like not being in control."

"No, he does not," Bennett agreed.

"Well, I should retire for the evening," Winston said as he picked up one of the glasses of port. "I have work I need to see to."

Bennett arched an eyebrow. "You do not wish to rejoin the ladies?"

"Good gads, no," Winston huffed. "I would prefer the silence of my bedchamber to the incessant chatter of our sisters."

As Winston walked off, Bennett could almost see his brother's shoulders weighed down with burdens. His brother had always been more serious in nature than him, but now Winston seemed dreadfully unhappy.

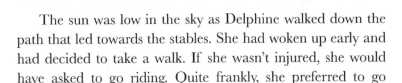

The sun was low in the sky as Delphine walked down the path that led towards the stables. She had woken up early and had decided to take a walk. If she wasn't injured, she would have asked to go riding. Quite frankly, she preferred to go riding.

As she approached the stables, a groom dropped a cloth into a bucket and asked, "Would you care to ride, my lady?"

"No, thank you," she replied. "I just wanted to come meet the horses."

The groom opened the door. "You are more than welcome. Let me know if you require any assistance."

Delphine stepped into the stables and started walking down the center aisle. There were many magnificent horses but one caught her eye above the rest. It was a black horse that was in the back stall.

"Good morning," she said in a gentle voice. She wanted to make her presence known without scaring the horse.

The horse shook its head in response.

She came to a stop in front of the stall, being mindful to keep enough distance between her and the horse. "Why is no one riding you?" she asked.

The groom spoke up from the door. "I would keep your distance from that one, my lady. Hercules is headstrong."

Delphine smiled. "I can handle headstrong." She turned her attention back towards the horse. "I have discovered your name so it is only fair that I tell you mine. It is Delphine."

Hercules' ears seemed to relax as he listened to her. He didn't seem as tense as he was when she first approached him.

She glanced down and saw a basket of apples. She reached down and selected a large red one. Holding it steady in her hand, she brought it closer to Hercules.

"Would you care for a treat?" she asked.

The horse moved closer and gobbled up the offered treat.

When the horse didn't move right away, Delphine slowly brought her hand up and gently stroked his neck. "I assure you that I am no threat to you, Hercules."

Bennett's voice came from further down the aisle. "How were you able to beguile Hercules so easily?"

"I did not beguile him," she replied as she continued to pet Hercules, "I merely bribed him with an apple."

"I have tried that before, but Hercules won't let me touch him- or anyone for that matter," Bennett said. "He was my late uncle's horse."

Delphine brushed Hercules' hair out of his eyes. "He is a beautiful horse."

"That he is," Bennett agreed, joining her by Hercules' side. "I have attempted to ride him multiple times, but with no success."

"He must miss your uncle terribly," Delphine observed.

"It is hard not to," Bennett responded. "Uncle Richard was a man that most people wished to emulate. He was strong, determined, but had the kindest heart. I hope that one day I can carry on his legacy."

Delphine turned towards Bennett. "You will."

He regarded her with apprehension. "I know you mean well, but you did not meet my uncle. He truly was a remarkable man, difficult to emulate."

"That may be true, but I have grown to know you these past few days, and I know what kind of man *you* are," Delphine said. "All those attributes you said your uncle had, you have them and more. Besides, did your uncle ever save the life of another?"

"Not that I am aware of," he replied. "But he was a good man."

Delphine reached out and placed a hand on his sleeve. "So are you, Bennett. I daresay that you aren't giving yourself enough credit."

Hercules leaned forward and nudged her hand off of Bennett's sleeve.

"I do believe someone is jealous," Bennett remarked.

Delphine shifted back towards Hercules. "Do you think Hercules will let me ride him?"

Bennett shook his head. "Not in your condition."

"I don't mean now," Delphine said. "But in the future."

"Does this mean you aren't as anxious to return home?" Bennett asked, almost eagerly.

Delphine grinned. "I do need to eventually return home, but this time with you- and your family- has been nice," she said. "And I especially enjoyed last night's meal."

"Did you now?" Bennett asked, taking a step closer to her. "Elodie did not share your sentiments. I caught her sneaking down to the kitchen when I retired to bed."

"That doesn't surprise me, considering she claimed she saw the haggis move on more than one occasion," Delphine joked.

Bennett chuckled. "It is far too easy to goad Elodie."

Delphine brought her hand up to Hercules' neck. "You shouldn't tease your sister so."

"You are defending her?" Bennett asked. "Did you forget that she has a terrible habit of spying on us?"

"Elodie is struggling to find her place, just as we all are."

Bennett leaned against the side of the stall and studied her for a moment. "Not only can you play the bagpipes, but you also have won over Hercules. Which is not a small feat."

Keeping her eye on Hercules, Delphine shared, "My

father purchased a stud once who seemed to hate everyone and anything. He spent much of his time alone and far away from the other horses. Being young, I worried that this horse didn't have any friends so I decided to be his friend."

"You wanted to be friends with a horse?"

Delphine shrugged. "I was friends with a goat so I didn't see a big difference in the two," she said. "I named him Lord Cranky Bottom."

Bennett smirked. "What are the odds! I was just thinking I should call my next horse that. Although, I fear that name is become increasingly common."

"If you aren't nice, I won't continue my story," Delphine said, a smile playing on her lips.

He waved his hand, indicating that she should continue.

With a satisfied look, Delphine continued. "I would bring a basket of apples with me and sit on the edge of the far fence," she said. "Whenever Lord Cranky Bottom came near, I would hold up an apple and wait for him to approach. The first attempts felt like hours, but slowly he began to trust me. Eventually, he would come when I called to him."

Bennett turned his head towards Hercules. "I do not think Hercules will ever like me enough to let me ride him."

"Hercules is still mourning the loss of his owner. You must be patient with him," Delphine encouraged.

"My father thinks we should sell him and be done with him," Bennett admitted.

Delphine's eyes grew wide. "Is that what you want?"

"No," he replied. "Hercules meant a great deal to Uncle Richard, and I could not bear to part with him."

Reaching down, Delphine picked up an apple and extended it towards Bennett. "Give Hercules an apple."

"I have tried but—"

She spoke over him. "Try again," she urged. "Only this time, remember that you are both mourning the loss of your uncle."

Bennett accepted the apple but didn't look convinced. "Why should that make a difference?"

"Horses can sense changes in our emotions," Delphine replied.

Holding up the apple in his hand, Bennett leaned closer to Hercules. "Go on, then. Eat the apple."

Hercules eyed the apple but did not make a move to eat it.

"I tried to tell you. Hercules hates me," Bennett said as he lowered the apple to his side.

Delphine moved to stand next to Bennett. "Don't give up. Hold the apple up again and tell Hercules why you miss your uncle so much."

Bennett huffed. "Hercules is just a horse, Delphie."

"Try for me, please."

With a shake of his head, Bennett held the apple up once more and shared, "I miss going to my uncle for advice. He would take the time to sit down with me and make me feel as if I had just asked the most profound question." His lips curled into a smile. "He had the unique ability to make people feel heard."

Hercules shifted towards Bennett and promptly ate the apple from his hand.

Bennett looked at her in surprise. "How in the blazes did you know that would work?" he asked, bringing his hand up to the horse's neck.

"Much like people, horses can sense vulnerability and react to it," Delphine said.

Hercules turned his head towards Delphine and nudged her.

Delphine laughed. "It would appear that Hercules wants more apples from me."

"I think we should adjourn for breakfast before my mother comes in search of us," Bennett suggested.

"I am rather famished," she admitted.

Bennett offered his arm. "Have any more of your memories returned?"

"No, I'm afraid not," Delphine said as she accepted his arm. "I may not ever know why I was running in the woodlands."

"Do you know of anyone that meant you harm?"

Delphine considered his question before saying, "I would suppose it would have been awfully convenient for my cousin if I hadn't survived. But he has never given me a reason to think he might hurt me."

"Can you think of no one else? An angry suitor, perhaps? Or a vindictive tenant?" Bennett pressed.

"I cannot think of one," she replied. "I consider myself to be a fair landlord and I do hope no one is angry enough at me to try to kill me."

Bennett patted her hand. "Of course not, but with your permission, I was hoping to hire a Bow Street Runner to make some inquiries on your behalf."

"What kind of inquiries?" Delphine asked.

"The kind that would explain why you were found unconscious, and missing a shoe in the woodlands," Bennett said. "It could be nothing, but I just want to ensure you are safe when you eventually return home."

Home.

Why did that word seem so misplaced?

As they approached the manor, Bennett glanced over at her with a concerned look on his face. "I hope I did not upset you."

"No, I was just woolgathering."

"Anything you wish to share?" Bennett asked.

No.

How could she tell him that she was beginning to feel more at home with him than she had ever felt at her country estate?

Knowing he was still waiting for a response, she replied, "I was just thinking about how relieved my staff will be when I return home."

"And your goats," Bennett said, his voice laced with amusement.

She grinned. "You may mock me, but my goats adore me."

"Why wouldn't they?" he asked. "You are a remarkable person."

A blush tinged her cheeks at his compliment, though she tried to maintain her composure. "I do hope there will be some haggis left over for breakfast."

"You might have to fight Elodie for it."

"I do not think it would be much of a fight," Delphine quipped. "I remember that haggis was served the first time I was able to dine with my father."

Bennett's eyes crinkled around the edges. "My family is rather odd in the fact that we have eaten together as a family for as long as I could remember."

"I am envious of that," Delphine admitted. "My father would sit on one end of the table and my mother on the other. I sat in the middle of the two and we would each speak of our day. At least until we ran out of things to say. Then I would just stare at my food and attempt to ignore the deafening silence."

"That sounds rather lonely."

"It was," Delphine responded, her words filled with emotion. How could she explain how lonely she had been as a child? And now, as an adult. She had more freedoms, but more constraints as well. She felt as if she were in a prison of her own making.

Bennett came to a stop on the gravel path and gently turned her to face him. "If it helps, our family meals often ended in fighting."

"That does help a little," Delphine remarked.

"And I learned quickly to duck when Elodie would reach

for a roll," Bennett shared with a chuckle. "She had an impressive aim for her age."

Delphine sighed wistfully. "It still sounds rather idyllic."

Bennett put his finger under her chin and raised it until she was looking at him. "Your past is your past; I cannot change that. But I can change your future," he said. "You came into my life for a reason, and I don't intend to ever let you go."

Delphine held his gaze, trying to decipher his words, wondering if he meant something more. Did she dare allow herself to hope for a deeper connection between them? The sincerity in his eyes made her heart ache with the possibility of a different future, one where she wasn't alone.

"No matter what happens, I will always be your friend," Bennett said, his eyes searching hers.

Her heart sank.

Friend.

The word echoed in her mind, extinguishing any flicker of hope she had dared to entertain. How foolish she had been to imagine he felt differently about her.

Mustering up a smile, Delphine replied, "I feel the same."

She thought she saw a fleeting look of disappointment in Bennett's eyes, or perhaps it was just her imagination. Maybe it wasn't only her heart playing tricks on her.

Bennett withdrew his hand. "We must make haste if we want any leftover haggis," he said, his words light and playful.

Delphine had been adamant that she didn't want to wed for the foreseeable future. But the more time she spent with Bennett, she was starting to come to the realization that maybe- just, maybe- she didn't want to be alone anymore.

Chapter Nine

As Bennett guided Delphine towards the dining room, he couldn't help but notice her uncharacteristic silence. Had he unintentionally said or done something to upset her? The thought troubled him because he cared greatly for her. Being with her felt like a respite, a chance to be his true self without pretense.

Concern gnawed at him as he stole a glance at her and noticed her gaze was fixed ahead. He decided that the silence had gone on for too long. "You are being awfully quiet," he remarked.

Delphine offered him a weak smile. "I suppose I am," she responded. "I am thinking about the soiree that your mother is planning."

"There is no need to worry about that. She just wants to show you off to our friends," Bennett said.

"What if they find me lacking?"

Bennett thought that was rather a ridiculous notion. "Why would they find you lacking?" he asked.

Delphine bit her lower lip before saying, "I have never had a party in my honor before. What if I say or do something—"

He came to a stop in the entry hall and turned her to face him. "You are overthinking this, Delphie. You are enough."

"Not to my father," Delphine sighed, the pain evident in her eyes. "I was never enough for him. It didn't matter how hard I tried to be the person he wanted me to be. I always failed, time and time again." She hesitated. "That is why I work tirelessly to ensure the estate and my business thrive. I need to prove to myself that I am just as capable, if not better, than my father."

Bennett leaned in closer, his voice filled with sincerity. "Well, if you ask me, he was a muttonhead to not appreciate what he had right in front of him."

"You say that now…"

He spoke over her, determined to make his point. "I will say that *always*," he stated firmly. "What I know about you is simple. You make me laugh, and I prefer to be around you because of the person I become when I'm with you."

"That is the way you make me feel as well," Delphine admitted.

"Then it is a good thing that we have found one another, is it not?" Bennett asked.

Delphine's eyes lit up. "I suppose it is."

Winston's voice came from down the corridor. "Brother, a word?" His words weren't as much of a question as a command.

Bennett turned to face his brother. "Whatever is the matter?" he asked, noting the solemn look on Winston's face.

"I will explain in the study with Father," Winston replied before disappearing down the corridor.

Attempting to make light of the situation, Bennett shifted his gaze back towards Delphine. "Well, it would appear that my presence is needed in the study. I shall join you for breakfast shortly."

Delphine nodded. "Very well, but you mustn't hurry on

my account." She lowered her voice. "Winston seemed rather upset."

"No doubt he is just looking for an excuse to spend time with me," he joked. "I can't help it that my family just adores me too much."

Her lips twitched slightly. "I am not sure if that is it."

"All will be well. I promise," Bennett reassured her.

Delphine didn't quite look convinced of his words, but she didn't press him. "I will be in the dining room," she announced before departing the entry hall.

With a determined stride, Bennett headed towards the study. What was so urgent that Winston had to speak to him at that precise moment?

Entering the study, Bennett's eyes fell upon a tall man with dark hair, deep-set eyes and rumpled clothing.

Winston closed the door before he provided the introductions. "Father. Bennett. Allow me to introduce you to Jasper. He is the Bow Street Runner that I was telling you about."

His father rose from his chair and studied Jasper. "I haven't met a Bow Street Runner before but I thought you all wore red waistcoats."

"That is only when we wish to be identified, my lord," Jasper said, his voice deep and commanding. "I prefer anonymity, especially in the case of your sister."

"Have you met my sister?" his father asked.

Jasper shook his head. "I have not been properly introduced to Lady Sarah, if that is what you are asking. But I have been to the cottage she is residing at and I have seen her."

Bennett stepped forward. "Is she safe?"

"I'm afraid not," Jasper said. "With her inheritance—"

With a furrowed brow, Bennett asked, "What inheritance?"

"Your uncle, Richard, left Sarah a small inheritance of one hundred pounds per annum," his father shared. "It isn't much to us, but it is a substantial sum to her."

"Why did you not say anything until now?" Bennett asked.

His father exchanged a glance with Winston. "I informed Winston of this, but I didn't think it was pertinent."

"Not pertinent?" Bennett asked. "No wonder Isaac is trying to find Sarah. That money rightfully belongs to him."

"It shouldn't! It should go to the care of Sarah and her son, considering her husband is a blackguard," his father exclaimed.

"Blackguard or not, Sarah and Isaac are wed, and he is entitled to that money," Winston interjected.

Bennett crossed his arms over his chest. "How did Isaac even learn of the inheritance?"

"When Richard died, his solicitor went in search of Sarah and informed Isaac of the inheritance," his father explained.

"Can Isaac not access the inheritance?" Bennett asked.

Winston leaned back against the desk. "Uncle Richard was a smart man and he wanted to ensure that Sarah was taken care of. The inheritance came with a stipulation. Sarah must be present to collect the money."

Bennett frowned. "Well, that surely does complicate things. Does Sarah know about the inheritance?"

"She does, but her main concern is keeping her son safe and far away from Isaac's heavy hand," his father replied. "If Isaac finds Sarah, I do believe he will kill her."

"If he does, then he won't have access to her inheritance," Bennett pointed out.

His father grew solemn. "Then she will have a fate far worse than death."

Jasper spoke up, drawing their attention. "I will keep Lady Sarah safe. Which is why I intend to move her to another cottage."

"That is highly inappropriate," his father growled.

The Bow Street Runner appeared unconcerned by his father's terse tone. "I will not be residing in the cottage with them, but I will remain close to keep them safe."

His father rose from his seat and walked over to the drink cart. "Where is this cottage?"

"I will not say," Jasper replied.

Picking up the decanter, his father asked, "Surely you do not think we will tell anyone?"

Jasper stood his ground. "I do not want to take any chances. Once I can ensure Lady Sarah is safe from her estranged husband, I will bring her home."

"And how, pray tell, are you going to do that if you are remaining with my sister?" his father asked as he poured himself a drink.

"I am not the only Bow Street Runner on this case, my lord," Jasper replied. "But you must prepare yourself that Isaac will come here looking for his wife."

His father brought the glass up to his lips. "I do not like this."

Jasper took a step forward. "You don't have to like it, but it will keep Lady Sarah safe. Now, if you will excuse me, I have a job to do."

"Before you go," Bennett began, "I was hoping to speak to you about our guest, Lady Dunrobin. I found her in the woodlands, unconscious and missing a shoe. Her memories of why she was there have not returned. I was hoping you, or an associate of yours, could make some inquiries into the matter. I want to ensure she is safe when she recovers and returns home."

Jasper's expression grew grim. "I will send for a Bow Street Runner at once to conduct an investigation," he said with a decisive nod.

After the Bow Street Runner departed from the study, Lord Dallington turned to Winston and said, "I hope Jasper is as good as you say he is."

"No, he is better," Winston said. "He is a little rough around the edges but he is good at what he does."

Bennett uncrossed his arms and asked, "What are we expected to do when Isaac comes looking for his wife?"

"We tell him the truth- that we have no idea where she is," Winston replied.

His father tossed back his drink and placed the glass onto the tray. "With any luck, that coward will stay far away and this will be a moot point."

"Do you believe that?" Winston asked.

"No, I don't," his father replied in a dejected tone. "I have never met Isaac before. Quite honestly, I have never felt the need. But from what Sarah has told me, my heart aches for what she has had to endure these past few years."

Bennett could hear the anguish in his father's voice and suspected he felt partially responsible for his sister's circumstances.

Turning towards him, Winston said, "This conversation is over. You should join Delphine in the dining room for breakfast."

"Will you not join us?" Bennett asked.

Winston gave him a knowing look. "Even if I did, you would hardly notice my presence since you seem rather beguiled by Delphine."

"Delphine is a guest in our home," Bennett defended. "I am trying my best to make sure she feels comfortable here."

Winston smirked. "That is quite admirable, Brother. But do you not think your interest extends beyond being the perfect host?"

"If you are implying I wish to pursue Delphine, you would be wrong," Bennett said. "Besides, Delphine has no designs to marry at this time and lose the freedoms afforded to her."

Putting his hands up in surrender, Winston responded, "Forgive me. I spoke out of turn."

His father returned to his seat. "Now off with both of you. I have work that I need to see to before my meetings this afternoon."

As the two brothers exited the study, Bennett said, "I intend to ask Delphine to go boating with me on the lake. Would you care to join us?"

"No, I have far too much work to see to," Winston replied.

Bennett eyed his brother with concern. "You work far too hard," he said. "When are you going to have some fun?"

"Fun?" Winston repeated back. "I don't have time for fun. I must make something of myself before it is too late."

"Too late for what?" Bennett pressed.

Winston huffed. "You are the heir, the golden child. You have nothing to prove. But I..." His voice trailed off. "I must make it on my own. Build my own legacy."

Bennett couldn't disagree with his brother more. Just because he was the heir didn't mean he didn't have responsibilities. "You are wrong about one thing. I have everything to prove. Every decision that I make affects people's livelihoods."

With a sigh, Winston said, "I am sorry. I did not mean to make light of your situation. We both have troubles that keep us up at night."

"If you do not enjoy working as a barrister, you can always return home and—"

Winston's sharp voice cut him off. "No, absolutely not! I will not live in your shadow for the remainder of my days," he declared before storming off.

Bennett watched Winston's retreating figure and he wished- and not for the first time- that he could find a way to help his brother. Something was bothering him, but Winston was not one to ask for help. But if someone was going to make something of himself, it was his brother. He was sure of that.

Delphine sat at the long, rectangular table in the dining room as she ate the food that had been placed in front of her.

The only sound was the creaking of the floorboards when the footmen shifted in their stances.

She was alone… again. This is what she was familiar with. She had eaten alone long before her mother had grown sick. Her mother preferred taking a tray in her chambers, leaving her to dine alone. In silence. Yet, it had never bothered her- until now.

Delphine had greatly enjoyed her time with the Lockwood family. Their constant bantering back and forth only endeared them more to her. She had always wondered what it would be like to be in a family that expressed love for one another, and now she knew.

Her mother loved her; she was sure of that. But her mother had always been busy with her own pursuits to give Delphine much heed. They had grown somewhat closer before her mother passed away, and she cherished that time she had with her.

With a glance around the elegantly furnished dining room, Delphine let out a sigh. She would miss this manor when she departed for home.

A footman stepped forward with a cup of chocolate and gently placed it in front of her.

"Thank you," Delphine murmured before reaching for the cup.

As she took a sip, Elodie stepped into the room and came to an abrupt halt. "You are here," she said.

Delphine eyed her curiously. "Is everything all right, Elodie?"

Elodie glanced over her shoulder, as if she were looking to retreat. "Bennett told me that I can't say anything too outlandish around you."

"Why would he say that?"

"He is worried that I might offend you," Elodie responded.

Placing her cup back onto the saucer, Delphine said,

"Well, I am not one to get easily offended so you do not need to worry. Please join me for breakfast."

Elodie visibly relaxed. "Thank you. I knew I liked you for a reason." She walked over to the table and waited for a footman to pull out a chair. "I am surprised you are up so early. Normally, I am the first one down to breakfast."

"I'm afraid I couldn't sleep so I toured the stables," Delphine said. "I met Hercules."

"Hercules is quite the ornery horse. Which is why I adore him so much."

Delphine reached for her fork and knife. "I think he is sweet."

"I wouldn't go straight to sweet, but I would say he is misunderstood, especially by my father," Elodie shared. "He wants to sell Hercules since no one can ride him."

"That would be a shame," Delphine said.

"What good is a horse that can't be ridden?"

Delphine had to admit that Elodie had a point, but she still felt that someone should fight for Hercules. "I will speak to your father about purchasing Hercules, assuming he is in earnest about selling him."

"Why would you want Hercules?"

She shrugged one shoulder. "Whyever not?" she asked. "I could always use him as a stud since he is such a magnificent horse."

Elodie placed a napkin onto her lap. "I have many fond memories of my uncle riding Hercules. He adored that horse."

"That is what Bennett shared, as well."

"Oh, you saw Bennett this morning?" Elodie asked.

Delphine nodded. "I ran into him at the stables and he escorted me back to the manor," she shared. "He should be joining us shortly."

Elodie picked up her knife and held it up. "If that is the

case, I will need to protect my plate from Bennett since he likes to steal food."

"Whatever for?"

"I don't know," Elodie replied. "I suppose he likes how I butter my toast with expert precision."

Delphine grinned. "How does one butter toast with 'expert precision'?"

Elodie lowered the knife to the table. "I perfected the method when I was at boarding school," she replied. "I ensure that the butter reaches all the edges so every bite is equally rewarding."

"That is odd," Delphine couldn't help but say.

"How do you butter your toast?"

Delphine shrugged. "I take a knife and spread a small amount of butter on my toast. It is not an overly complicated process."

Elodie looked less than impressed by her admission. "But if you do not spread the butter to the edges, you are depriving yourself of deliciousness."

"It is just toast," Delphine remarked.

Picking up a piece of toast from her plate, Elodie said, "I would take offense, but you are from Scotland. You must not eat a lot of toast there."

"We eat toast in Scotland."

Elodie huffed. "Then I just feel bad for you."

A deep chuckle came from the doorway, interrupting their conversation. "Only you love toast that much, Elodie," Bennett said.

"Everyone should love toast," Elodie stated with a tilt of her chin.

Bennett walked closer to the table and snatched a piece of toast from Elodie's plate. After he took a bite, he said, "Your buttering technique is excellent, Sister."

Elodie gave Delphine a knowing look. "I told you," she

said. "My brother is uncivilized and steals food from plates. You should guard your food with your life."

"Don't be so dramatic," Bennett joked. "It is just a piece of toast. I shall get you another. Two, in fact."

"I don't want another piece of toast. I want *that* piece of toast," Elodie said.

Bennett finished the piece of toast and brushed his hands together to get rid of the crumbs. "You are being overdramatic."

Elodie settled back in her seat. "Why is it that when a woman does something a man doesn't like then they are called 'overdramatic'?"

Delphine shifted in her seat to face Bennett. "Elodie does have a point," she acknowledged. "You did eat her toast and that was wrong of you."

Bennett didn't look the least bit repentant, despite his next words. "I am sorry, Sister." He paused. "But you should eat faster."

"Mother says the opposite," Elodie declared. "A young lady should eat at a slow pace so she may engage in the conversation around her."

"I daresay that Mother is wrong," Bennett said.

Elodie put a finger up to her lips. "Shh… she might hear you. Mother has hearing like a hawk."

Bennett gave his sister an amused look. "Since when did you care about upsetting Mother with your words?"

"I do not intentionally try to upset Mother, but the placement of my words can be problematic sometimes," Elodie admitted nonchalantly.

Delphine spoke up. "I think it is admirable that you express yourself so freely."

Leaning closer to her, Bennett lowered his voice. "Do not encourage her," he said. "Elodie says- and does- the most outlandish things."

"It is true, but no one seemed to care when I was just the

niece of a marquess," Elodie admitted. "Now that I am a lady, I am held to a higher standard."

Melody entered the room and joked, "Poor Elodie. What a burden she must bear."

Elodie frowned. "It is easier for you," she said. "From the moment you were born, you have acted the part of a lady, destined for great things. Whereas I would prefer to live a quiet life in the countryside for the remainder of my days."

"You, quiet?" Bennett teased. "I daresay that the sheep grazing two fields over can hear you when you are outside."

Shifting her gaze towards Delphine, Elodie asked, "Why are you friends with him?"

Delphine felt her lips twitch. "I have no choice since he saved me from certain death."

"Ah, so it is because of guilt that you are friends," Elodie reasoned. "That does explain a lot."

Bennett puffed out his chest. "You just don't like the fact that I am a hero. It must gnaw at you that I am the bravest one of all."

Elodie rolled her eyes. "You were riding through the woodlands and you happened upon Delphine. It was sheer happenstance."

"Yes, but the woodlands are a treacherous place and I had to use my incredible strength to carry her out of the ravine," Bennett responded. "I am surprised that I was not given the Order of the Garter, but I suppose that is only because the Prince Regent has not heard about my heroic deeds."

Melody lifted her brow. "The Order of the Garter is the most senior order of knighthoods in Britain."

"I am aware, and it changes nothing," Bennett said.

"You are delusional, Brother," Elodie remarked.

Bennett smirked. "You are just jealous and that is all right for you to admit. It must be exhausting to have a brother like me. One who is so accomplished."

"You say the most bacon-brained things," Elodie muttered.

Turning towards Delphine, Bennett asked, "Would you care to go boating with me this afternoon?"

"Do you think that is wise?" she asked.

Bennett bobbed his head. "I do. It is only a short carriage ride to the lake and I promise that I won't make you row the boat." He paused and a mischievous glint came to his eyes. "Unless I get tired. Then you will have to row us back."

"How chivalrous of you," Melody quipped.

Putting his hand up, Bennett said, "Good point. I promise that I won't make Delphine row or tip over the boat so either of us have to swim."

"That is a relief because I would not care to swim back to shore in a gown," Delphine said.

"If that is the case, Elodie can't come with us," Bennett said. "She has a tendency to stand up in the boat and cause it to tip over."

Elodie let out a groan. "That was one time, and it was your fault. You dared me to stand in the boat."

"You could have refused my dare," Bennett remarked.

"And admit that I couldn't do it? Never!" Elodie exclaimed. "Regardless, I stood up perfectly fine until you started rocking the boat. That is the only reason why the boat tipped."

Bennett shot his sister an amused look. "You are just angry that you had to walk back to shore."

"Indeed I was, and Mother was none too pleased either since I soiled another gown," Elodie admitted with a sigh.

Delphine finished eating her breakfast and placed the fork and knife onto the plate. "Despite what Bennett says, you are welcome to join us this afternoon." She glanced between Melody and Elodie. "Both of you."

Elodie gave her brother a smug smile. "Thank you,

Delphine. You are most generous- unlike my brother. I do believe I will join you, but I will go in another boat."

Melody interjected, "Should we invite Winston?"

"Yes, but I doubt he will come," Elodie replied. "He has been so busy working on a case."

Delphine turned towards Bennett and noticed that he was watching her. Rather than look away, he leaned closer to her and said, "You do not need to fear boating. I promise I will keep you safe."

"I know," she replied. And it was the truth. She trusted Bennett, wholeheartedly. He would never let any harm come to her.

A smile tugged at the corners of Bennett's lips, his eyes crinkling with amusement. "Although, if we did fall into the water, it would give me another opportunity to save you," he teased.

"I hope it does not come to that," Delphine remarked as she held his gaze.

Delphine had to admit that she rather enjoyed staring into Bennett's blue eyes. They seemed to dance with amusement, drawing her in, and keeping her transfixed. How was it that he could smile so freely, as if he had never experienced any pain?

Elodie's voice broke through her musings, reminding her that they were not alone. "If you will excuse me, I need to go practice the pianoforte. Mother is insistent that I play every day. Like a performing monkey."

Melody laughed. "You are hardly a performing monkey."

Pushing back her chair, Elodie rose. "You are lucky. You have a beautiful voice and can charm even a deaf man. Whereas I play the pianoforte- just like every other debutante."

"You play other instruments," Melody pointed out.

"I do, but Mother won't let me play those instruments in

front of guests," Elodie said. "Off to my prison. At least I have boating to look forward to this afternoon."

After Elodie had departed from the dining room, Bennett stood up and announced, "I need to review the accounts until our outing this afternoon."

Delphine rose. "I think I would like to go listen to Elodie practice. She is quite talented, whether she believes it or not."

Bennett offered his arm. "Allow me to escort you, my lady."

As she accepted his arm, Delphine shifted her gaze to Melody. "Would you care to join me?"

"No, thank you," Melody replied. "I think I would prefer to go on a ride this morning. It is such a fine day."

With a solemn look, Bennett said, "Be sure to take along two grooms."

"I always do, Brother," Melody remarked.

Appearing satisfied with his sister's response, Bennett started to lead Delphine out of the dining room. How she loved any reason to be close to him. She wished she could slow down time or stop it altogether. For every moment that passed, she was closer to returning home.

Chapter Ten

A delightful lavender scent drifted off Delphine's person as she sat next to Bennett in the coach. It shouldn't affect him, but it did. Greatly. It took a great effort on his part not to lean closer to her and bask in her nearness.

Fortunately, sanity prevailed. That, and his sisters were sitting across from him in the cramped coach.

He glanced over at Delphine and noticed that she was staring out the window. There was a line between her brow as she appeared deep in thought. He wished he could wipe away every worry, every concern, but it was not his place to do so.

In a few days, she would return home and that was for the best. At least, that was the lie he kept telling himself. He wasn't quite ready to say goodbye to her.

Elodie's voice filled the coach, captivating everyone's attention. "We are almost there," she announced.

Reaching up, Melody adjusted the straw hat on her head as she turned to address her sister. "I am taking you at your word that you won't tip over the rowboat."

"I assure you that I won't since I have no desire to have Mother lecture me about soiling another gown," Elodie responded.

Bennett chuckled. "How is it that you soil so many gowns?"

"I'm not quite sure," Elodie said. "The most unfortunate things happen to me. It is hardly my fault."

"Then, precisely, whose fault is it?" Melody asked.

Elodie shrugged. "The universe."

Melody shook her head. "When are you going to stop blaming everyone- and everything- but yourself for your misfortune?"

"Perhaps I will stop when Mother and Father accept that I wish to be a spinster forever." Elodie paused. "I shall live in Delphine's castle with her and I will be her apprentice."

"You, an apprentice?" Bennett asked.

With a tilt of her chin, Elodie replied, "Yes, I would be the greatest apprentice of all time. People would write stories about me and perhaps even make up folk songs."

Bennett knew he was going to regret this question, but he decided to ask it anyways. "What will you be an apprentice of, Sister?"

"Does it matter?"

"Yes, it does, actually," Bennett replied, "Being an apprentice means you intend to learn specific skills.

"Then I shall learn the art of running a business," Elodie shared.

Bennett gave Elodie a disbelieving look. "Is that something you are truly interested in?"

"I had never considered running a business until I met Delphine," Elodie said. "But why not?"

"Father would never allow you to do such a thing," Bennett declared.

Elodie's lips twitched. "Then I shall run far away and open the greatest business of all time."

Bennett did not think Elodie was the least bit serious, but he decided to press her anyways. "And what type of business would that be?"

"I haven't quite decided yet, but I will figure that out when I apprentice with Delphine," Elodie stated.

Melody chimed in, "Being an apprentice would require you to be teachable."

"I am very teachable. Everyone says so," Elodie declared.

Bennett furrowed his brow. "Who, pray tell, is 'everyone'?"

Elodie waved a dismissive hand in front of her. "The list is far too extensive for me to go into it now, but suffice it to say, you would know some of the people."

"I do think you are making that list up," Bennett remarked.

"How dare you make such an outlandish accusation!" Elodie exclaimed, feigning outrage.

Shifting her gaze from the window, Delphine said, "I would love to have Elodie come live with me."

Elodie gave her brother a smug look. "Did you hear that, Bennett? Delphine said she would love to have me come live with her."

"I heard it, considering we are inside of a coach," Bennett teased. "But Mother would never let you go live with Delphine. She wants you to find a husband and settle down."

"We both know that is never going to happen," Elodie remarked.

"Whyever not?" Bennett asked.

Elodie gestured towards her sister. "Melody will be the diamond of the first water this Season, and she will have her pick amongst suitors. But I…" she hesitated, "I want more out of life."

Delphine placed her hand on Bennett's sleeve. "Elodie is always welcome to live at my castle with me. It would be fun."

"Trust me, you don't want to live with Elodie," Bennett said.

"Why is that?" Delphine asked.

He leaned closer and whispered, "She has the terrible habit of thinking she is always right."

A smile came to Delphine's lips. "Ah, it is a family trait then."

Melody giggled and her hand came up to cover her mouth.

"I should warn you that Elodie loves goat cheese," Bennett said. "She would eat up all of your profits."

Elodie huffed. "I could not eat that much goat cheese."

The coach came to a halt, its weight shifting as the footman descended from his perch. Moments later, the door swung open, and Bennett emerged, extending a hand to assist the ladies.

As they began to walk towards the lake, Delphine's gaze swept over the body of water. "Frankly, I had imagined it to be much larger," she commented.

"My mother refers to this as a pond, but Bennett insists it is a lake," Elodie explained.

Bennett's eyes scanned the expanse of water before him. "I like to call it 'Lockwood Water.' Isn't it lovely?"

"It is indeed lovely," Delphine agreed.

"When I was younger, I learned how to swim here," Bennett shared. "Most parts are shallow enough to stand up in."

Elodie increased her stride and reached the rowboats first. "The first ones out to the middle wins."

"The winner of what?" Bennett asked.

"I don't know, but you are wasting your time asking such foolish questions," Elodie said. "Come along, Melody."

Bennett rushed forward and held his hand out to help his sister into the rowboat. "Careful," he encouraged as she stepped down.

Elodie jumped into the boat and reached for the oars. "Since you are here, Brother, can you push us off?"

"Of course," Bennett said.

After he gently pushed the boat into the water, he reached back and assisted Delphine into another waiting rowboat. He waited until she was situated before he pushed the boat off from shore.

Not long after, Bennett heard Elodie's triumphant shout. "We won!"

"It was never a competition!" he retorted playfully.

Elodie's laughter rang out. "That is just what a loser would say."

Bennett looked heavenward. "My sister is..." His words trailed off.

"Delightful? Entertaining?" Delphine inquired.

"Those were not the words I was going to use," Bennett said. "What if a potential suitor offers to take her on a boat ride? I have no doubt she would insist on rowing the boat."

Delphine gave him a knowing look. "If a gentleman is so easily chased off by Elodie, was he truly the one for her?"

With a glance at his sisters, Bennett said, "I do hope my sisters choose well. I can't abide the thought of either of them being miserable."

"You must trust them to make the right decisions for themselves," Delphine stated.

Bennett let out a sigh. "That did not work out in my Aunt Sarah's case. She married someone far below her station and has dealt with the repercussions ever since. Her husband beat her, relentlessly in fact, and then turned his heavy hand onto their son. Fortunately, they were able to escape with their lives, but at what cost?"

"That is awful," Delphine said. "Dare I ask what has become of them?"

Bennett felt his jaw tighten. "She is somewhere safe- for now. And I won't let anything happen to her or her son."

"I know you won't," Delphine said, her eyes filled with approval. "You are a good man, Bennett."

"And you are a good woman, Delphine," Bennett responded.

She laughed, but he was serious. "I'm being sincere."

"As am I," Bennett said. "I have never met someone quite like you."

"I shall take that as a compliment."

Bennett grinned. "You should."

A silence descended over them as he rowed the boat and he realized that he felt a sense of contentment that he had never felt before. It was like everything he needed was in this boat. Which was absurd. Was it not?

Delphine turned her head towards his sisters and smiled. "I find it interesting just how truly unique Elodie and Melody are, despite being twins."

"It is true," Bennett said. "They both see the world very differently."

"How do you see the world?"

Bennett furrowed his brow. "I must admit that I am more of a pessimist now," he admitted. "But I do believe that people are inherently good and are searching to be loved and accepted."

Delphine pressed her lips together. "How is it that you believe in love so freely?"

"I was fortunate that my parents showered love upon me from the day I was born," Bennett replied.

"I envy you," Delphine sighed. "I grew up in a very different environment."

Bennett stopped rowing and met her gaze. "I'm sorry."

She offered him a weak smile. "I have no right to complain. I had everything I ever wanted..." Her voice trailed off.

"But nothing that you truly needed," Bennett said, finishing her thought. "But now you get to decide your own future."

"For which I am most grateful"

Bennett grinned. "Do you truly live in a castle?"

"I do, at least when I am visiting Scotland," she replied.

"I hope to see it one day."

Delphine returned his smile. "You will always be welcome in my home," she said. "You, and your family."

Bennett leaned forward in his seat, unable to resist being closer to Delphine. "And you will always be welcome in my home."

"It has been nice to be around your family, especially your parents. It is rather obvious that they love one another," Delphine said.

"They do," Bennett agreed, growing pensive. "I fancied myself in love once." He wasn't quite sure why he had admitted that so freely.

Delphine cocked her head. "What happened?"

Bennett frowned at the painful memories. "When I first saw Lady Mary at a ball, I thought it was love at first sight, and I immediately set out to make her acquaintance. We danced a set and I was determined to make her my own. It wasn't long after that I decided I would offer for her."

He paused, knowing how foolish he must sound to her. "The morning I intended to call upon her, I read an article in the newssheets. It was about how this young woman had been spotted leaving Lord Whitmore's townhouse."

Bennett ran a hand through his hair. "I confronted her about it and she admitted that she was with child. Lord Whitmore had no designs to marry her so she hoped to marry me before the *ton* discovered her secret."

"How awful," Delphine murmured.

"I felt betrayed and confused. I had cared for her, but she had only meant to use me," Bennett said. "The worst part is that if she had only come to me and explained her plight, I might have still married her."

Bennett continued. "I felt like a fool and I departed for our country home that very day. I couldn't stand the thought of being around Lady Mary for one more day."

Delphine leaned forward in her seat, her eyes full of

compassion. "She was wrong to take advantage of your kind heart."

"The funny thing is that I still believe in love," Bennett admitted. "When I marry, it will be for love. I won't settle for anything less."

"As well you should," Delphine said. "It is no less than you deserve."

"But not you?" Bennett asked.

Delphine settled back in her seat, her expression giving nothing away. "I have always led myself to believe that love was a weakness. I had been so adamant, but now I find myself questioning that belief."

Bennett gripped the ends of the oars tighter, resisting the urge to reach for Delphine's hand. Despite his efforts, he longed to feel her touch.

Elodie's voice interrupted his musings. "Shall we race?" she asked eagerly.

Turning his head, he saw Elodie and Melody were a short distance away. How did he not notice them approach?

But he already knew the answer.

Delphine.

When he was around her, nothing else seemed to matter. He was starting to reveal far too much of himself to her. But he had no regrets about doing so.

Delphine sat in her bedchamber as she waited for the dinner bell to ring so she could make her way down to the drawing room. Her hair was piled high atop her head and she was dressed in a borrowed jonquil gown.

Until she had met Bennett, she had been content with her life. But now… she was not quite so sure. She had feelings for him, but they were unrequited. Which was fine by her. She had no intention of giving her heart to anyone. She had been doing just fine on her own and couldn't risk losing all that she had worked so hard to obtain.

So why did her heart seem to beat only for Bennett?

Rising from the settee, she walked over to the window and stared out into the darkness of night. Only fools fell in love, giving the other person power to hurt you, over and over again. For isn't that what marriage was?

Delphine sighed. Perhaps her view of marriage had been tainted from watching her parents. They seemed to take great pleasure in making the other person miserable. It had almost seemed like a game to them.

And yet, Lord and Lady Dallington were nothing like her parents. The affection they held for one another was evident in every glance, every word and every touch. What would it have been like to be raised by parents that truly had loved one another? Would they have showered her with love?

Maybe, just maybe, that is why she was so drawn to Bennett. He treated her with such kindness that her heart was softening towards him. A heart that she thought was impenetrable. But was love not a weakness? She had always thought so, but now she wasn't so sure.

Delphine couldn't risk showing a crack in her façade. Her cousin was trying to take away her title and she had to be strong. All the time. She would not lose her legacy over a trifling thing such as love.

Love?

Did she love Bennett?

No.

She couldn't.

She wouldn't.

But she did.

Delphine leaned her shoulder against the window frame. Perhaps it was best that she leave Brockhall Manor sooner rather than later. The longer she stayed here, the longer she doubted her decision to remain alone.

A knock came at the door and her heart took flight. Had Bennett arrived to walk her down to the drawing room?

She straightened from the wall and rushed over to the mirror. Once she confirmed she looked presentable, she walked over to the door.

With a smile on her face, she opened the door, but it faltered when she saw Elodie. "Good evening," she said as she attempted to hide her disappointment.

Elodie gave her a knowing look. "Were you expecting someone else?"

She was, but she didn't dare admit that. Not to Elodie. "No, of course not," she said, opening the door wide. "I am very happy that you are here."

"May I come in?" Elodie asked.

"Yes, please do," Delphine responded as she moved to the side.

Elodie stepped into the room and turned to face her. "I was hoping we could speak privately for a moment."

Delphine eyed her curiously. "Is everything all right?"

"It is," Elodie rushed to assure her.

After she closed the door, Delphine gestured towards the settee at the end of her bed. "Would you care to sit?"

Elodie sat down and clasped her hands in her lap. In a solemn voice, she asked, "What are your intentions towards my brother?"

Delphine reared back. She hadn't expected that from Elodie. Although, in fairness, she never quite knew what to expect from her. "Pardon?"

"I have been watching you two and I suspect that you both have grown to care for one another," Elodie responded. "Is it true?"

"I… um… I don't know what to say," Delphine replied.

"It is a simple enough question. Do you care for Bennett?"

Delphine pressed her lips together, unsure of how she wanted to answer. She didn't want to lie, but she couldn't afford to tell the truth. "I do care for Bennett but not in the way you are thinking. He is my friend."

Elodie lifted her brow. "You two did not appear to be just friends when you were in that boat earlier."

Coming to sit down next to Elodie on the settee, Delphine said, "I do not know what you are referring to."

"You two acted very familiar with one another."

"That is what friends do," she attempted.

With a shake of her head, Elodie said, "I can't tell if you are lying to me or actually believe what you are saying."

"Elodie…"

She put her hand up, stilling Delphine's words. "I know what I have seen, and it is evident that you two have affection for one another. Do not insult me by saying otherwise."

Delphine should never have underestimated Elodie and thought it was best to just admit what she was feeling. "Frankly, I don't know what I feel. I have never felt like this before and it frightens me."

"What are you frightened about?"

She tossed up her hands. "About everything!" she exclaimed. "I never set out to develop feelings for Bennett."

"But this is wonderful news. You and Bennett can marry—"

Delphine spoke over her. "No, I have no designs for marriage at this point in my life," she asserted.

Elodie blinked. "But you care for Bennett and he cares for you."

"That may or may not be true, but I cannot marry. If I did, I risk losing everything I have worked so hard to obtain," she shared. "For once I am married, no one will take me seriously. I will just be Bennett's wife. They will expect him to run the estate, my business… everything. And I will be left with nothing to do."

"Bennett wouldn't let that happen," Elodie asserted.

"I'm sorry, but I have seen it happen before," Delphine said. "I am not the first woman who has inherited a title, and I won't be the last. My estate may be entailed, but not the business. My husband will have full control over that."

Elodie's eyes grew determined. "You could defy convention, could you not?" she inquired.

"I don't know," she sighed.

"Do you truly intend to walk away from Bennett?"

Delphine felt a stab in her heart at that thought. "I wish to remain his friend, assuming he feels the same."

Elodie jumped up from her seat. "Friend? Surely you are not this blind. You two can't seem to stop staring at each other."

"I'm sorry, but…"

"No!" Elodie exclaimed. "I won't let this happen. You love him. I know you do!"

As her eyes grew downcast, Delphine felt embarrassed that Elodie had been able to see right through her. "I don't know if what I feel is love. Perhaps, but it changes nothing."

Elodie's mouth dropped. "It changes everything!"

Bringing her finger up to her lips, Delphine said, "Shh. You must keep your voice down. I don't want anyone to overhear our conversation."

"Just so you know, everyone else knows." Elodie paused. "Well, everyone but you and Bennett."

"I know you are trying to help, but I am a countess. If I marry Bennett, I would lose a part of myself."

"I disagree. You would gain a partner and a helpmate. You wouldn't have to go about it on your own anymore."

Delphine gave her a knowing look. "Did Bennett ask you to come speak to me about this?"

Elodie shifted uncomfortably. "No, but I know he cares for you."

"Care, not love," Delphine said. "There is a difference and

it isn't fair that you came here to speak for him. He might be content with being my friend."

"What if he isn't?"

Delphine lifted her brow. "Your brother wants a love match and I can't give him that. He deserves to be happy."

"You have made him far happier than I have ever seen," Elodie declared. "Bennett can't seem to stop himself from smiling when he is around you."

"That is the way Bennett is," Delphine attempted.

"No, it isn't," Elodie assured her. "He is happy, truly happy, for the first time. And it has everything to do with you."

Delphine smiled. "You are a good sister, but should you not at least ask Bennett what he wants first?"

Their conversation was interrupted by a sudden knock at the door.

Delphine crossed the room and opened the door, revealing Bennett. He had a boyish grin on his lips that was doing inconvenient things to her heart.

He bowed. "Good evening," he said. "May I escort you down to supper?"

"Actually, you could escort us both down," Delphine responded as she opened the door wide.

Bennett glanced over her shoulder and asked, "Why is Elodie in your room?"

Elodie smirked. "Are you afraid I am going to reveal your secrets?"

"I have no secrets," Bennett replied.

"No?" Elodie asked as she came to stand next to Delphine. "What about Mr. Swanson and—"

Bennett cut her off. "There is no need to rehash that story."

Winston's voice came from down the hallway. "I think Delphine has a right to know, considering you almost died."

"I did not almost die," Bennett remarked. "I only received a few stitches from that bull."

"What bull?" Delphine asked.

Winston leaned his shoulder against the door frame. "Our Bennett here decided that he wanted to be a matador after seeing them perform in Spain."

Bennett turned towards Delphine and explained, "I had a little too much to drink and my friends dared me to challenge a bull to a fight. I took a red quilt and I went over to Mr. Swanson's field. As I went to climb over a fence, a bull rushed towards me and I fell backwards, hitting my head on a rock."

Delphine frowned. "You could have been killed."

"Not me," Bennett said with a cocky smile. "I am far too handsome to die."

Elodie let out an exasperated sigh. "Dear heavens, do you ever hear yourself speak?" she asked before brushing past her brother.

Winston straightened from the wall. "I must side with Elodie. You do say the most idiotic things."

As Winston walked away, Bennett chuckled. "And that is how I rid myself of my siblings."

"You are awful," Delphine said lightly. She was secretly pleased that they were alone and could speak freely.

Bennett offered his arm. "You look lovely this evening, Delphie."

"Thank you," she said as she placed her hand on his sleeve. "But I still have questions about why you thought it was a good idea to challenge a bull to a fight."

"It wasn't my finest moment," Bennett joked. "I had seen a matador perform in Spain on my Grand Tour and I thought it would be fun to try."

Delphine pursed her lips. "Why stop with bulls? You could always pick a fight with a tiger at the menagerie."

"Point taken, my lady," Bennett said as they started down the stairs. "I promise I will not pick any fights with animals that are bigger or stronger than me."

"Good," Delphine responded.

Bennett's eyes held amusement as he said, "I am flattered that you are so concerned for my wellbeing."

Delphine grinned. "You have a low bar for being flattered."

"I won't deny that," Bennett said. "But it is not every day that such a beautiful young woman cares what becomes of me."

A blush came to her cheeks at his words. "You flatter me now."

Bennett came to a stop at the bottom of the stairs and gently turned her to face him. "I hope you know that I find you to be quite beautiful." He held her gaze. "And your bravery runs deep. You are a unique blend of strength and beauty."

Delphine's breathing grew ragged and she couldn't seem to force herself to look away. He made her feel safe and protected. She couldn't ever remember feeling that way with anyone before.

And that is when she knew- without a doubt- that she had fallen in love with Bennett.

Chapter Eleven

Absently clutching his drink, Bennett sat in the study, fixated on the crumpled note lying before him. Doctor Anderson had sent word that he intended to call upon Delphine tomorrow morning, in hopes that she could travel home.

But he didn't want her to return home.

He wanted her to stay here… with him.

Bennett leaned forward in his seat and placed his drink down onto the table. He cared for Delphine- there was no denying that- but she had made her thoughts about marriage abundantly clear. Was it even possible to get her to change her mind?

He hoped so.

And if he failed, could he just watch her ride off, knowing he had lost her forever?

Bennett ran a hand through his hair and let out a deep, resounding sigh. When had life gotten so complicated? He finally found a young woman that cared little for his title or his wealth and wanted nothing from him. Which was part of the problem. What did he have to offer her?

Winston entered the study and studied him for a long moment. "Why do you look like death?"

"I do not look that bad," Bennett grumbled as he settled back into his seat.

"You look rather perturbed."

Bennett frowned. "What is it that you want?"

Winston gave him a knowing look. "Your question just proves my point. The only time you don't joke around is when you are upset."

"I am fine."

"You are not fine."

Bennett's frown deepened. "It is too late to be having this conversation. Will you not drop it?"

Winston sat on the settee and pointed to his glass. "I could, but I won't. You hardly touched your drink, and your cravat is hanging around your neck. Something is clearly upsetting you."

Leaning his head back, Bennett looked up at the ceiling. "I do not want to talk about it."

"Is it Delphine?"

Yes.

His thoughts were always about Delphine.

But Bennett didn't dare admit that. Not to his brother. Not to anyone. If anyone discovered how much he cared for Delphine, it could ruin everything.

Knowing that Winston was still waiting for a response, Bennett said, "It is late, and I am tired."

As he went to rise, Winston put his hand up, stilling him. "Before you go, you should know that Jasper sent word that Aunt Sarah is somewhere safe."

"That is a relief."

Winston nodded his agreement. "Furthermore, the other Bow Street Runner has arrived at the village and is keeping a watchful eye out for Isaac."

Shifting in his seat, Bennett asked, "How do we contact this Bow Street Runner?"

"We don't," Winston replied. "But I was told by Jasper that he is close by, watching, and waiting."

"Do you know this particular Bow Street Runner?"

Winston shook his head. "Jasper did not disclose any additional information of the Bow Street Runner and I am a smart enough man not to ask."

"Do you think Isaac would be stupid enough to come here to speak to Father?"

"For the money, yes," Winston replied.

"You think he cares more about money than his own wife and son?" Bennett asked.

Winston grew thoughtful. "Regardless of what I think, Isaac is dangerous. And that does not bode well for Sarah or anyone for that matter," he said. "Father even instructed White to hire additional footmen and to post them around the manor."

"That will be sufficient," Bennett responded, rising from his seat. "If you will excuse me, it is late."

"Late?" Winston repeated. "You are starting to sound like an old man. Soon you will tell people that your bones are creaking."

"I am not that old yet."

Winston's expression grew solemn. "I am worried about you."

He stared back at his brother incredulously. "You are worried about me?" he repeated. "I am more worried about *you*."

"There is no reason to worry about me," Winston asserted.

"I could say the same thing, but we both know we are lying," Bennett said, challenging his brother to argue with him.

Winston leaned back in his seat, his expression resigned. "All right, but just know that I am here to listen," he responded.

"Thank you, but I can manage on my own," Bennett said before he departed from the study. He knew his brother was just trying to help, but this was something that he had to handle on his own. Delphine would eventually leave Brockhall Manor, and he would need to learn to live without her.

As he stepped into the entry hall, he saw a tall, broad-shouldered footman standing guard. This must be one of the new footmen that White had hired. He hoped that the presence of additional footmen would keep Isaac away from their family, including Aunt Sarah and her son.

"Brother!" Elodie called out from the top of the stairs.

Bennett turned and saw Elodie descending the stairs in her white wrapper and slippers. "Whatever are you doing up at this late hour?"

"I am hungry," Elodie said. "I am going to the kitchen for a biscuit. Would you care to join me?"

"For a biscuit, always," Bennett responded.

Elodie came to a stop at the bottom of the stairs and gave him a curious look. "Why do you look so disheveled?"

"Says the girl who is wearing a wrapper and a cap on her head," Bennett teased.

She smiled. "Fair enough," she replied. "Let's go find the biscuits that Mrs. Meek left out for me."

"How do you know she left out biscuits for you?"

A mischievous look came into his sister's eyes. "This is not the first time I have raided the kitchen for biscuits."

"Dare I ask how often you do such a thing?"

"It may or may not be a nightly endeavor," Elodie replied with a slight shrug. "But you mustn't tell Mother. I have dresses that I must fit in for the upcoming Season."

Bennett chuckled. "You poor thing."

"You laugh, but you could not handle the pressures of being a woman," Elodie declared. "We are defined by our looks, not our minds. All of our training and education is for the sole purpose of finding a suitable match."

He heard the pain in her voice and he reached out to place a comforting hand on her shoulder. "You, dear sister, have nothing to worry about. You will have hordes of suitors flocking around you."

Elodie grew quiet. "And if I don't want that?"

"What do you want?" he prodded.

"That is the problem," she replied. "I don't know what I want, but I hope I can find it, when I need it."

Bennett dropped his hand to his side. "This conversation would be much better if I had a biscuit in my hand."

As they began walking down the corridor, Elodie broke the silence. "You were awfully quiet during dinner this evening. Is everything all right?"

"Everything is fine," he assured her, though the truth was far from that. He didn't feel like discussing it with his sister. He just wanted a biscuit. Not a reminder that Delphine was going to leave soon.

Elodie glanced at him as if sensing his thoughts. "You could ask her to stay. There would be no shame in that."

"Elodie…" he started.

She stopped and turned to face him. "I may be many things, but being blind is not one of them. I know you care for Delphine."

"It is complicated," he admitted.

"Then you must strive to do everything in your power to 'uncomplicate' it," Elodie said firmly.

Bennett knew his sister was only trying to help but that didn't mean he needed- or wanted- her help. "If only it was that easy, Sister."

Elodie gave him a knowing look. "What if I told you that Delphine was not entirely immune to your charms?"

"She told you this?"

"Not in so many words," Elodie replied.

Bennett grew solemn. "Delphine is a countess and has her own responsibilities. Furthermore, she has been rather forthright about how eager she is to return home to her own country estate."

Elodie bobbed her head in agreement. "Yes, but people can change."

"Not that much," Bennett said, gesturing towards the servants' entrance. "We should eat a biscuit before it grows too late."

His sister appeared as though she wanted to inquire further, but thankfully she relented. "Very well," she said. "The thought of a biscuit is much too appealing at the moment."

Bennett walked over and opened the door that led to the servants' stairs. "Biscuits make everything better," he said before he followed his sister down the stairs.

Once they arrived in the kitchen, Elodie walked over to a plate that had a cloth covering it. "Mrs. Meek leaves me three biscuits and I will be happy to share one with you."

"That is most gracious of you," Bennett joked.

Elodie removed the cloth and extended a biscuit to her brother. "If you bring forth some stimulating conversation, I might give you another half."

Bennett leaned against the counter. "This may come as a surprise, but many young women find me to be a delight."

"You are an earl. They will say anything to snag you, including listening to your drivel," Elodie said.

He smirked. "You make it nearly impossible to like you."

Elodie held her biscuit up. "The truth hurts, dear brother, but there is one young woman that has no intention of snagging you. And I think you need her as much as she needs you."

Bennett brushed the crumbs off his hands as he remarked, "I know you mean well, but…"

"I just have one question for you," she said, speaking over him.

He gave her an expectant look. "I may come to regret this, but I find myself curious as to why you care so much."

Elodie reached for the last remaining biscuit and broke it into two pieces. "What would you do for a chance at love?"

"Love?" Bennett repeated. "No one said anything about love."

Extending him the half of a biscuit, Elodie replied, "You didn't have to."

Bennett stared at his sister, unsure of how to respond. He couldn't possibly love Delphine. Could he? But the more he thought about it, the more he was forced to accept his feelings ran deeper than he realized.

And that thought both terrified and excited him at the same time.

Delphine sat at the dressing table in her bedchamber as she stared at her reflection in the mirror. The doctor should be arriving soon and all she felt was dread. No doubt he would inform her that she was ready to travel home. And isn't that what she had wanted from the moment most of her memories had returned to her?

But it was different now.

She was different.

Despite not knowing how she had ended up in the woodlands in the first place, she felt perfectly well. Her headaches were gone, her stiff neck had eased and she no longer experienced any shortness of breath when walking.

This was ridiculous. It wasn't as if she wouldn't see Bennett again. She would see him- and his family- this Season. But it would be different. No matter how much she wanted to convince herself that it would be the same, she couldn't deny the truth.

She would be forced to watch Bennett be surrounded by young women, all vying for his attention. Not that she would blame any of them. Bennett was the best of men and would make a fine husband.

A knock came at the door.

"Enter," Delphine ordered.

The door opened, revealing a young maid. "Doctor Anderson has come to call, my lady. He is waiting for you in the drawing room."

Rising, Delphine said, "Please inform him that I will be down shortly."

"Very well," the young maid responded with a slight curtsy.

Delphine ran a hand down her pale blue gown before she headed out the door. As she entered the corridor, she saw Bennett standing there, waiting for her, and her heart leapt at the sight of him. Just as it always did.

He smiled when his eyes landed on her. "Delphie," he greeted. "Good morning." Why did it seem like whenever he said her name she felt her soul take a breath?

"Good morning," she responded.

"I have come to escort you down to breakfast," Bennett said as he offered his arm.

She placed her hand on his as she replied, "Breakfast shall have to wait. Doctor Anderson has called upon me."

"He is here- already?" Bennett asked in a voice that almost sounded panicked. But that was impossible. Why would Bennett not be pleased by that news?

"Apparently he is an early riser," Delphine replied.

As Bennett started leading her down the hall, he remarked, "I do hope you still plan on attending the soiree, considering it is being held in your honor."

Delphine bobbed her head. "I have no intention of leaving before then. I do not wish to insult your mother, especially since she has been most gracious to me."

"Furthermore, there is much that I haven't shown you at Brockhall Manor," he said as he waggled his eyebrows.

"Now you have piqued my interest."

"Good, because we have a chapel here that dates back hundreds of years," Bennett said. "It is where my cousin, Edwina, got married, and it is where I hope to..." His words trailed off.

Delphine glanced over at him. "Where you hope to what?" she prodded.

"Get married," Bennett rushed out.

"Oh," Delphine murmured, unsure of what else she could say. She wanted Bennett to be happy, but she wasn't quite sure how she felt about him marrying someone else. Not that she wanted to marry him. No, she was quite adamant about that. So why was the thought so appealing to her?

Bennett led her down the stairs towards the drawing room. In a hushed voice, he said, "No matter what happens in there, you can always stay here as long as you would like."

"I do not wish to overstay my welcome."

He came to a stop just outside of the drawing room and gently turned her to face him. "You, my dear, could never do such a thing."

Delphine stared up at him as she found herself admitting, "Out of all the people that could have found me in the woodlands, I am glad that it was you."

"As am I," Bennett said, taking a step closer to her.

A clearing of a throat came from the drawing room, causing them to jump apart. Delphine hadn't realized how close she had been to Bennett until that precise moment.

Turning her head, she saw Doctor Anderson was standing in the doorway with his leather satchel in his hand.

"I do apologize for interrupting, but I'm afraid I do not have much time," the doctor said. "I just need to examine you for a moment to see if you are fit for travel."

"Of course, Doctor," Delphine responded.

The doctor stood back and gestured towards the drawing room. "It will just be a moment, my lord," he said as he addressed Bennett.

With a parting glance at Bennett, Delphine entered the drawing room and came to a stop in the center of the room. A maid sat in the corner, working on her needlework, not giving them much heed.

Doctor Anderson approached her with a kind look in his eyes. "I see that you and Lord Dunsby have grown rather close. He is a fine man."

"Yes, he is," Delphine readily agreed.

The doctor came to a stop in front of her and his eyes studied hers. "How are you feeling?"

"I am well."

"Any headaches?"

"No."

He cocked his head. "What of your memories?" he asked. "Have all of them come back yet?"

She winced. "I'm afraid I still cannot remember how I ended up in the woodlands in the first place."

The doctor gave her an understanding look. "You must be prepared that those memories may never come back."

"Ever?"

"I'm afraid so," Doctor Anderson replied. "I have seen it with soldiers on the battlefield or with patients that have experienced some form of trauma. Many consider it to be a mercy to forget such a thing."

Delphine pressed her lips together, not believing it was a mercy to forget one's memories. "Quite frankly, I do not. I want to remember those memories."

"Be patient with yourself, but you may never have the answers that you seek," the doctor said. "Fortunately, your story did not end in the woodlands. It has only just begun."

"Does this mean I get to travel home?"

The doctor reached for his satchel. "Let me examine you for a moment and then I shall decide. Is that fair?"

Delphine bobbed her head before he did a thorough examination on her. Once he was finished, he placed his tools back into his satchel.

"You look the epitome of health, my lady, and, in my medical opinion, I do believe it is safe for you to travel home," Doctor Anderson said.

In a hesitant voice, she asked, "Are you sure?"

Doctor Anderson lifted his brow. "Is something wrong?"

Yes.

She wanted him to tell her that she couldn't go home. At least, not yet. She wanted to stay at Brockhall Manor for the time being. But she didn't dare say such a thing.

Delphine mustered up a smile. "No, everything is fine. Thank you, Doctor. I shall return home after the soiree."

The doctor tipped his head. "If you need anything, please do not hesitate to send for me," he said.

After Doctor Anderson departed from the room, Delphine dropped down onto the settee in the most unladylike huff. She had anticipated this, but she had hoped she was wrong. What was wrong with her? She had so many responsibilities back at her country estate, but she couldn't bear the thought of leaving Bennett.

Bennett stepped into the room and eyed her curiously. "Did you receive bad news?"

Delphine hesitated, struggling to collect her thoughts. She couldn't bring herself to tell Bennett the truth- not when he had never shown her any intention that he held her in high regard. They were friends, nothing more. "Yes... no..." she finally replied. "The doctor said that I could return home at once."

"Is that not what you hoped for?" Bennett asked as he came to sit down next to her on the settee.

Delphine straightened in her seat and clasped her hands in

front of her. "It was precisely what I hoped for," she lied. "I have much work to do before I depart for London."

"As do I," Bennett said.

"I imagine you do, being an earl and all," Delphine remarked.

Bennett smirked. "I could say the same thing about you since you are a countess and all," he teased.

A laugh escaped Delphine's lips. "I suppose we both have much to do." How was it possible that he could always make her laugh even when her heart was breaking?

All humor left Bennett's expression as he said in a soft voice, "Delphie…"

"Yes?" she prodded.

Bennett's eyes held vulnerability as he held her gaze. "I know we have not known each other for long but I…"

Lady Dallington's cheerful voice came from the doorway. "What wonderful news!" she exclaimed. "I just received word that Delphine will be returning home soon."

Delphine turned her attention towards Lady Dallington. "Yes, I intend to depart after the soiree."

"And you shall have use of our finest coach to return home," Lady Dallington said, walking further into the room.

"That is most generous of you," Delphine responded.

Bennett had risen when his mother had stepped into the room but he wouldn't meet Delphine's gaze. "Excuse me for a moment," he muttered before he swiftly departed from the room.

Lady Dallington's smile seemed to grow wider after Bennett had left. "We have much to do today since the soiree is tomorrow evening," she said. "The dressmaker has agreed to alter one of Melody's ballgowns to fit you."

"Thank you," Delphine said, her thoughts on anything but a ballgown. They were fixated on Bennett. What had he intended to say to her before they were interrupted?

Moving to sit next to her, Lady Dallington remarked,

"Now, on to the particulars. I was hoping that you and Bennett would dance the first set together."

"I have no objections." Which was the truth. The thought of dancing with Bennett was far too appealing to turn down. It had been far too long since she had been in his arms, his strong embrace making her feel safe and cherished.

Lady Dallington nodded in approval. "I think it might be prudent if you and Bennett practiced dancing a set together. That way it will look more natural." She waved her hand in front of her. "I will see to all the arrangements, including having some musicians brought in for the occasion."

"That is not necessary," she attempted.

"It would be no bother," Lady Dallington declared. "Now we do have the issue of the receiving line. It can be a nuisance but I do love seeing each and every one of my guests. And, of course, they will want to meet you. It is not every day that we have a bona fide countess arrive in our village."

Delphine shrugged. "I do not mind a receiving line."

"Good, good," Lady Dallington said as she rose. "Shall we have a bite of breakfast before we meet with the dressmaker?"

Rising, Delphine glanced at the empty doorway, wondering where Bennett had gone. "Perhaps I should look for Bennett."

"He will be fine. No doubt he is in the dining room," Lady Dallington asserted. "Besides, we have much more important things to dwell on."

As Delphine followed Lady Dallington out of the drawing room, her eyes roamed over the entry hall, looking for any sign of Bennett. But there was none. Where had he gone? She hoped she hadn't said or done anything that had upset him.

Lady Dallington stopped at a window and looked out. "Dear heavens, why is Bennett heading to the stables?"

Delphine's feet faltered and she knew this was her chance to speak to Bennett again. Alone. "I will go ask him," she said eagerly.

"There really is no need," Lady Dallington responded. "We can send a footman."

"No, I can do it," Delphine stated before spinning on her heel.

Without bothering to wait for Lady Dallington's response, she hurried out the back door and headed towards the stables.

Chapter Twelve

Bennett arrived at the stables and came to a stop in the aisle. He didn't want to go riding, but he just needed a moment to collect his thoughts. He had come so close to confessing to Delphine that he had feelings for her, but thankfully he was interrupted by his mother.

Why did Delphine have such a hold over him- over his thoughts- unceasingly? He couldn't seem to stop thinking about her. She was the object of his desire, but she only considered him as a friend. Which he would take. He just wanted her in his life… always.

He loved the way she looked at him, with a genuine interest in him. She didn't see his title or his wealth, but she saw him. Just him. And her eyes seemed to see everything he was, everything he wasn't and everything he might be one day.

Life had grown increasingly complicated when he had saved Delphine from the woodlands. Her mere presence made him content, and he couldn't help but smile when he was with her. She had been precisely what he had been looking for but hadn't realized it until she told him that she was going to leave.

Botheration.

She was going to leave him. Soon.

Bennett hung his head. He couldn't just let her walk away but what choice did he have? He could ruin everything between them if he offered for her. He knew she didn't want to marry now- and not just him, she didn't want to marry anyone. And he respected her more for it.

Yet a glimmer of hope flickered within him. What if he could change her mind about marriage… to him?

Another matter weighed heavily on his mind. Would Delphine even be safe if she returned home? Jasper had promised to send for one of his associates to investigate, but that would take time. Time that he did not have. Not if Delphine was adamant about returning home. The thought of her walking into a perilous situation made his heart ache.

Hercules nickered, drawing his attention. The horse seemed to be concerned about him, but that was highly unlikely. Hercules barely tolerated him, and only if he had an apple in his hand.

Bennett walked down the aisle towards Hercules and reached for an apple in the bucket. "Do you want an apple?" he asked, holding it up.

Hercules eyed him but didn't make a move to accept the offering.

He chuckled. "You are a stubborn thing," he remarked. "What are you waiting for? Eat the apple."

The horse leaned forward and accepted the apple.

Placing a hand on Hercules' neck, Bennett said, "You are lucky you are a horse. It is rather difficult to deal with ladyfolk."

Delphine's amused voice came from behind him. "Hercules is smart enough not to respond to that remark."

Bennett turned his head towards Delphine and asked, "Why are you not at breakfast?"

She took a step closer to him, but still maintained a proper distance. "I could ask you the same question."

"I am not hungry," he lied.

A look of uncertainty crossed her delicate features before she inquired, "Would you like me to go?"

No.

He wanted her to be with him forever.

Bennett forced a smile to his lips, hoping it was convincing enough. "You are welcome to stay, but you must be prepared for a stimulating conversation with Hercules."

His words seemed to set Delphine at ease and her face softened. "Oh? And what does Hercules wish to talk about?"

"Right now, he is very interested in apples," Bennett remarked.

Delphine reached into the bucket and pulled out an apple. "Well, I can help with that," she said as she came to stand next to him. She held her hand out with the apple.

Hercules eagerly ate it out of her hand.

She smiled as she regarded the horse. "Hercules is a magnificent horse. I will miss him when I am gone."

"What will you miss? His refusal to let anyone ride him or his stubborn streak?" he joked.

Turning to face him, she replied, "Hercules is a good horse. He will come around, but you must be patient."

"I am the epitome of patience, my lady."

Hercules nudged Delphine's shoulder.

She giggled. "It would appear that Hercules wants more apples," she said. "I do not fault him for that."

Bennett gave the horse a look of mock sternness. "You have had enough for today."

In response, Hercules tossed his head in complaint.

"You are better than me," Delphine said. "I would have given him another apple just to appease him."

"Then Hercules has trained you, and not the other way around."

Delphine ran her fingers down Hercules' neck. "Perhaps, but I just want Hercules to be happy."

Bennett eyed her curiously. "Why is his happiness so important to you?"

"He suffered a great loss when your uncle died, and deserves to be happy," Delphine replied.

He heard the anguish in her voice, prompting him to ask, "Are you happy, Delphie?"

She grew silent. "For so long, I thought I was, but it all changed when you saved me. I now know what true happiness is."

"What prompted that realization?"

Delphine held his gaze before saying, "I met you."

Bennett blinked, not knowing what he could say. He felt precisely the same way. His whole life had changed when Delphine had come into it. And it was for the better. How could he make her understand that he needed her in his life? This wasn't just some passing whim for him. Delphine was his future, he was sure of that.

An adorable blush came to her cheeks and she ducked her head. "I should join your mother for breakfast."

He couldn't let her go. Not after what she had just revealed.

"Delphie..." he started.

She looked up at him, her eyes holding vulnerability.

What could he say that would keep her here? Did he confess his feelings and hope that he hadn't misread the situation?

As he opened his mouth, Delphine spoke first, her words sounding rushed. "I... um... am very hungry. Starving, in fact."

Sensing her discomfort, Bennett thought it was best not to tease her, but he did need to say a few things before she left.

"I shall join you, assuming you don't mind," Bennett said.

Delphine gave him a weak smile but she didn't argue with him. "I would appreciate the company."

He held his hand out, gesturing that she should walk down the aisle first. He followed her out of the stables and quickened his pace to match her stride.

Bennett clasped his hands behind his back so he wouldn't do something foolish like reach for her hand.

Delphine's eyes remained straight ahead. "You have a lovely manor."

"That I do," Bennett agreed. But he didn't want to talk about Brockhall Manor. He wanted to talk about a possible future between them. "I do hope you have enjoyed your time here."

That was the right thing to say because Delphine seemed to perk up. "That I did," she responded enthusiastically. "I just adore your family."

"They can be rather difficult to deal with," Bennett said.

"Only to you," Delphine responded. "To me, they showered kindness upon me."

Bennett smirked. "Ah, so they have fooled you into thinking they are something that they are not."

Delphine shook her head. "You are most fortunate. Family is not something that one should take for granted."

"You are right," Bennett said.

She stopped on the gravel path and stared up at him. "I know I am, but I rather like hearing you say that. I have a feeling that you don't say those words very often."

"It sounds like you have been talking to Elodie about me," Bennett said.

Delphine shrugged. "Elodie does enjoy talking about you and whatever else comes to her mind."

Bennett unclasped his hands, dropping them to his sides. "What has she told you about me?"

"Are you worried, my lord?" Delphine teased.

"Quite frankly, I never know what is going to come out of Elodie's mouth."

Delphine patted his arm. "Do not be concerned. Elodie only says good things about you. It is obvious that she loves you very much."

"Yes, well, what is not to love?" Bennett quipped as he reached for the lapels of his jacket. "I am rather charming."

She rolled her eyes, just as he had intended. "You are far too cocky."

"No young lady has ever complained before."

"Not this again," Delphine sighed before she continued walking down the path.

He easily caught up to her and remarked, "It is perfectly acceptable to admit that I am charming."

Without sparing him a glance, she asked, "Are you charming? I'm afraid that I haven't noticed."

"Your words have hurt me deeply, my lady," he joked.

"I am confident that you will overcome it."

Bennett saw the manor was looming ahead and he didn't want to wait any longer to say what needed to be said. He reached for her arm and gently turned her towards him. "Before we go inside, I was hoping to say a few things."

Delphine pointed towards a window in the manor and said, "I should warn you that Elodie is spying on us."

Following her gaze, he saw Elodie right before she ducked down, but he could still see the top of her head. "That doesn't surprise me," he responded. "But it is most fortunate that she is terrible at eavesdropping. She never can quite help herself from getting caught."

"Does Melody ever eavesdrop?"

"Not that I am aware of, but if she does, she is clearly very good at it." Bennett took Delphine's arm and gently led her out of Elodie's sight. "There. Now we can speak freely."

Delphine bit her lower lip before asking, "What is it that you wish to speak to me about?"

Bennett smiled, hoping to set her at ease. "I have greatly enjoyed our time together."

"As have I."

Good. This was going well, he thought. Now he just needed to confess he held affection for her and hoped she felt the same.

But as Bennett went to open his mouth, a footman with a solemn look on his face approached them at a clipped pace. "Lady Dunrobin," he shouted, his voice sounding urgent.

Delphine turned towards the footman. "Yes?"

The footman came to a stop in front of them as he attempted to catch his breath. "Your husband has just arrived."

Rearing back, Delphine asked, "My husband?"

In a resolute voice, the footman responded, "Yes, and he is waiting for you in the drawing room."

Delphine felt her world was spinning around her as she tried to process what the footman had just told her. Husband? She was quite certain that she did not have one of those. So who was in the drawing room? And why was he claiming to be her husband?

None of this made sense.

Bennett's voice came from next to her but it seemed so far away. "Delphie, are you all right?"

She met his gaze and admitted, "I am not. I don't know what is going on but I don't have a husband."

"Then who is in the drawing room?"

Her eyes darted towards the manor. "I have no idea." And she meant it. A feeling of trepidation washed over her. "No gentleman was courting me. I am most certain of that."

"Did you have any suitors?"

"There were many gentlemen that tried to press their suit, but I was not interested in any of them," Delphine said.

"Surely there was someone," he pressed.

Delphine shook her head. "No, there wasn't. I have no desire to marry at this point in my life and I told everyone that."

"Perhaps you don't recall getting married."

She let out a disbelieving huff. "That is something one would certainly remember."

"But all your memories have yet to return," he remarked. "What is the last thing that you remember before you woke up here?"

"I was in the drawing room with my friend, Charlotte, and we were discussing the upcoming Season," Delphine replied. "And I was husband-*less*. I am sure of that."

Bennett gave her a pointed look. "Then you must go speak to this man that is claiming to be your husband. It is the only way to find the answers that you seek."

Delphine knew that Bennett was right. She couldn't ignore this problem and hope that it would go away. But deep down, she only felt dread. Something was not right.

"Would you like me to accompany you to the drawing room?" Bennett asked.

"Yes, please."

Bennett gestured towards the manor. "Shall we?"

Delphine noticed that he didn't offer his arm as he usually did, and her heart ached because of it. If she were truly married, it would be entirely inappropriate for him to escort her into the manor. But she needed his touch now more than ever.

"It will be all right," Bennett encouraged.

She frowned, feeling herself growing increasingly upset by his encouraging words. Though she knew he meant to help, she couldn't bear to entertain hope at the moment. "How?" she asked, her voice tinged with frustration. "There is a man claiming to be my husband and I have not the faintest idea of who he could be."

Bennett's response was gentle but firm. "The first step is to speak to him."

"And if I don't like what he says?" Delphine asked, her apprehension palpable.

His gaze softened with understanding. "You won't know that unless you speak to him," he assured her. "I promise you that we will figure this out."

Delphine's legs felt heavy. She no more wanted to go speak to this man than have a thorn in her boot.

"Come along, Delphie," Bennett said. "You can do this. I know you can."

She found comfort in Bennett's reassuring words, his belief in her lending her strength. Drawing upon reserves deep within her, she squared her shoulders, ready to face whatever lay ahead. "You are right," she said.

"I usually am," he teased.

She resisted the urge to smile. Now was not the time. There was nothing amusing about this situation that she found herself in. "You will stay with me?"

Bennett nodded. "Always."

"Then let us go," she said before she started walking towards the manor. The worst part was that she believed Bennett's words. He would stay with her… unless she did truly have a husband.

Then he would leave her.

Delphine dismissed that thought. She didn't have a husband so this was a moot point. It must be a misunderstanding. It had to be.

As they walked next to one another, she snuck a glance at Bennett and saw his jaw was clenched. She suspected that he held some affection for her, just as she did for him, but had she been wrong to fall for him?

No.

She loved him.

A footman held open the back door as they stepped inside. As they grew closer to the drawing room, Delphine's steps grew more determined. She didn't know who she would find in there but she didn't want to lose Bennett over this.

Bennett came to a stop in front of the drawing room and gave her an encouraging look. But his eyes held a pain that she hadn't seen before. A pain that she was sure she had caused.

Delphine entered the drawing room and she saw her neighbor, Mr. Simpkin, standing by the window. His dark hair glistened in the sun and his long sideburns highlighted his long, thin face.

As she opened her mouth to ask him what was going on, a familiar voice came from the settee. "Delphine!" Charlotte shouted, jumping up from her seat.

She had barely turned towards her dear friend when she found herself wrapped up in Charlotte's arms.

"I can't believe you are alive," Charlotte said, leaning back to look at her. "I was so worried about you."

Delphine stared at her friend in disbelief. "What are you doing here?"

Mr. Simpkin spoke up. "I'm afraid that is my doing," he replied. "When we received Lady Dallington's letter about your condition, I felt you might need a friend."

Charlotte dropped her arms and took a step back. "You are looking well. Far better than what I expected."

Knowing that introductions were in order, Delphine turned towards Bennett. "Lord Dunsby, allow me to introduce you to my friend, Miss Eden, and Mr. Simpkin, a neighboring landowner near my country estate in Skidbrooke."

Bennett bowed. "A pleasure."

Mr. Simpkin approached her, albeit cautiously. "Lady Dallington's letter was rather vague about your condition, but she shared that some of your memories have returned."

"They have," Delphine replied. "But I can't seem to recall how I ended up in the woodlands in the first place."

Mr. Simpkin exchanged a concerned look with Charlotte before bringing his gaze back to Delphine. "Do you by chance recall us eloping to Gretna Green?"

Delphine's mouth dropped open in astonishment as she found herself utterly stunned. "Heavens no! Why would I have ever done such a thing?"

"Because you didn't want to make a big ado out of it," Mr. Simpkin replied. "Once you learned of your father's intentions, you thought it was best if we wed at once."

"My father's intentions?" Delphine inquired. "What on earth are you talking about?"

Mr. Simpkin gave her a look that was filled with sympathy. "Your father wished for us to wed once you reached your majority. Your solicitor explained all of this to you before we departed for Scotland."

Delphine brought a hand to her head. "I don't recall any of this. Why would my father wish for me to marry you? You are just a member of the gentry."

"That may be true," Mr. Simpkin responded, his voice tinged with pride, "but your father saw the potential in us combining our lands. Together, we are one of the largest landowners in all of England."

"This doesn't make sense," she murmured. "If what you are saying is true, why did we elope to Gretna Green?"

"You were rather insistent in that regard since you did not want a large wedding," Mr. Simpkin said gently. He reached into his jacket pocket and withdrew a piece of paper, unfolding it with care. "Perhaps if you saw the marriage license."

She accepted the paper and hesitated for a long moment before she read it. It was as he had said. They were married in the eyes of the law.

And she was trapped.

This one paper confirmed that she now belonged to Mr. Simpkin.

Delphine felt her legs grow weak and she stumbled back. Bennett caught her and held her in his arms.

"Let me help you to the settee, my lady," Bennett said.

She let him lead her to the settee, feeling all of the fight drain out of her. She was a married woman now. She had no rights. No freedoms.

Mr. Simpkin was not an unkind man. His lands neighbored hers and he had always been friendly to her. He had never made an attempt to court her, but he would often seek her out at social events.

Bennett gestured towards the marriage license in her hand. "May I?" he asked.

Without saying a word, she extended him the paper so he could review it. If anyone could find a way out of this mess for her, it was him.

In a terse voice, Bennett said, "Everything appears to be in order."

"Quite right," Mr. Simpkin responded as he stepped forward for the marriage license. "Now that we have established that, it is time for us to depart. For home."

Home.

No. Her home was not with Mr. Simpkin.

Delphine started shaking her head. She refused to go with him. "I can't go with you. I hardly know you."

Mr. Simpkin simply smiled. "We are married, my dear. We can have a lifetime to get to know one another."

Charlotte sat down next to Delphine and reached for her hand. "I know this comes as a shock to you, but you wanted to marry Mr. Simpkin. You told me as much."

"I did?" Delphine asked. Why did that sound so far-fetched to her?

Her friend bobbed her head. "You called upon me after

you visited your solicitor's office and told me that you were eloping with him."

"If what you are saying is true, why didn't we post the banns and get married at our local parish?" Delphine asked.

Charlotte tightened her hold on Delphine's hand. "You didn't want to marry in the same chapel your mother attended."

Delphine had to admit that her friend did have a point. The chapel did hold unpleasant memories for her since her mother had insisted on going there until the end.

A young, blonde maid stepped into the room with a tea service in her hand. She placed it on the table in front of Delphine. "Would you care for me to pour, my lady?" she asked.

Delphine didn't respond but instead stared at the teapot. None of this made any sense. Why couldn't she remember marrying Mr. Simpkin or the circumstances leading up to it? Her mind was blank. But none of this explained how she ended up in the woodlands.

Bringing her gaze up, she addressed Mr. Simpkin. "How did I end up in the woodlands?"

Mr. Simpkin grew somber. "On the way back from Gretna Green, the carriage had an accident and we were both thrown out. When I came to, we couldn't find you and we feared you were lost to us. To me."

Delphine had enough of this. She couldn't take it anymore. The life that she knew was over and she just wanted to be alone.

Rising, she put a hand to her forehead. "Excuse me, but I find this to be a little overwhelming," she said. "I need a moment alone."

Without waiting for their responses, she rushed out of the room, hoping this was just a terrible nightmare that she would awake from soon enough.

Chapter Thirteen

Bennett watched Delphine as she fled from the room and he resisted the urge to follow after her. To comfort her. But it wasn't his place. Not anymore. She was a married woman.

As his eyes remained fixated on the empty doorway, he heard Miss Eden say, "Excuse me. I will go see to Delphine."

Miss Eden hurried out of the room, leaving him alone with Mr. Simpkin. Which is the last place he wanted to be.

Mr. Simpkin cleared his throat. "I want to thank you for taking such good care of my wife."

My wife.

Those words cut him deeply.

Bennett turned his head to meet Mr. Simpkin's gaze. "How was it again that you came to lose Lady Dunrobin?" he asked, his words curt.

Mr. Simpkin gave him an apologetic look. "There was a carriage accident and we were all rather disoriented."

"Disoriented enough to leave your wife to die in the woodlands?" Now his words were accusatory.

"We looked for her—"

"Not hard enough, if you ask me."

Mr. Simpkin stiffened. "I didn't ask you, my lord," he said. "Once my wife has collected herself, we will be on our way."

Bennett knew it wasn't his place to keep Delphine here, but he wasn't ready to say goodbye either. He didn't trust Mr. Simpkin and he needed time to see if anything could be done to help Delphine.

"You might wish to speak to Lady Dunrobin, considering my mother is holding a soiree in her honor tomorrow evening," Bennett said.

Mr. Simpkin looked displeased by what he had just revealed. "I shall speak to her at once. I do not wish to offend Lady Dallington, especially since she has bestowed such kindness upon my wife."

"I think that is wise," Bennett said. "Now if you will excuse me, I am needed elsewhere."

Not bothering to wait for a response, Bennett walked purposefully out of the drawing room and ran right into Elodie.

His hands went out to steady her as she fell backwards. "You are terrible at eavesdropping," he remarked.

Elodie looked up at him with wide eyes. "Is it true?" she asked. "Is Delphine married?"

"Apparently so," he replied, his jaw clenched.

"What are we to do?"

Bennett shrugged. "I don't know, but I am going to speak to Winston. He might have an idea or two on what to do."

"I'll come with you."

With a shake of his head, Bennett said, "No, I do not need your help on this."

Elodie placed a hand on her hip. "What am I to do then?"

Bennett placed his hands on her shoulders. "You are a clever young woman. I am sure you will find something to occupy your time."

"If you don't allow me to come with you, I will just eavesdrop outside of the door," Elodie said.

"Fine," Bennett said, dropping his hands to his sides. "I am not in the mood to continue to debate this with you."

Elodie smiled triumphantly. "If it helps, I have confirmed that Winston is in his bedchamber."

"That does help," Bennett said before he started heading towards the grand staircase. He couldn't quite believe that Delphine was married, a fact she seemed neither eager about nor able to recall.

He could just accept the fact that Delphine was married and move on, but he couldn't bring himself to do so. He had to find a way to assist her, and that is where Winston came in. With his extensive knowledge of the law, he was their best hope.

Bennett reached Winston's door and knocked.

"Enter," Winston ordered.

Opening the door, Bennett gestured for Elodie to enter first before following her into the room. His gaze fell upon an empty whiskey bottle on the desk, and he raised a questioning eyebrow at his brother.

Winston leaned forward in his seat, disposing of the bottle in the dustbin. "What is it that you want?" he asked.

"I need your help," Bennett said.

"With what, exactly?" Winston asked.

Running a hand through his hair, Bennett attempted to quiet the flurry of thoughts racing through his mind. He needed to keep his wits about him, especially in this moment. Delphine needed him more now than ever.

In the calmest voice that he could muster up, Bennett revealed, "Delphine is married and her husband just showed up."

Winston kept his face expressionless as he asked, "What do you want me to do about that?"

Bennett walked across the room and sat on the edge of the bed. "Delphine doesn't remember getting married and is rather distressed at the moment."

"Did she want the marriage?" Winston asked.

Elodie spoke up. "It does not appear so," she replied.

Winston leaned back in his seat. "Tell me everything that you know," he said.

"Mr. Simpkin claims they were married in Gretna Green and they suffered a carriage accident when they were returning home, which is how she ended up in the woodlands on our property," Bennett said.

"Does Mr. Simpkin have a marriage license?" Winston asked.

Bennett nodded. "He does."

Winston grew thoughtful. The only sound echoing through the room was the steady ticking of the mantel clock. "The good news is that marriages in Scotland can be voided but only for a few reasons, such as insanity, adultery or abandonment. Perhaps we can argue to the Court that Delphine doesn't remember entering into the marriage."

"Do you think that would work?" Elodie asked.

"If Delphine wishes to go down this path, it is not an easy one. It will be expensive and could take years to get her marriage voided," Winston said. "And there is no guarantee that the Court will side with her."

"But there is a chance?" Bennett asked.

Winston tipped his head. "It is possible, considering Delphine is a countess in her own right. She does wield some influence."

Bennett rose from the bed and clasped his hands together. "I shall go tell Delphine at once!" he exclaimed. "She will be overjoyed to hear this."

Putting his hand up, Winston asked, "Are you sure this is what *she* wants, and not just you?"

"Of course she would want this," Bennett asserted. "She doesn't want to be married to Mr. Simpkin. Not that I blame her. He is not a man to be trusted."

"She said this to you?" Winston asked.

Bennett shifted uncomfortably in his stance under his brother's critical eye. "Not in so many words, but I know Delphine. Mr. Simpkin could never make her happy."

Winston pressed his lips together before asking, "And you could?"

"This isn't about me!" he exclaimed. "A man showed up here claiming to be Delphine's husband. A man who is entirely below her station."

Winston rose from his seat. "All right, but you must be pragmatic about this," he said. "Just because Delphine doesn't remember getting married, that doesn't mean she didn't do so of her own free will."

"Why would she marry that blackguard?" Bennett asked.

"How do you know he is a blackguard?" Winston countered.

Bennett scoffed. "He left Delphine in the woodlands to die," he said, his voice rising. "What kind of man does that to his wife?"

Elodie bobbed her head in agreement. "I agree with Bennett."

"Regardless, he didn't do anything criminal," Winston said. "Carriage accidents happen all the time and people die as a result of it."

Bennett felt his anger start to rise. How could Winston justify Mr. Simpkin's cowardly behavior?

Winston must have sensed the tension in the room because he gave Bennett a knowing look. "You are letting your emotions get ahead of you."

"My emotions have nothing to do with this," Bennett grumbled.

His brother was not easily fooled. "Just promise me that you aren't going to go off half-cocked until we attempt to resolve this amicably."

Bennett knew he needed to be rational about this, but he found he didn't want to be. He was angry. Hurt. The thought of Delphine being married to anyone but him was excruciatingly painful.

What if they couldn't void the marriage? Could he stand by and let Delphine be miserable for the remainder of her days? Did he even have a choice?

Elodie's voice came from next to him. "Do not give up hope."

"You didn't see Delphine's face when she looked at the marriage license. She looked defeated," Bennett said. "I know she doesn't love him."

"Marriage isn't always about love," Winston attempted. "Many people in her position use it to elevate their status in Society."

"And there is the rub! Mr. Simpkin is just a landowner, and Delphine is a countess. This marriage did nothing to elevate her status," Bennett stated.

In a calm voice, Winston responded, "Yes, but we still need to speak to Delphine. This decision lies with her and her alone."

Bennett narrowed his eyes at his brother. "Whose side are you on?"

"Yours, always," Winston replied. "I'm just trying to be pragmatic about this."

"How are we going to speak to her without Mr. Simpkin knowing?" Bennett asked.

Elodie smiled. "Leave that to me," she said as she walked towards the door. "Meet me in the kitchen in thirty minutes."

"What do you intend to do?" Bennett pressed.

"Just trust me," Elodie remarked before opening the door.

After his sister departed, Bennett sank back onto the bed, feeling the weight of the situation press down on his shoulders. It was hard to comprehend that this was actually happening. Poor Delphie. He had to remind himself that this wasn't about him. It was about her.

Winston stepped closer to him. "Do you think Mr. Simpkin forced Delphine into a marriage?"

"Meaning?"

"It isn't uncommon for men to abduct heiresses and force them to elope to Gretna Green," Winston responded.

Bennett clenched his jaw so tightly that he felt a muscle pulsating at the base of his ear. "It is entirely possible," he stated. "If I had my way, I would have already had him removed from our home."

Winston sat next to him on the bed. "I know you care for Delphine, but she is a married woman… for now. You will need to use some restraint when you are around her."

"Do not remind me," he muttered.

"You must take your heart out of this and apply logic to the situation," Winston advised.

Bennett glanced at his brother. "My heart isn't involved," he lied. "I am just merely concerned about Delphine."

Winston smirked. "My apologies, but your actions suggest otherwise."

"I just want what is best for Delphine," Bennett admitted. Which was the truth. He only wanted her to be happy. She deserved that much.

"We both do," Winston said.

Bennett sighed. Winston was right. He loved Delphine. And he would fight for her, even if it looked impossible for them to be together.

Delphine felt the tears form in her eyes as she rushed to her bedchamber on the second level. She didn't want anyone to see her cry. If they did, they would feel pity for her. And she didn't want anyone's pity.

Nothing seemed to make sense. Why had she married Mr.

Simpkin? He said it was her father's wish, but that meant nothing to her. Her father had no control over her now that he was dead.

If Mr. Simpkin hadn't had the marriage license in his hand, she wouldn't have believed it. It just seemed so far-fetched that she married a man that she hardly knew. A man who was so far below her station.

Delphine arrived at her bedchamber and opened the door. She started pacing in the room, not knowing what she could do to help herself. She was a married woman and every freedom she had enjoyed was now gone.

She belonged to Mr. Simpkin.

No.

She could not accept this. There had to be a way out of this precarious situation that she found herself in.

A soft knock came at the door before it opened, revealing Charlotte.

With a concerned look on her face, Charlotte asked, "May I come in?"

Delphine stopped pacing. "Yes, please do." She was most grateful that her friend was here since she needed her now more than ever.

Charlotte closed the door behind her and approached Delphine. "How are you?" she asked.

"My whole life is over!" Delphine exclaimed as she tossed up her hands. "What was I thinking when I married Mr. Simpkin?"

"It was a logical choice on your part," Charlotte said.

Delphine shook her head. "That doesn't make any sense," she asserted. "I didn't want to marry anyone at this stage in my life."

"That is true, but by marrying Mr. Simpkin, you are now one of the largest landowners in all of England."

"I care little about that," she declared.

Charlotte sat down on the settee and patted the seat next to her. "Come sit," she encouraged.

Delphine begrudgingly walked over to the settee and sat down.

"To begin with you should stop calling your husband 'Mr. Simpkin.' His given name is George," Charlotte said. "He is a good man and has always treated you with kindness."

"Kindness, yes, but he never once attempted to court me, which makes this all the more confusing," Delphine admitted.

Charlotte's eyes held compassion. "Let's start at the beginning," she suggested. "What is the last thing you remember?"

Bringing a hand to her forehead, Delphine said, "I was in the drawing room with you and we were discussing the upcoming Season. But I have no recollection of marrying Mr. Simpkin or how I ended up in the woodlands."

"George," Charlotte corrected.

She shook her head. "No, he is not George to me. I do not know him well enough to call him by his given name."

"You have known him most of your life," Charlotte pointed out. "He may be many years older than you, but you have always been neighbors."

Delphine jumped up from her seat. "Yes, and not once did my father tell me that I was to marry him."

"Your father wanted to wait until you reached your majority before he informed you of his intentions."

"But, why?" Delphine asked as she started pacing.

Charlotte shrugged. "I cannot speak on that, but you did decide it was in your best interest to marry Mr. Simpkin. By doing so, you had the protection of his name and you didn't have to endure the marriage mart."

"But I am a countess. I didn't need the protection of *his* name," Delphine insisted. Why couldn't she remember any of this? As she tried to force herself to recall these memories, all she was met with was darkness.

Her friend moved to the edge of her seat. "It will be all right," Charlotte assured her.

"How can you be so calm about this?" Delphine asked, her voice coming out much louder than she had intended. "My life is over."

"Aren't you being a tad bit dramatic?" Charlotte asked.

Delphine stopped and turned to face her friend. "I eloped to Gretna Green and I don't remember any of it. I think I have earned the right to be dramatic."

Charlotte tipped her head. "Good point, but what is done is done," she said. "And Mr. Simpkin is here to take you home."

"Home?" she repeated. "Where is home? Are we to reside at his country estate or mine?"

"Does it matter?"

Delphine blinked, bewildered by how calm her friend appeared while her entire world seemed to be crumbling around her. "Of course it matters! I don't want to leave my home to live with…" Her words came to an abrupt stop. "Have we been… intimate?"

"I cannot say," Charlotte replied.

"How would I know?" Delphine asked. "I don't feel any different so that must mean I'm still an innocent."

Charlotte grinned. "I am not sure if it works that way."

With a groan, Delphine sat down next to her friend. "What am I to do?"

"Why don't you go speak to Mr. Simpkin?" Charlotte suggested. "You might feel better once you do so."

"And if I feel worse?"

Charlotte gave her an understanding look. "When Mr. Simpkin received word that you were still alive, he promptly came to retrieve me because he was worried you might react this way," she said. "His first thought- and his only thought- was your wellbeing."

Delphine reached for her friend's hand. "I am grateful that you are here."

"I wouldn't be anywhere else," Charlotte said. "You are my dearest friend and I was devastated when Mr. Simpkin informed me of the carriage accident. He even started planning your funeral."

"How morbid," Delphine said.

"But that is all behind us," Charlotte said. "Now that you are alive, Mr. Simpkin wishes to host me for the Season. Just think of the fun that we shall have."

Delphine pressed her lips together. "What of your mother?"

"My mother thinks it is a grand idea since it saves her the expense of traveling to London," Charlotte said. "You are a married woman so it is more than acceptable."

"Yes, but, if I am indeed a married woman…"

"You are."

"… then what is the point of going for the Season?" Delphine asked.

Charlotte looked at her in disbelief. "There are so many things to do in London and just think of the social events. We shall have a grand time. Trust me!"

"I do trust you, but I would rather be at home, ensuring that my estate and business are thriving," Delphine said.

Charlotte waved a hand in front of her. "You do not need to worry about that anymore. Mr. Simpkin will see to all of that."

With a frown, Delphine said, "I doubt that Mr. Simpkin knows anything about goat cheese or the other specifics about the business."

Charlotte gave her a chiding look. "Why are you insistent on calling him 'Mr. Simpkin'?" she asked.

"Because that is how I think of him."

"He is your husband."

Her frown deepened. "Do not remind me."

A knock came at the door, interrupting their conversation.

"Enter," Delphine ordered.

The door opened and Elodie stepped into the room with a smile on her face. "I am sorry for disturbing you, but the cook has a few questions for you about the menu for the soiree. I'm afraid it is rather urgent."

Delphine thought it was rather odd that the cook was asking to speak to her, but she suspected that Elodie was up to something. "Very well," she said, rising. "I shall be down in a moment."

Knowing that introductions were in order, Delphine turned towards her friend. "Allow me to introduce you to Lady Elodie. She has been most attentive to me during my stay at Brockhall Manor."

Charlotte tipped her head at Elodie. "My lady," she greeted. "I am Miss Charlotte Eden. I grew up with Delphine."

"You are most welcome here," Elodie said before shifting her gaze back to Delphine. "Shall we?"

"You are accompanying me?" Delphine asked.

"Yes, my mother insisted since the menu for the soiree is of the utmost priority," Elodie replied.

It was now evident that Elodie had a plan of some sort because the menu for the soiree had already been planned by Lady Dallington days ago. But why was Elodie trying to get her to go down to the kitchen? Regardless, she had every intention of finding out.

Turning towards Charlotte, Delphine said, "I shall be back shortly. If you would like, a maid can show you to the library."

Charlotte perked up. "The library?"

"Yes, and it is quite exquisite," Delphine shared, knowing her friend shared in her love of books.

"Then I shall not miss you one bit," Charlotte joked.

Delphine laughed before she followed Elodie out of the room.

Once they were walking down the corridor, Elodie lowered her voice and shared, "Winston and Bennett want a word with you."

"Then why not just send a servant to fetch me?" Delphine asked, wondering what all the secrecy was about.

Elodie glanced over at her. "This is not a conversation that we want to be overheard."

Delphine furrowed her brow. "Why is that?"

"You will see," Elodie murmured as she came to a stop by a door. She opened it up, revealing the servants' staircase. "Be careful."

As Delphine descended the creaky stairs, she wondered what Winston and Bennett wished to discuss with her. Perhaps they had devised a plan to get her out of her predicament. Was that even possible?

Reaching the bottom step, she found Bennett standing in the kitchen. Their eyes locked, and her heart skipped a beat. How she loved this man. But she could do nothing about it. She was bound to Mr. Simpkin.

Was her fate sealed?

No.

She refused to give up. Not now. She had once thought it was a wishful fantasy to fall in love, but now she knew different. She had changed. And it was all because of Bennett.

Chapter Fourteen

Bennett watched as Delphine approached and he resisted the urge to close the distance between them. As much as he wanted her close, he knew that he had no right to actually do so. He just needed to be patient and trust Winston.

His eyes roamed around the empty kitchen and servants' hall. He wasn't sure how Elodie had managed to accomplish such a feat but he was pleased that she had done so. This was not a conversation that he wished to be overheard.

Delphine came to a stop in front of him and offered him a shy smile. "My lord," she greeted.

"My lady," he responded, though he didn't enjoy the newfound formality between them. "Thank you for coming."

A furrow appeared between her brows. "I am not quite sure why I am here."

Elodie came to stand next to Delphine. "Winston has found a way to help you divorce your husband."

Delphine turned her astonished gaze to Winston. "You have?"

Winston put his hand up. "There are a few things we must discuss first," he replied. "Do you remember anything about your wedding?"

With a shake of her head, Delphine replied, "I don't remember anything, including the events leading up to it."

"Could Mr. Simpkin have abducted you and forced you to wed?" Winston asked.

"I am acquainted with Mr. Simpkin, and he has never done anything that would lead me to believe he would do such a thing," Delphine replied. "He has only treated me with kindness in passing."

Winston crossed his arms. "Which begs the question, did you want this marriage?"

"Absolutely not!" Delphine declared, her eyes darting towards Bennett. "Mr. Simpkin claims that it was my father's intention that we were to wed, but I don't know if that is true. He would have never wanted me to marry someone so far below my station."

A solemn look came to Winston's expression. "We could argue that you never consented to the marriage, thus making it void. But that is assuming there were no witnesses that would argue against that fact."

"Would that work?" Delphine asked.

Winston dropped his hands to his sides. "It might, but it will take some time for the Court to hear your case. Until then, you will remain a married woman and Mr. Simpkin will have control over your business. But not your estate. That is entailed and it remains with the title." He paused. "At least, I assume it is entailed?"

Delphine nodded. "It is entailed, as with all my properties, and will be passed to my heir, male or female."

"That is good," Winston said, relief evident in his voice.

Bennett watched as Delphine's shoulders slumped ever so slightly. He could tell that she was trying to be strong, knowing how fiercely independent she was. Yet, he could only imagine the unbearable weight she was feeling. He wanted to offer comfort, to reach out to her, but propriety held him back.

Elodie spoke up. "Can Delphine remain here with us while you go argue her case in front of the judge?"

"That is assuming Mr. Simpkin allows it," Winston replied. "He stands to lose a great deal if this marriage is voided."

"He loses nothing! It was all mine to begin with," Delphine asserted.

Winston bobbed his head. "Yes, but it would go a long way if you could get Mr. Simpkin to cooperate with us. If we have his support to void the marriage, it will be uncontested, and the Court will no doubt rule in your favor."

Delphine grew quiet. "Why can't I remember any of this?" she asked, frustration evident in her voice.

"You must be patient with yourself," Bennett encouraged. "It will come back to you."

Shifting her gaze towards him, Delphine inquired, "What if it doesn't? I will always be left wondering what truly happened."

"I would advise you to take one day at a time and take comfort in knowing that truth always has a way of revealing itself," Bennett replied.

Winston interjected, "Bennett is right, and that is something I rarely say. Our first step is for Delphine to talk to Mr. Simpkin and see where he stands."

"And if he doesn't go along with the dissolution of our marriage?" Delphine asked.

"Then we fight," Winston responded firmly. "I have also taken the liberty of sending our fastest rider to Gretna Green to see if he discovers anything that might be in our favor."

Bennett could see the worry in Delphine's expression and it tugged at his heartstrings. He wanted to say something that might offer her the least bit of comfort. "It will be all right," he assured her.

"How?" Delphine asked. "I thought I had been so careful

but I did something intolerably stupid. And I don't even remember doing it."

He went to take a step closer to her but stopped himself. "I promise that we will figure this out… together."

Delphine's eyes grew sad. "Please," she murmured, her voice tinged with vulnerability, "don't make promises that you can't keep."

As she spun on her heel and hurried out of the kitchen, ascending the servants' stairs, Bennett watched helplessly. He knew she was right. Despite his desire to assist her, there were some things beyond his control. And that frustrated him to no end. He wanted to fix this. He *needed* to fix this.

Winston placed a hand on Bennett's shoulder. "We will find a way to help Delphine. I promise you that."

"What if we can't?" Bennett asked, letting the doubt creep back in. Now that Delphine wasn't here, he didn't have to pretend to be strong. "What if the judge doesn't rule in her favor and she is stuck in an unwanted marriage?"

His brother withdrew his hand. "There is always that chance, but you are overlooking one crucial detail."

"Which is?"

Winston smirked. "I am a very competent barrister and I have yet to lose a case."

Elodie walked over to the counter and retrieved a biscuit off a plate. "I forgot to tell Delphine that I asked the cook to leave out some biscuits for us."

"I think biscuits were the least of her concerns," Bennett remarked.

"Pity," Elodie replied before taking a bite.

Bennett couldn't resist goading his sister. "What purpose do you have in being here?" he joked.

Elodie held her hand out towards the biscuits. "I ensured there were refreshments available during our discussion."

A door opened and their portly cook stuck her head in. "May we come in now?"

"Yes, please," Elodie encouraged.

Mrs. Meek stepped into the kitchen. "I need to start preparing supper for this evening. I understand that we are to be having more guests."

Elodie nodded. "Unfortunately, yes. With any luck, we can scare them off before dinner."

Bennett gave his sister a pointed look. "We don't want to scare Mr. Simpkin off or he might insist that Delphine accompany him."

"You make a good point," Elodie remarked. "Although, I was planning on wearing a sheet over my head and pretending that I was a ghost."

"What purpose would that serve?" Bennett asked.

Elodie looked at him like he was a simpleton. "Everyone is afraid of ghosts. One look at me and Mr. Simpkin would be racing out the door."

Bennett chuckled. "You would have the same effect without the sheet."

His sister playfully narrowed her eyes at him. "I thought you were a gentleman," she said. "Besides, I'd think you would be nicer to me since I am helping you with your Delphine situation."

With a smile, Bennett responded, "I am sorry if I insinuated that your face scares people."

"There. Was that so hard to admit?" Elodie asked with a tilt of her chin.

Winston reached for a biscuit as he said, "If you will excuse me, I need to brush up on my Scottish law."

Turning towards his brother, Bennett expressed his gratitude, his tone carrying the weight of sincerity. "Thank you, Winston."

"Don't thank me yet," Winston said. "It is rather difficult to void a marriage, but not impossible."

"If anyone can do it, it is you," Bennett stated.

A pained look came to Winston's eyes before he blinked it

away, making Bennett wonder if he had imagined it in the first place. "I appreciate the vote of confidence, but let's not get ahead of ourselves."

As he went to respond, Winston walked off, not bothering to spare him a glance.

Elodie's eyes remained on Winston's retreating figure. "Winston seems more troubled than usual."

"That he does," Bennett agreed.

"Do you know why that is?" Elodie asked as she met his gaze.

Bennett shook his head. "I was hoping you knew. After all, you do like to eavesdrop on private conversations."

His mother's voice came from the direction of the stairs. "There you two are. I have been looking everywhere for you," she said. "Why are you down in the kitchen?"

"For the food," Elodie replied, holding up a biscuit.

Not looking convinced, his mother responded, "The truth, please."

Bennett glanced around the kitchen as the servants were milling around. "We were discussing a way to help Delphine," he admitted.

Approval shone in his mother's eyes. "Wonderful!" she exclaimed. "I assume that Winston was involved in the conversation."

"He was," Elodie confirmed.

"Then carry on," his mother said with a wave of her hand. "For how can Delphine marry you if she is already married?"

Bennett sighed. "Mother…" he started.

She laughed. "Everyone is thinking it, my dear. I am just the only one who is brave enough to say it."

"It is true," Elodie agreed.

Bennett didn't have the energy to continue this conversation. But as he started to walk away, his mother shared, "I have asked the maids to prepare the guest chambers for Mr. Simpkin and Miss Eden."

"Did Mr. Simpkin agree to stay until after the soiree?" Bennett asked.

His mother looked rather pleased with herself. "He did," she replied. "I will have you know that I can be rather convincing when I want to be."

Bennett knew that his mother could have been a barrister if she had so desired. She had an innate ability to convince people to do her bidding.

Elodie walked over to the pot that hung in the hearth. "What are we having?"

"Haggis," Mrs. Meek replied.

Her face fell. "Again?"

Mrs. Meek gave her an amused look. "Do not worry. I will set aside a plate of mutton for you."

"Will you do the same for me?" his mother asked.

"Yes, my lady," Mrs. Meek said.

Bennett glanced between his sister and mother. "Haggis is not terrible," he remarked. "It is one of Delphine's favorite dishes and I want to give her a reason to smile."

His mother stepped forward and patted his cheek. "I am pleased that I raised such a thoughtful son."

"He is only thoughtful when it comes to Delphine," Elodie insisted. "He implied that my face scares people."

"That wasn't very nice," his mother chided him.

Bennett grinned, not feeling the least bit repentant. "If the cap fits…"

Delphine made her way towards the library, seeking out Charlotte for support during this tumultuous time. The thought of her friend's presence brought her great comfort. They had been inseparable for as long as she could recall.

Upon entering the library, Delphine found Charlotte seated on a settee, engrossed in a book, while Mr. Simpkin stood by the window, his expression pensive.

Catching sight of Delphine, Charlotte lowered her book and greeted her with a playful twinkle in her eyes. "You are back. Did you solve the menu crisis for the soiree?"

"It wasn't a crisis, per se, but food is very important at soirees," Delphine replied. A twinge of guilt pricked Delphine as she kept the truth from her friend, but she knew it wasn't the time or place to delve into the depths of the matter.

"I wholeheartedly agree," Charlotte replied, tucking a piece of her blonde hair behind her ear. "Sometimes I feel as if I go just for the food."

Mr. Simpkin had turned towards them and met Delphine's gaze. "I understand that you wish to stay until after the soiree."

Delphine nodded. "It is true," she replied. She wanted to stay much longer, but she didn't think it was prudent to say such a thing. Not here. Not now.

"Then we shall stay," Mr. Simpkin said.

"Thank you," Delphine muttered. She didn't like the fact that Mr. Simpkin was granting permission for her to stay. Did she not have her own voice?

Mr. Simpkin watched her for a moment before asking, "Would you care to take a walk with me in the gardens?"

No.

She didn't want to go anywhere with Mr. Simpkin. But she reluctantly admitted to herself that it would be a good opportunity for them to speak frankly.

Delphine mustered up a smile. "That would be nice," she lied.

Mr. Simpkin stepped forward and offered his arm.

She glanced down at his arm, having no desire to be that

close to him. However, propriety won out. She placed her hand on his sleeve and allowed him to lead her out of the library.

Once they were in the corridor, Mr. Simpkin asked, "How are you faring?"

"I am well," she responded.

"I can only imagine how scared you were to wake up and not have your memories to comfort you," Mr. Simpkin said. "I wish I had been there for you."

Delphine could hear compassion in his voice and she found herself relaxing in his presence. "It was rather scary, but most of my memories returned fairly quickly."

"Yet you can't remember our wedding," Mr. Simpkin said.

She shook her head. "No, but I am trying."

Mr. Simpkin patted her hand. "I know you are," he said. "Lady Dallington informed me that the doctor told you to be patient and your memories should return."

"But what if they don't?"

"You mustn't focus on the 'what ifs,'" he replied. "That is not a path that is the least bit helpful."

As Mr. Simpkin led her down the stairs, Delphine said, "I daresay that it is a familiar path for me."

He grinned. "You are not alone. I have found myself being guilty of that a time or two as well. But I try to be a little better than I was the day before."

"That is a good philosophy to have."

His grin dimmed. "My father demanded perfection from me, even at a young age, and I never quite measured up."

"I can relate to that since my father was the same way."

"Perhaps that is why they got along so well," Mr. Simpkin remarked.

Delphine could hear the hurt in Mr. Simpkin's voice and she assumed his admission cost him a great deal. "At least you didn't disappoint your father the day you were born. My father was rather upset I was born a useless female."

Mr. Simpkin turned towards her with astonishment on his features. "What an absurd notion. You are a formidable woman."

"Thank you, but my father didn't want to pass his title to a woman," Delphine shared. "Or his business, for that matter."

"Well, you have proved him wrong by thriving," Mr. Simpkin praised.

Delphine offered him a grateful smile. "I appreciate that," she said. "I have worked hard to ensure my estate and business are profitable."

"It is more than just profitable," Mr. Simpkin declared. "You are providing livelihoods for hundreds of people. You should be proud."

A footman held open the back door as they stepped out onto the veranda.

Mr. Simpkin led her down onto one of the gravel paths. "I hope you do not mind, but I took the liberty of speaking to your man of business."

"You did?" she asked, her back growing rigid.

"Yes, now that we are married, you don't need to concern yourself with such things," Mr. Simpkin replied. "I shall oversee the estate and business."

Delphine came to a stop on the path and turned to face him. "You had no right to speak to Mr. Hawthorn," she declared. "He is *my* man of business, not yours."

Mr. Simpkin had the decency to look ashamed. "I upset you," he said. "That was not my intention."

"Then what was?" she demanded.

"I wanted to assure you that your estate and business were in good hands while you resided at Brockhall Manor," Mr. Simpkin said. "I imagine that it has been weighing heavily on your mind."

Delphine reluctantly admitted that he did have a point. "I suppose it has been."

His eyes crinkled around the edges. "You and I are very similar in that regard. We value duty above all else."

"I do," she sighed. "I suppose I should thank you for making inquiries, but it was wholly unnecessary."

"You and I are a team now," Mr. Simpkin said.

Delphine stiffened. She didn't take issue with Mr. Simpkin as a person, but she didn't want to remain married to him. There was no team, at least in her mind. She could handle whatever came her way, and she didn't need his help. Quite frankly, she didn't *want* his help.

Mr. Simpkin gestured towards a bench that was further down the path. "Would you care to sit?"

"Yes, thank you," Delphine replied before she walked over to the bench.

As she settled in, Mr. Simpkin took a seat beside her, leaving little space between them. Discomfort prickled within her. This proximity was unsettling, unlike the reassuring warmth she felt in Bennett's presence.

Fortunately, her unease was short-lived as Matilda approached, her hooves clacking on the gravel path.

Mr. Simpkin regarded the goat with curiosity. "What is that goat doing here?"

"Matilda has claimed this bench as her own," Delphine informed him. "It might be best if you move over to make room for her. If not, she will just sit on your lap."

"You are going to let a goat dictate your actions?" Mr. Simpkin asked in an appalled voice.

"Matilda tends to do as she pleases," Delphine said. "It is best if you just accept that fact and move on."

Mr. Simpkin looked displeased by her remark but he shifted on the bench to allow more space between them.

Matilda jumped up onto the bench and rested her head in Delphine's lap.

As she began to pet Matilda, Mr. Simpkin said, "I do hope you have more control over your goats."

"Do you not care for goats, Mr. Simpkin?"

"It is George, if you don't mind," he replied. "And no, I do not care for goats. But they serve their purpose."

Delphine gave him a curious look. "Is there a particular reason why you don't like goats?"

Mr. Simpkin looked down at Matilda, the disdain evident in his eyes. "I tolerate them, but I do not treat them as pets."

"That is a shame," Delphine said. "I had a pet goat when I was younger, and I am still quite fond of her."

A silence descended over them and Delphine was grateful. She wasn't quite sure how to start the conversation about voiding their marriage. But she needed to be brave and do so. She refused to stay married to a man that she was only acquainted with.

But as she went to open her mouth, Mr. Simpkin spoke first. "I know you don't remember marrying me, but I promise to make you happy."

Delphine's hand stilled on Matilda, knowing it was the perfect moment to broach the subject. "About that," she hesitated, "I was wondering, hoping, really, that you would consider speaking to the judge about voiding our marriage."

Mr. Simpkin stared back at her. "I beg your pardon?"

"We hardly know one another—"

He spoke over her. "Then let us resolve that issue, shall we?" he asked. "What do you wish to know about me?"

Delphine pressed her lips together before saying, "You are many years older than me and never once expressed a desire to court me. What changed?"

Mr. Simpkin grew solemn. "Before your father died, he came to me and proposed the idea of a marriage between you and me. He wanted to ensure you were taken care of, but he knew you would balk at the idea."

"Which is true," Delphine said. "I would have been furious had I known he had such a conversation with you."

"That is precisely why he asked me to wait until you

reached your majority before making his intentions known," Mr. Simpkin shared.

Delphine had so many questions for him, but she asked the one that was most pressing for her. "And when you came to tell me of my father's intentions, I just agreed to it?"

Mr. Simpkin chuckled. "Not at first," he replied. "You reacted very similarly to how you are right now. In fact, you told me that you had no desire to marry- at least at this stage in life- and asked me to leave. But I was persistent."

"I'm sorry. I just find it so hard to believe," she admitted.

"That is why I brought Charlotte with me," he said. "But it is true. All of it. You agreed to marry me in name only."

Delphine lifted her brow. "In name only?" she repeated. That hardly rang true, considering she knew she needed an heir… eventually.

"Yes, this is merely a business transaction. At least, that is how you put it to me," Mr. Simpkin said. "Although, I am hoping to convince you otherwise since I have admired you for many years. But in order to do so, you must give me a chance." His eyes seemed to plead with her. "Will you, Delphine?"

She was at a loss for words. Mr. Simpkin's plea was so heartfelt, but her heart had already been claimed by Bennett. She had no doubt that he would not be pleased with her response.

"I can't," Delphine said. "I'm sorry."

Mr. Simpkin's face fell. "I understand, but that doesn't mean I won't stop trying to win your affection." He rose from his seat. "When I received word that you were safe at Brockhall Manor, I thought of little else but you. I feel as if we have been given a second chance and I intend to make the most of it."

"Mr. Simpkin…"

"George," he corrected.

"… I just don't feel the same."

He smiled warmly. "I know, and that is all right. I have a lifetime to convince you to fall in love with me." He bowed. "My dear."

As her eyes remained on Mr. Simpkin's retreating figure, she knew if she continued down this path of voiding their marriage, it would be a fight. It was evident that he wasn't about to let her go.

But didn't she owe it to her heart to at least try?

Chapter Fifteen

Bennett stood in front of the parlor window, watching Delphine in the gardens. She sat on a bench, gently stroking Matilda, her expression one of sadness and pensiveness. He felt the need to go to her, to offer his support, but he had convinced himself not to do so.

His mother's voice came from the doorway. "You should go to her," she said.

"And say what exactly?" Bennett asked as he turned to face her. "She just finished conversing with her husband."

She walked further into the room. "I have no doubt that Delphine is scared, and she needs a friend."

"Friendship is not what I am seeking," Bennett admitted.

His mother did not look the least bit surprised by his declaration. "Perhaps not, but that is what she needs right now," she said as she came to stand beside him. "Winston informed me about what Delphine intends to do with her marriage. Voiding a marriage is not an easy path."

Bennett understood this all too well. He did not need reminders of the difficulty involved. It was weighing heavily on his mind. "I know, but Delphine wants to go forward with it."

"She is a brave young woman," his mother acknowledged. "If she is successful, her reputation will be in tatters."

"I do not think she has even considered that," he said as he dropped down onto a chair.

His mother lowered herself down into a chair next to him. "What is it that you want?" she asked.

"I don't rightly know," he confessed.

"That is not the answer I was hoping for," she said.

Bennett didn't have time for this. He wanted nothing more than to be alone so he could wallow in his self-misery. "What is it that you want from me, Mother?"

His mother regarded him with a compassionate gaze. "As a mother, I want you to have everything your heart desires. I want to take away every pain, every heartache and only allow you to experience joy. But that is impossible. You must experience each if you want to appreciate the other." She paused. "How you respond to your suffering is what will define you."

"That is easier said than done," Bennett remarked.

Rising, his mother said, "Right now, more than anything, Delphine needs a friend. Can you be that for her?"

"I want to, but I'm afraid that I won't be able to set aside my feelings for her," Bennett replied.

"If you can't be with her during the bad times, what makes you think you deserve to be with her through the good?"

Bennett knew his mother made a very good point. He had been so consumed with his own thoughts and feelings that he hadn't considered what Delphine was truly going through. And that ended now. He would be a friend to her- the greatest of all friends.

He jumped up from his seat. "I can be her friend."

His mother gave him a knowing smile. "I know you can, my dear," she said. "Now, go before I give you even more unsolicited advice."

"Thank you," Bennett said before he hurried out the door.

He knew the odds were stacked against Delphine, but he refused to give up. Not on her. Or himself. They might not have a future together, but all he wanted was for her to be happy.

As he passed by the drawing room, he heard giggling coming from within. He came to a stop, wondering what was so amusing.

Bennett stepped into the room and saw Mr. Simpkin and Miss Eden sitting on the settee, engaged in a conversation. By the looks of it, they were both rather enjoying themselves.

He cleared his throat, wanting to make his presence known.

Miss Eden's eyes went wide at the sight of him and she quickly rose. "Lord Dunsby," she said as she moved to create more distance between herself and Mr. Simpkin.

Mr. Simpkin did not look the least bit ashamed and simply asked, "My lord, is there something we can help you with?" His words were curt, despite the awkward situation.

"No," Bennett replied, his response blunt and to the point.

With a glance at Mr. Simpkin, Miss Eden said, "Excuse me. I think it would be best if I go rest before supper."

Bennett stood to the side as Miss Eden departed from the drawing room.

Mr. Simpkin stood and regarded him with disdain. "Now that Miss Eden is gone, I was hoping we could speak for a moment."

"What is it that you wish to speak about?" Bennett asked as he walked further into the room. He had a feeling that this conversation was meant to be private.

"I know what you are trying to do with my wife, and it ends now," Mr. Simpkin asserted. "I refuse to go along with voiding our marriage. We are legally wed, and I will not lose her."

Bennett could hear the determination in Mr. Simpkin's

voice but if he wanted to have a frank conversation, so be it. "Do you love her?"

Mr. Simpkin huffed. "Love?" he asked. "What does love have to do with marriage? Delphine and I agreed to wed in name only. It was a strategic move on both our parts."

"What does Lady Dunrobin get out of the marriage?"

"She has the protection of my name," Mr. Simpkin stated.

Bennett lifted his brow. "What kind of protection is that?" he asked. "You are only gentry and I doubt that you have made any mark in Society."

Mr. Simpkin bristled. "With Delphine's lands, I am one of the largest landowners in all of England."

"All I am hearing is that *you* benefit greatly from the marriage," Bennett responded. "Lady Dunrobin is a clever young woman. Why would she have gone along willingly with this marriage when it is so clearly not in her favor?"

With narrowed eyes, Mr. Simpkin asked, "Are you accusing me of forcing Delphine into this marriage?"

Bennett shrugged. "I suppose I am."

"That is preposterous!" Mr. Simpkin exclaimed. "We eloped to Gretna Green and even Charlotte was there to witness the happy occasion."

"Miss Eden was there?" Bennett asked. "At your anvil wedding?"

Mr. Simpkin gave him a decisive nod. "Yes, she was one of the witnesses."

That revelation did not sit well with Bennett. If they had truly eloped, why would they go through the trouble of bringing someone with them? None of that made any sense. And why was this the first time he was hearing that Miss Eden had accompanied them

Bennett took a step closer to Mr. Simpkin and crossed his arms over his chest. "Was Miss Eden injured in the carriage accident?"

"No. Thankfully she was spared of all harm," Mr. Simpkin said.

"Then how was it that you came to lose Lady Dunrobin, considering Miss Eden hadn't been 'disoriented'?" Bennett asked. "She could have helped look for her friend."

Mr. Simpkin's expression grew guarded. "Have you been in a carriage accident, my lord?" he drawled. "The aftermath is one of chaos and everyone is just grateful to have survived the ordeal."

"That didn't answer my question."

Taking a purposeful step towards Bennett, Mr. Simpkin said, "I don't answer to you. All you need to know is that my wife was thrown out of the carriage and we did everything in our power to find her."

"I'm beginning to suspect that wasn't true," Bennett responded, challenging him.

Mr. Simpkin pursed his lips. "You know nothing about me and yet you stand here, judging me."

Bennett uncrossed his arms and held Mr. Simpkin's gaze. "If you had cared at all for Lady Dunrobin, you wouldn't have left the woodlands until you had found her. That is what an honorable gentleman would have done."

"You are lecturing me on honor now?" Mr. Simpkin scoffed. "I have seen the way you look at Delphine. You care for her."

"My feelings are irrelevant," Bennett responded.

Mr. Simpkin moved to stand in front of him. "That is why you want to void my marriage. You want Delphine for yourself!"

Bennett stood his ground, not the least bit cowed by Mr. Simpkin's attempt to intimidate him. "I want Lady Dunrobin to be happy."

"With you?" Mr. Simpkin demanded.

Leaning closer, Bennett replied, "What I want is not

important. I just want to ensure that Lady Dunrobin has been treated fairly."

Mr. Simpkin's nostrils flared. "I am warning you to stay out of our lives."

"Is that a threat?"

At those words, the tall, broad-shouldered footman that had been standing guard out in the entry hall stepped into the drawing room.

Mr. Simpkin's eyes shifted towards the footman. "At least I can fight my own battles, my lord," he mocked.

Bennett chuckled dryly. "Yet you can't seem to keep track of your wife."

"I should challenge you to a duel for saying such a thing," Mr. Simpkin stated.

"Name the time and your seconds," Bennett responded.

Mr. Simpkin took a few deep breaths, his eyes narrowing with each inhalation, before stepping back. "You are not worth my time or notice," he grumbled.

"And I contend that you are not worthy of Lady Dunrobin's notice, considering she is far too good for you," Bennett declared.

Mr. Simpkin glared at him, the tension in the room becoming palpable. "Consider yourself warned," he spat as he stormed out of the room.

Bennett found that the more he learned of Mr. Simpkin, the less he liked him. He was beginning to wonder if Mr. Simpkin had spent any time looking for Delphine after this supposed carriage accident.

And some things were not making sense.

Winston entered the room and asked, "Is there a reason why Mr. Simpkin just snapped at me?"

"It might have to do with the fact that I asked him a few questions about his so-called wedding," Bennett said. "Mr. Simpkin revealed that Miss Eden accompanied them to Gretna Green."

Winston grew thoughtful. "That is odd."

"I thought so as well," Bennett responded. "And why had no one mentioned it until now? It just seems like something one would share."

"Perhaps our rider can provide some insight when he returns from Gretna Green," Winston said.

Bennett bobbed his head. "You were wise to send someone to ask questions surrounding their marriage."

Winston smirked. "I am not wholly incompetent at my job."

"I never implied you were," Bennett said. "I know of your reputation and how hard you work as a barrister."

The smirk faded from Winston's lips. "Yes, well, no amount of hard work will make up for what I have done."

Bennett eyed his brother curiously. "What have you done?"

Winston visibly tensed. "It is in the past, where I wish it to remain."

"Winston…" Bennett started.

Putting his hand up in front of him, Winston said, "Leave it alone, Bennett. We have more important matters at hand." He dropped his hand to his side. "I am calling in every favor that I have to help Delphine."

"Thank you," Bennett said, not knowing what else he could say. He was truly grateful for his brother's help.

Winston acknowledged Bennett's words with a tip of his head. "Have you spoken to Delphine about whether or not Mr. Simpkin will assist with voiding their marriage?"

"There is no need. Mr. Simpkin was rather clear that he intends to remain married to Delphine," Bennett shared.

"That is what I had assumed would happen, considering Mr. Simpkin stands to lose a great deal if the marriage is voided," Winston said.

Bennett glanced over at the window and saw that

Delphine was no longer on the bench with Matilda. He wondered where she had gone.

Winston's voice drew back his attention. "In case you were wondering, I saw Delphine walking to the stables."

"Why would I wonder such a thing?" Bennett asked, wondering how his brother had been able to see right through him.

Winston grinned. "You are a terrible liar, Brother," he said before departing from the room.

It only took Bennett a moment to realize that he needed to go after Delphine. He told himself that it was only to ensure she was well, but he wanted to see her. Even if it was for a moment.

Delphine leaned against the fence as she watched Hercules gallop back and forth, appearing to not have a care in the world.

She would miss this place. She had greatly enjoyed her time at Brockhall Manor and she didn't want it to come to an end.

But all good things must come to an end.

Even if she was successful in getting her marriage voided, she still had her own estate and business to run. And she took her responsibilities most seriously. She always had. However, could she just walk away from Bennett, the only man that she had ever loved?

Life had not always been kind to her, but what if the universe was correcting a wrong? What if this was her chance to be happy? The kind of happiness that she had only read about in books. The kind of happiness that she never thought she deserved.

Bennett came to stand next to her. "There you are," he said. "I have been looking for you."

Delphine's heart leapt at the sight of him, knowing she would never tire of being in his presence. She smiled. "Well, here I am."

"Yes, you are," he replied as he returned her smile.

She turned her gaze back towards Hercules. "Have you ever wondered what it would be like to be a horse?"

"No, not once, actually," Bennett responded, his words light.

"I just wonder what it would be like to be able to run free and to not feel the crushing weight of responsibilities that we inevitably must bear," Delphine said.

Bennett glanced over at her. "You are being rather cheerful this afternoon," he teased.

A laugh escaped Delphine's lips. "I suppose I am," she replied. "I was born into this life, and I have never thought to question it. But what if there is more to life?"

"Now that is a question that I have asked myself often," Bennett said, growing solemn. "What have you deduced?"

Delphine shrugged one shoulder. "Frankly, I am still trying to figure it out, but it has been a nice reprieve to be here at Brockhall Manor. With you."

Bennett's lips twitched. "It is a good thing I saved you then."

In her heart, she knew that Bennett had saved her in more ways than one, but she wasn't strong enough to admit such a thing. Not under these circumstances.

Hercules wandered over to where she was standing and whinnied.

"What is it that you want?" Delphine asked the horse.

Bennett chuckled. "I don't know why you ask such questions. Hercules is a horse. He is not going to answer you."

"He answers in his own way, and in his own time," Delphine said. "One should not force such things."

"I had not taken you for a horse expert."

"No, you misunderstood me. I do not claim to be a horse expert, but I see a kindred soul in Hercules."

Bennett grew silent. "If that is the case, I want you to have him."

Her eyes went wide. "You cannot be in earnest," she said. "I know Hercules reminds you of your uncle."

He turned to face her, a solemn look on his face. "He does, but Hercules seemed to come alive again when you came around. I want you to have something that will remind you of your time at Brockhall Manor." He paused. "And me."

"I don't need a horse to remind me of you," she admitted softly.

"Perhaps you might even be able to ride Hercules one day," Bennett said.

It was a tempting thought as her gaze drifted towards Hercules. She did admire this horse greatly, but could she do such a thing? "Are you truly in earnest because…"

He spoke over her. "I insist."

"Should you not at least speak to your father first?" Delphine asked.

Bennett gave her a pointed look. "My father has wanted to sell Hercules for a long time now and make him someone else's problem."

"At least let me buy Hercules from you."

He put his hand up in front of him. "I do not want your money, Delphie."

Delphine resisted the urge to smile at the use of his nickname for her. He had been so formal since Mr. Simpkin had arrived, and she understood his reasonings for it. One cannot be too familiar with another man's wife.

She knew there was only one thing she could say right now, and she hoped it expressed her gratitude. "Thank you, Bennett. I accept your gift."

"Good, because I do believe Hercules will be much happier with you," Bennett said.

"I hope so," she murmured.

A comfortable silence descended over them as Bennett leaned his forearms on the fence and stared out towards the fields.

Delphine felt no words needed to be said and she just enjoyed being near Bennett. He made her feel content in a way that no one else ever had.

After a long moment, Bennett asked, "Do you remember Miss Eden accompanying you to Gretna Green?"

"No, I do not recall that, but surely you are mistaken," Delphine replied. "Why would she travel with us to Scotland?"

"Mr. Simpkin informed me of this," Bennett said.

Delphine furrowed her brows. "If that is the case, I am sure there was a perfectly acceptable reason why she came along."

"Perhaps you could ask her," Bennett proposed.

"I will," Delphine said. "I just wish I could force myself to remember."

Bennett removed his arms from the fence and turned to face her. "I know you think Mr. Simpkin is not capable of nefarious intentions, but I do not trust that man. He had too much to gain by marrying you."

Delphine winced as she admitted, "He does not want to void our marriage."

"I know," Bennett said. "He told me as much when we spoke earlier in the drawing room."

"He wants our union to be a love match," Delphine shared.

Bennett eyed her curiously. "Is that what you want?"

With a huff, Delphine asked, "How could you ask such a thing? I thought I made it very clear that I wish to void this marriage."

"I just wanted to make sure. I don't want to make you do anything that you do not wish to do," Bennett said.

As Delphine went to respond, she saw Charlotte approaching them with a blue bonnet in her hand.

She put her hand up in greeting. "Charlotte."

Charlotte stopped in front of Delphine and extended her the bonnet. "I saw that you weren't wearing a hat and I thought you might like one."

"Thank you," Delphine said as she accepted the bonnet.

Bennett bowed. "Miss Eden."

With a tip of her head, Charlotte acknowledged Bennett but she didn't look pleased to see him by the small frown that played on her lips.

"If you will excuse me, I have work that I must see to," Bennett said before he started to walk off towards the manor.

Charlotte's gaze followed Bennett. "I do not know why you insist on spending time with Lord Dunsby."

"We are friends," Delphine replied.

"You are a married woman. Your friendship with Lord Dunsby could get the gossips' tongues wagging," Charlotte pointed out.

Delphine shook her head. "Lord Dunsby saved my life. I will forever be in his debt."

"It just seems like you two are rather close, and I am worried about you," Charlotte remarked.

"There is no reason to worry about me," Delphine assured her friend. "We are just friends, nothing more."

Charlotte gave her a knowing look. "I have known you a long time, and I have never seen you so smitten. You can hardly keep your eyes off Lord Dunsby when you two are in the same room."

"Nothing untoward has happened between us."

"I am not implying that it has, but I just want you to be careful," Charlotte said. "You are a wife to Mr. Simpkin now."

Delphine did not need to be reminded of that fact. She

just wished that she could close her eyes and end this nightmare.

Charlotte's next words were gentle. "I am sorry. I am being a terrible friend right now."

"No, you aren't," Delphine responded. "Everything you are saying is true, but I just wish I could remember."

"You will," Charlotte encouraged.

Delphine offered her a weak smile. "The doctor said my memories might never return."

Charlotte seemed to consider her words before asking, "Do you remember anything about traveling to Gretna Green?"

"Not a thing," Delphine responded. "Lord Dunsby claims that you accompanied us to Scotland. Was that true?"

"Yes, you asked me to come and be a witness," Charlotte replied.

Delphine pressed her lips together before asking, "I did?"

Charlotte's eyes held understanding. "It was a whirlwind decision on your part, and I was not about to question it," she said. "Besides, I wanted to be there for you, especially after everything you have done for me over the years."

Delphine let out a frustrated sigh. Why couldn't she just remember? She glanced up at the position of the sun. "I am surprised you are not resting right now."

"As am I," Charlotte replied. "Naps are the most important part of the day, but I saw you out here hatless. And being the good friend that I am, I knew I had to remedy that."

"You are a good friend," Delphine said.

Charlotte glanced over her shoulder before she lowered her voice. "I can see why you have been taken with Lord Dunsby. He is rather handsome."

"I have not been taken with him," Delphine lied.

"No, of course not," Charlotte rushed out with an exaggerated wink.

Delphine shot her friend a frustrated look. "You are not

being the least bit helpful right now," she stated. "Lord Dunsby and I are just—"

"Friends," Charlotte said, cutting her off. "I wouldn't mind being friends with him, too."

The thought of Charlotte flirting with Bennett did not sit well with her. Rather than engage her friend, she asked, "Shall we return to the manor so we can rest before dinner?"

"I think that is a fine idea since I was considering laying on this grass and taking a nap," Charlotte said.

"I am sure your bed is far more comfortable than the ground."

As they walked back towards the manor, Charlotte asked, "Do you think if I wander around the woodlands, a handsome lord will rescue me, as well?" Her eyes held a mischievous glint.

Delphine rolled her eyes. "You are awful," she said, her words light.

Charlotte grinned. "I'm sorry. I know I shouldn't joke about such things, especially after I lectured you so thoroughly, but I am in need of a husband. A handsome, wealthy husband."

"What of love?"

Her friend's smile dimmed. "What of it?"

"Do you not want to marry for love?" Delphine asked.

Charlotte looked away, but not before Delphine saw a pained look on her face. "Love is of little consequence for me."

Delphine came to a stop on the path and turned to face her friend. "Where is this coming from?" she asked. "You have always spoken of love as a requirement for marriage."

"I suppose we all have to grow up at some point," Charlotte said dejectedly before she continued walking towards the manor.

Remaining rooted in her spot, Delphine wasn't quite sure what to make of Charlotte's thoughts on marriage. Her friend had always encouraged her to marry for love, insisting they both deserved love matches.

What had changed in Charlotte to cause her views to radically shift?

Delphine would drop it… for now. But she could tell her friend was hurting and she refused to do nothing to help her.

Chapter Sixteen

Seated in the study, Bennett gazed into the dancing flames of the crackling fire, a glass of port held loosely in his hand. He was not looking forward to dinner with Mr. Simpkin. He'd found that the man grated on his last nerve and he would be happy to wipe the smug look off his face.

He had little doubt that Mr. Simpkin had forced Delphine into an unwanted marriage. For how could she have ever agreed to marry that man? He was not a man to be trusted, especially since he had abandoned Delphine in the woods to die on her own.

Perhaps he should challenge the interloper to a duel and be done with it.

But that would not solve the problem.

Delphine was still married to that horrible man. But not for long. He would do everything in his power to see it voided by a judge.

Winston stepped into the room and gave him an incredulous look. "You are having port before dinner? Are you a heathen?"

Bennett leaned forward and placed his nearly full glass onto the table. "I thought I would try something different."

"Did it work?"

"No," he replied. "I am still miserable."

Winston gave him an amused look. "Voiding a marriage takes time. Are you going to be miserable the entire process?"

"Most likely."

"Assuming we are successful, then what?" Winston asked.

Bennett knew precisely what he wanted to do in that situation. "I want to marry Delphine," he asserted.

Winston grinned. "I assumed as much, but I am glad to hear you say it out loud."

"Just because I want to marry her doesn't mean she wants to marry me," Bennett said. "She is fiercely independent."

"That she is, but you are just as good as anyone," Winston hesitated, "except for Mr. Simpkin."

Bennett chuckled. "That man is awful."

"I won't disagree with you there," Winston said.

A knock came at the door and the tall, broad-shouldered footman stepped into the room. "My lords, might I have a moment of your time?"

Bennett exchanged a look with Winston before replying, "Very well." He wondered why the newly hired footman that had been standing guard in the entry hall wished to speak to them.

The footman closed the door, ensuring their conversation remained private. "My name is Grady, and I work with Jasper."

Realization dawned on Bennett. "You are the Bow Street Runner that we were told was to watch over us."

"That I am, and I did not intend to make my presence known, but I do believe I have some information that you might be interested in," Grady said.

Winston spoke up. "What is it?"

Grady grew solemn. "I watched Miss Eden enter Mr. Simpkin's room this afternoon and she remained there for well over an hour."

Bennett lifted his brow. "Are you sure?"

"I know what I saw and I kept time on my pocket watch," Grady replied firmly.

Winston's expression grew thoughtful. "That is most helpful," he said. "In Scotland, a woman can petition for divorce if her husband is found committing adultery."

"Which will take the least amount of time in the Court? Voiding a marriage or divorce?" Bennett asked.

"Depends on the judge," Winston replied before turning back towards Grady. "Did either of them see you?"

Grady shook his head. "I know how to be discreet."

The sound of the dinner bell echoed throughout the main level.

"I should be returning to my post before anyone discovers that I am missing," Grady said. "I hope for your discretion as well."

After the Bow Street Runner departed from the study, Winston asked, "Shall we join everyone in the drawing room?"

"I suppose we must."

Winston's eyes held amusement. "It is fun seeing you this miserable."

Bennett didn't know if he should take offense to such a statement. "Why is that?"

"Everything has always come so easy to you, has it not?" Winston asked with a knowing look.

"That is not the least bit true," Bennett defended.

Winston put his hands up. "You have always been the heir, the golden child, and I had the misfortune of being born after you."

Bennett took a step closer to his brother. "I hope you know I don't think that way. I am proud of everything that you have accomplished."

"It is hard to be a second son," Winston admitted. "We are pushed aside until we are needed."

"I always need you, Brother," Bennett stated.

Winston didn't look convinced. "You and I are on very different paths, but that doesn't mean I am envious of your position. I must work harder to make something of myself."

"And you have."

His brother huffed. "We should hurry. We don't want to keep anyone waiting."

As Bennett followed Winston from the study, he wondered- and not for the first time- how he could help his brother. But he didn't even know what he was grappling with. He heard snippets of his pain, but his brother never explained the cause of it.

He had just arrived in the entry hall when he saw Delphine descend the stairs. She was dressed in a stunning blue gown adorned with a delicate white net overlay. Her hair was elegantly piled atop her head, and a coral necklace graced her neck.

In that moment, Bennett could not recall ever beholding a more breathtaking sight. But it wasn't just her outward beauty that captivated him. It was something deeper, something intangible. Delphine possessed a charm and grace that transcended mere appearance. She was everything he desired in a companion, and he found himself hoping that he could be the man worthy of her affection.

Mr. Simpkin came to stand next to him and lowered his voice. "She is mine, all mine," he taunted.

"Not for long," Bennett asserted.

"Your plan to void our marriage won't work," Mr. Simpkin mocked. "You will fail."

Bennett smirked. "You do not know me very well then," he said. "I am very good at getting what I want."

Mr. Simpkin leaned closer to him. "So am I, my lord."

After Delphine stepped down onto the marble floor, Mr. Simpkin approached her with his arms wide open. "My dear, you look lovely. The vision of perfection."

Delphine visibly tensed as Mr. Simpkin went to kiss her on the cheek. "Thank you," she murmured.

Mr. Simpkin remained close and offered his arm. "May I escort you to the drawing room?" he asked.

She looked down at his arm with hesitancy in her eyes before placing her hand on his sleeve.

With a triumphant glance at Bennett, Mr. Simpkin led Delphine into the drawing room.

Winston's voice came from behind him. "I can see why you do not like that man."

"I assure you that it is not just for one reason," Bennett said as he turned to face his brother. "I object to his whole person."

Elodie and Melody descended the stairs and they both were wearing the same pale green gowns.

Winston shook his head. "Mother does not like it when you two wear matching gowns. I know because she has told you as much- multiple times, in fact."

They came to a stop on the last step and Melody smiled. "We thought we would have some fun at Mr. Simpkin's expense."

"I will allow it," Bennett said.

Winston glanced between his sisters. "Dare I ask what you intend to do?"

Melody leaned forward and placed a hand to the corner of her mouth. "It is best that you don't know."

"I am surprised that Elodie talked you into this," Winston said, addressing Melody.

Elodie reached up and brushed back one of the curls that framed her face. "It was actually Melody's idea."

"I find that hard to believe," Winston remarked.

Melody's lips twitched. "I can be a little devious when I want to be," she stated.

Bennett knew that Melody spoke true. She was oftentimes reserved, but she had a quiet strength that he had always admired. She could hold her own with Elodie and remain true to herself.

His mother stepped out of the drawing room and let out an exasperated sigh. "Good heavens, Elodie and Melody," she said. "What am I going to do with you?"

But as his mother approached them, her face softened, and a hint of amusement played in her eyes. In a hushed voice, she asked, "What is the plan?"

"The plan?" Bennett asked.

His mother bobbed her head. "How do you intend to goad Mr. Simpkin?" She paused. "Wait, do not tell me. It is best if I am surprised. My reaction will be more genuine."

Melody cast a concerned look towards the drawing room. "How is Delphine?"

"Mr. Simpkin remains rooted at her side and is insistent that he answers for her," Lady Dallington revealed. "It is vexing for me, but Delphine is handling it with grace."

Bennett wanted to go in and save Delphine from Mr. Simpkin, but it wasn't his place to do so. Botheration. How he hated that Mr. Simpkin had the upper hand, but it would change soon enough.

The butler stepped into the entry hall and announced that dinner was ready to be served.

As they walked towards the dining hall, Elodie matched Bennett's stride and asked, "How are you, Brother?"

"I am well," he lied.

Elodie gave him a look that implied that she didn't believe him. "Just say the word and I will put parsnip in Mr. Simpkin's bed. He will develop a terrible rash and will be miserable for days."

The worst part was that Bennett knew Elodie was in earnest. He could easily imagine Elodie grinding up parsnip leaves so she could sprinkle them on Mr. Simpkin's bed.

"I appreciate what you are trying to do but this isn't your fight," Bennett said.

"I disagree," Elodie responded. "We are family, and we stick together."

As they entered the dining room, Bennett was surprised to see Mr. Campbell in the corner as he fiddled with the bagpipes.

Elodie leaned closer to him and explained, "Melody thought an encore was appropriate."

Bennett wasn't sure what his sisters were up to, but he found himself very curious.

Delphine was in a hell of her own making. She was sitting between the man that she loved and the man she was married to. And the worst part was that Mr. Simpkin was being overattentive, not giving her a chance to even speak up. He was taking away her voice, and she did not like that. But she didn't wish to cause a scene. Not here.

Charlotte sat across from her and gave her an encouraging look. If anyone understood what she was going through, it was her friend.

Her eyes shifted towards Elodie and Melody. She could scarcely tell them apart since they were wearing matching gowns and had worn their hair in a similar fashion. She wondered what game they were playing.

Lady Dallington spoke up, drawing her attention. "I do hope everyone is excited for the soiree tomorrow evening."

Delphine nodded. "I am," she replied. "I feel as if I haven't danced in ages."

Mr. Simpkin cleared his throat. "Are you sure that is wise?" he asked. "You are still recovering from your injuries."

"I am fine," Delphine assured him.

"Well, I must insist that you refrain from dancing," Mr.

Simpkin said. "We wouldn't want to jostle your brain any more than it has been."

Delphine pursed her lips together as she tried to quash the growing irritation she felt for Mr. Simpkin. "You do not need to concern yourself with me."

"I'm afraid that is impossible for me to do since we are married," Mr. Simpkin said.

"You do not need to remind me- again," Delphine responded. "I am fully aware of our situation."

Mr. Simpkin smiled, and it grated on her nerves. "I am not without a heart, my dear. I would be happy to dance one set with you."

Delphine no more wanted Mr. Simpkin's hands on her than she wanted a thorn in her boot. His touch was not the least bit comforting and she found herself looking for reasons to avoid it.

The footmen stepped forward and placed soup in front of them.

Mr. Simpkin glanced down at his bowl, giving it a look of trepidation. "This looks interesting," he muttered.

Elodie perked up in her seat. "We asked our cook to prepare some traditional Scottish dishes in honor of Delphine's last dinner with us," she said. "The soup is Cullen Skink and is primarily made from smoked haddock."

"That is most kind of you," Delphine acknowledged. "I greatly enjoy Cullen Skink. It brings back fond memories for me."

Mr. Simpkin took a sip of his soup before saying, "It is not as awful as I expected, considering the Scottish are not known for their food. But I still do not care for it."

Delphine resisted the urge to roll her eyes at such an idiotic remark. "You seem to forget that I was raised in Scotland and I have a fondness for their food."

"Yes, but surely you must agree that their food is far too hearty for everyday eating," Mr. Simpkin said.

She had been raised to be a lady, but her patience was being tried by Mr. Simpkin. She wanted to release her sharp tongue on him, but that would resolve nothing.

Mr. Simpkin must have taken her silence for acceptance because he continued. "I recently acquired a French cook that makes the most splendid meals. I have no doubt that you will greatly enjoy those."

"I have my own cook," Delphine said.

"Not any longer," Mr. Simpkin said. "I dismissed your household staff."

Delphine's mouth dropped open. "I beg your pardon?"

Mr. Simpkin waved a dismissive hand in front of him. "There was no need to employ two household staffs and I am partial to my own servants."

"You had no right," Delphine said, placing her spoon down. "Some of those people have been working for my family for generations."

"Yes, and I fear that they have grown far too complacent," Mr. Simpkin stated.

Delphine drew in a steadying breath, reminding herself to remain patient until her marriage was nullified. Once that happened, she could move on with her life, and Mr. Simpkin would be out of it.

Bennett caught her eye and winked, providing her with much needed reassurance. She could do this, and she knew she wasn't doing it alone.

Melody interjected, "While we eat, I thought we could listen to the bagpipes."

"That is a fine idea, Sister," Elodie said enthusiastically.

The sound of bagpipes filled the air and Delphine found the familiar music to be rather soothing. She could almost forget that she was married to a jackanapes.

While Delphine ate her soup, she realized that she wasn't being entirely fair to Mr. Simpkin. He wasn't inherently awful, but she found his persistent attempts to win her affection to be increasingly tiresome.

As the footmen stepped forward to collect the bowls, Mr. Simpkin opened his mouth to no doubt say something that would irritate her. But as he started to speak, the sound of bagpipes filled the room, drowning out his words.

Mr. Simpkin closed his mouth and the bagpipes seemed to soften as if in response to his silence.

Bennett rose as a footman placed a tray of food in the center of the table. "I hope everyone enjoys haggis."

Delphine heard Mr. Simpkin let out a groan and she was amused. It was evident that he was not a fan of haggis. She suspected that was the reason it was being served this evening.

Elodie picked up her plate and extended it towards Bennett. "I do love haggis. It is my favorite."

Delphine was well aware that Elodie did not enjoy haggis but she was pretending to goad Mr. Simpkin. Which was fine by her.

Once everyone was served, Bennett returned to his seat and picked up his fork and knife. "I asked our cook to ensure there was plenty of sheep lung in this meal. I know that Delphine is especially partial to that ingredient."

Mr. Simpkin looked down at his plate with disgust. "How can you eat this?" he asked.

"It is delicious," Delphine said before taking a bite.

Pushing his plate away from him, Mr. Simpkin announced, "I'm afraid that I have lost my appetite."

In a low voice, Delphine chided, "You are being rude to our hosts."

Lord Dallington put his hand up. "We are not ones to take offense," he said. "I am not fond of haggis either."

Mr. Simpkin went to respond just as the bagpipes started growing louder.

Delphine saw Mr. Simpkin's lips move but she didn't hear

the words that he uttered. She was beginning to suspect that was the point of the bagpiper.

The music came to an end and Elodie and Melody started clapping.

"That was wonderful," Elodie gushed. "Will you continue to play?"

The bagpiper nodded his head before he continued playing a traditional Scottish song.

Mr. Simpkin leaned towards Delphine and asked, "Would you care to take a turn around the gardens after dinner?"

That was the last thing that Delphine wanted to do. The more she learned about Mr. Simpkin, the less she liked him.

Fortunately, Lady Dallington chimed in. "We usually play card games in the parlor after dinner. It is a family tradition."

Mr. Simpkin looked disappointed but was wise enough not to argue with their host. "Very well," he said. "We can always go on a tour of the gardens tomorrow."

Bennett glanced down at Delphine's plate and asked, "How are you enjoying your haggis?"

"It is delicious," Delphine replied. "It was most thoughtful that you had the cook prepare this dish again."

"I remembered how much you liked it last time," Bennett said with a smile.

Delphine held his gaze for a moment before returning to her plate of food. How she wished that Bennett was her husband, and she could flirt with him as often as she wished.

Mr. Simpkin attempted to speak again, but his words were once more lost amidst the lively tunes of the bagpipes. Annoyance flickered across his face, indicating that he had finally realized the deliberate interference orchestrated by the bagpiper.

Charlotte, who had been quietly eating her haggis, leaned forward in her seat to meet Delphine's gaze. "Do you recall when your father would insist on being woken up by the bagpipes?"

"That was an unfortunate time for everyone, especially the person playing the bagpipes," Delphine said. "My mother would often throw her pillows out the windows in an effort to get him to stop playing."

"Your father had his own way of doing things," Charlotte commented.

"That he did," Delphine agreed. "But he did ensure I appreciated my Scottish heritage. For that, I am most grateful."

Winston joined in on the conversation by asking, "Do you prefer living in Scotland or England?"

Delphine considered his words for a moment, ensuring she gave it proper thought. "That is a tricky question. I consider them both my home. However, I could do without the house spiders in Scotland."

"I hate spiders," Melody muttered with a shudder.

"Then you would loathe the house spiders," Delphine asserted. "They enter the homes through gaps under the doors and chimneys. Their spiderwebs are enormous and almost look like a bedsheet. The worst part is that you can hear them as they move across the floor at night."

Melody turned towards her mother with wide eyes. "I do not wish to ever visit Scotland."

"I am sure that Delphine is just exaggerating," Lady Dallington said.

Bennett shook his head. "I'm afraid she's not," he confirmed. "I have seen many house spiders when I have visited Scotland. When they drop down onto a table, you can hear a palpable thud."

Elodie was pushing the haggis around the plate as she shared, "Spiders do not bother me, but I do not like rats."

"No one likes rats," Winston remarked.

The butler stepped into the room and met Delphine's gaze. "Pardon the interruption but Mr. Vincent Paterson is here to call upon you."

Delphine stared back at him in disbelief. "My cousin is here?"

"Yes, my lady," the butler confirmed.

As she struggled to think of one valid reason as to why Vincent was here, Mr. Simpkin revealed, "I should note that I invited Mr. Paterson here."

She turned towards him. "Why would you do such a thing?" she demanded. "Vincent has been trying to take my title since I inherited it."

Mr. Simpkin smiled at her, no doubt in an attempt to disarm her. "Mr. Paterson is only here to ensure that you are well."

"I doubt that."

"It is true," Mr. Simpkin said. "When I returned from Scotland without you, your solicitor insisted that I show proof that you had died before he proceeded with transferring your assets to me. Mr. Paterson also had a vested interest in securing proof so he might inherit your title."

Mr. Simpkin continued. "Before we could dispatch riders to look for your body, we received word from Lady Dallington about your condition. You can only imagine how relieved we both were."

"Yes, I can only imagine," Bennett muttered under his breath.

Mr. Simpkin did not react to Bennett's remark but rather held Delphine's gaze. "Mr. Paterson is here to confirm that you are indeed alive and well."

Delphine wasn't quite convinced that was all it was, but she should go greet her cousin. She shoved back her chair and said, "I suppose I should get this over with."

Rising, Bennett asked, "Would you like me to accompany you?"

Before she could reply, Mr. Simpkin spoke on her behalf. "Need I remind you that I am Delphine's husband, and *I* will accompany her."

"I find it odd that you are constantly reminding people that you are married to Delphine," Bennett said dryly.

"I wouldn't have to do so if you didn't continually overstep your bounds," Mr. Simpkin responded with a clenched jaw.

Delphine glanced between Mr. Simpkin and Bennett with a stern look. "Are you two quite finished?" she asked.

Mr. Simpkin placed his hand on her sleeve. "Come along, Dear," he encouraged. "Let us go speak to Mr. Paterson."

"I would like Lord Dunsby to join us as well," Delphine said as she remained rooted in her spot.

Her husband looked displeased by her request but thankfully he didn't question her decision. "If you insist," he replied.

As they departed the dining room, Delphine didn't quite know what to expect from Vincent. They had been at odds for so long, and he had never once shown any interest in her well-being. He only cared about taking her title.

So why was he here?

And what did he hope to gain?

For one thing she knew about Vincent, he did nothing by chance.

Chapter Seventeen

Bennett followed Delphine from the dining room and noticed that she was tense. Not that he blamed her. From what she had told him of Mr. Paterson, it was evident they held no real affection for one another, despite being cousins.

As they stepped into the entry hall, he saw a tall man with slicked back black hair and a crooked nose.

"Cousin," Mr. Paterson exclaimed, his arms out wide. "It is so good to see you looking so well."

Delphine came to a stop a short distance away from her cousin. "Is it?" she asked. "Dare I ask why you are truly here?"

Mr. Paterson shifted his gaze to Mr. Simpkin. "Did you not tell her that I was coming?"

"No, I'm afraid it slipped my mind," Mr. Simpkin replied.

Turning back towards Delphine, Mr. Paterson said, "I was instructed by Mr. Shelden to confirm that you are indeed alive and well."

Delphine held her hands out. "As you can see, I am alive," she assured him. "You may return home now."

Mr. Simpkin stepped forward. "Delphine, you are being

rude to your cousin," he chided. "You should at least allow him to stay the night."

"It isn't my place to do so since we are guests in Lord Dunsby's home," Delphine remarked.

Mr. Paterson put his hand up. "It is no bother at all," he said. "I have already retained a room at the boarding house in the village."

"Very good," Delphine responded as she turned to leave.

Reaching forward, Mr. Paterson gently grabbed her arm, stilling her. "I know that we have never seen eye to eye before, but I am glad that you are alive."

Delphine pursed her lips before saying, "Eye to eye?" she questioned. "You have been trying to steal my title since I first inherited it."

"Yes, but that doesn't mean I wish to see you dead," Mr. Paterson said. "We are family, after all."

Yanking back her arm, Delphine responded, "You say that as if it means something, Vincent."

Mr. Paterson sighed. "You have always had a flair for dramatics."

Delphine gestured towards the door, her jaw firmly set. "You may go. And for your sake, do not come back."

Appearing amused by her dismissal, Mr. Paterson turned his attention towards Bennett. "I must assume that you are Lord Dunsby." He bowed. "Thank you for saving my cousin."

"It was my pleasure," Bennett replied, not wishing to engage Mr. Paterson any further. It was rather obvious that Delphine didn't want him here.

"I hope that she has behaved herself while she was a guest in your home," Mr. Paterson said.

Bennett tipped his head in acknowledgement. "She has been the epitome of grace and decorum."

"Just not when I am around," Mr. Paterson quipped.

Delphine placed a hand on her hip. "It is late and you

have interrupted us during dinner. We should return before the others come looking for us."

"Very well, but I shall return tomorrow to continue our delightful conversation," Mr. Paterson said. "We have much that still needs to be said between us."

"Yet I cannot think of one thing," Delphine remarked.

Mr. Simpkin spoke up. "We shall look forward to speaking to you tomorrow," he said with a bow.

Delphine turned her heated gaze towards Mr. Simpkin. "You do not get to speak for me," she stated firmly.

"But I am your husband," Mr. Simpkin said.

"You say that as if it is supposed to mean something," Delphine declared. "I am perfectly capable of speaking for myself."

Mr. Simpkin clenched his jaw. "Yes, Dear," he muttered.

Bennett resisted the urge to smile at Delphine's defiant stand against her husband. It was about time.

Delphine gestured towards the footman. "Will you show Mr. Paterson out?" she asked. "I'm afraid he has overstayed his welcome."

The footman walked over to the door and opened it. "Mr. Paterson?" he asked with a stern look.

Mr. Paterson made an exaggerated bow. "Cousin, as usual, I have enjoyed our chat," he said before departing from the manor.

Once the door was closed, Delphine turned to face her husband. "How dare you invite him here!" she exclaimed. "He is not a man to be trusted."

"I told you that your solicitor…" Mr. Simpkin started.

She spoke over him. "I know what you told me, but you should have asked me first," she said.

Mr. Simpkin looked displeased. "You are my wife and I do not have to ask permission from you."

"I am only your wife until we void this farce of a marriage," Delphine said.

Putting his hand up, Mr. Simpkin responded, "You are angry. I shall give you a few moments to calm down before we continue this conversation."

Bennett winced, knowing that Mr. Simpkin had misspoken. He had learned over the years that no woman ever liked to be told to calm down. In fact, it tended to make them angrier.

Delphine's eyes narrowed. "I think you should go as well."

"I beg your pardon?" Mr. Simpkin asked.

"I do not want you here," Delphine replied.

Mr. Simpkin's eyebrows puckered. "Where do you want me to go?" he asked.

"I do not care, just not here."

Taking a step back, Mr. Simpkin said, "I think it is for the best if I retire for the evening. I do hope you will be in a more agreeable mood tomorrow."

Bennett watched as Mr. Simpkin spun on his heel and headed up the stairs. Once the man disappeared down the corridor, he addressed Delphine. "Are you all right?"

"No," she replied. "Vincent is a terrible person and I want him nowhere near me."

"I figured that out rather quickly," Bennett said.

"Yet Mr. Simpkin invited him here and failed to warn me," Delphine responded, her eyes sparking with anger. "He had no right."

Bennett nodded. "I agree."

"I have tried being nice to Vincent, and to put our past behind us, but I have learned I mustn't let him interfere in my life," Delphine said. "He is just looking for a reason to strip me of my title."

He took a step towards her, but still maintained a proper distance between them. "What are you going to do tomorrow?"

"I am going to refuse to see Vincent," Delphine replied.

"What of Mr. Simpkin?"

Delphine frowned. "Quite frankly, I do not know what to do with him, especially since I do not wish to be around him."

Bennett knew that what he was about to say would change everything between them, but he was willing to risk it. "Then stay with me," he paused before adding, "at least until we have voided your marriage."

"I do not think that is wise."

"Whyever not?" Bennett asked.

Her gaze grew downcast. "People would talk," she said.

"Then let them talk." Bennett was tired of other people dictating his actions. He wanted Delphine as his wife, more so than anything he had ever wanted before. But he wouldn't force her to do anything that she was uncomfortable with.

Delphine brought her gaze up, holding him transfixed. "I need to return home and reinstate my household staff since Mr. Simpkin wrongly dismissed them."

"I could go with you," Bennett suggested.

She offered him a sad smile. "You are kind to offer, but I need to do it on my own. It is my responsibility and mine alone."

Bennett fisted his hands into tight balls to resist the urge to touch Delphine. "I have no doubt that you can manage your own estate. I thought you might want me to accompany you for the journey."

"What you are proposing is rather scandalous, my lord," Delphine said.

"Good. I try to do at least one thing a day that is scandalous," he joked. "It keeps me young."

Delphine considered him for a long moment. "What if I came back after my affairs were in order?" she ventured.

Bennett smiled. "I would like that greatly."

Her eyes sparkled with warmth as she returned his smile. "Good, because I have no doubt that I will greatly miss Elodie and Melody."

"Only them?" he asked.

"Oh, yes, I shall miss Winston as well," Delphine shared.

Bennett was enjoying his time bantering with Delphine, which had become one of his favorite pastimes, but he did need to inform Delphine about one thing. And it was important.

In a solemn voice, Bennett said, "A footman saw Miss Eden enter Mr. Simpkin's bedchamber this afternoon. With this information, Winston believes we could petition for a divorce, assuming the judge does not grant a ruling to nullify it."

Delphine reared back, visibly shaken. "Charlotte wouldn't do such a thing," she insisted. "The footman must have been mistaken."

Bennett cast a glance towards Grady, who remained steadfast in his position guarding the entry hall. "I'm afraid not," he said.

"No. If word ever got out, Charlotte would be ruined," Delphine said. "Surely there must be a reasonable explanation for her visiting Mr. Simpkin's bedchamber."

"Is there ever a good enough reason for a young woman to visit a man's bedchamber… alone?" Bennett asked.

Delphine's eyes grew determined. "I will not petition for divorce based upon adultery," she declared. "I won't do that to my friend."

"What if the judge does not approve voiding your marriage?" Bennett asked.

"He will," Delphine stated.

As he was about to argue with her, his mother's voice came from the doorway, interrupting their conversation. "We are about to have dessert," she informed them. "Will you two be joining us?"

Delphine bobbed her head. "Dessert sounds wonderful."

The last thing Bennett wanted was dessert but it was evident that Delphine was done with this conversation.

Offering his arm to Delphine, he asked, "May I escort you back to the dining room?"

Delphine placed her hand on his sleeve. "Thank you, my lord," she replied.

Bennett had to respect the fierce loyalty that Delphine had for her friend, but she had to think of herself right now.

Delphine sat at the dressing table while the maid styled her hair. She yawned and she made no attempt to hide it. She had the most restless night of sleep because she couldn't silence the relentless thoughts in her head.

She wondered if Charlotte could truly be having an affair with Mr. Simpkin. She wanted to believe Bennett, but it seemed so far-fetched. Charlotte had never done anything that was the least bit scandalous and visiting a gentleman's room would ruin her reputation. It just didn't make any sense.

Not that it mattered. She harbored no affection for Mr. Simpkin and was looking forward to their marriage being voided. She knew it might take some time, but some things were worth the wait. And Bennett was one of those things. She would do anything to be with him. He had her whole heart, and she didn't want it back.

A smile came to her lips as she recalled their conversation from the night before. He had offered to escort her home, knowing it would come at great risk to both of their reputations. Bennett hadn't declared his intentions for her, but she knew he cared for her. She could see it in his eyes and hear it in his voice.

The maid dropped her hands and took a step back. "Do you like your hair, my lady?"

Delphine turned her head to admire the fancy coiffure in the mirror. "I do," she replied. "Thank you."

A knock came at the door.

"Enter," Delphine ordered.

The door opened and Charlotte stepped into the room. "Good morning," she greeted with a smile.

"Good morning," Delphine said.

Charlotte glanced at the maid before inquiring, "I came to see how you are faring this morning. You were rather quiet after meeting with your cousin."

Delphine let out a groan. "I cannot stand Vincent."

"Did he say anything that upset you?"

"Everything out of his mouth upsets me," Delphine huffed. "I have never met a more vexing man."

Charlotte sat down on the settee and asked, "Do you believe that he just came to ensure you are well?"

Delphine shook her head. "No. He has never cared for my wellbeing before. Why start now?"

"Maybe he had a change of heart?" Charlotte suggested.

"I doubt that," Delphine responded. "He has been a nuisance since the moment my father died. He does not think a woman should hold a title."

Charlotte leaned back against the settee. "Well, you have certainly proved him wrong. Your estate is flourishing and you have a true knack for business."

"That may be true, but Mr. Simpkin informed me that he dismissed my entire household staff," Delphine said. "I need to go right his wrongs and hire them back."

"Do you not intend to live with your husband?" Charlotte asked.

"No, because I am hopeful that a judge will void our marriage," Delphine responded.

Charlotte sucked in a breath. "Have you thought through the repercussions of that decision? Your reputation would be ruined."

"It is better than being married to Mr. Simpkin," Delphine said.

"But you agreed to the marriage," Charlotte pressed.

Rising, Delphine smoothed down her pale blue gown. "I do not have any such memories of that."

Charlotte gave her a knowing look. "Is this because you care for Lord Dunsby?"

"My feelings for Lord Dunsby are inconsequential," Delphine replied. "I do not wish to tie myself to Mr. Simpkin for the remainder of my days."

"Why do you insist on calling him 'Mr. Simpkin'?" Charlotte asked.

"That is his name, is it not?"

Charlotte frowned. "You may not remember wanting to marry Mr. Simpkin, but I do. It was not a passing whim for you."

Delphine wanted to believe that was true, but it made no sense. How did she benefit from marrying Mr. Simpkin? She already had a title so she didn't need the protection of his name. How she wished she could remember those memories.

"I just think you should give Mr. Simpkin a chance to prove himself," Charlotte said. "He may not be an earl, but he is a good man."

She cocked her head. "I hadn't realized you were friends with Mr. Simpkin."

Charlotte bristled. "We are merely acquaintances," she asserted.

Delphine could tell that her friend was not telling the whole truth and she decided to press her. "Lord Dunsby claims a footman saw you enter Mr. Simpkin's bedchamber yesterday. Is there any truth to that?"

Her friend blinked, looking stunned. "Someone witnessed that?" she groaned. "I thought I had been most careful."

"So it is true?"

Her friend nodded. "Yes, but it is not what you think," she said. "Mr. Simpkin asked to speak to me privately about what he could do to win your affections."

Delphine lifted her brow in disbelief. "In his bedchamber?"

Charlotte winced slightly. "Yes, but it was because Mr. Simpkin didn't want Lord Dunsby to overhear our conversation."

"You could have spoken in the gardens or anywhere else for that matter," Delphine said. "Do you not care for your reputation?"

"I do, but I suppose I got wrapped up in trying to help Mr. Simpkin win you over," Charlotte remarked.

Delphine gave her friend an odd look. "Why is it so important to you that I remain married to Mr. Simpkin?"

Charlotte reached for a pillow and held it in front of her. "I just want you to be happy."

"And you think I would be happy with Mr. Simpkin?"

She shrugged. "I think you would have been very happy with Mr. Simpkin had you not met Lord Dunsby."

Delphine walked over to the settee and sat down next to her friend. "I truly doubt that. Mr. Simpkin seems to want an obedient wife," she said. "And that is something I never will be. I am far too headstrong to yield to my husband's commands."

"But if you are successful and void your marriage to Mr. Simpkin, then you will marry Lord Dunsby and move far away," Charlotte remarked in a dejected voice. "What am I to do then?"

"That is assuming that Lord Dunsby offers for me."

"He will," Charlotte stated. "I can see in his eyes that he cares greatly for you. Just as you do for him."

Delphine offered her a reassuring smile. "Whatever happens, we will always be friends," she said.

Charlotte looked unsure. "You say that now, but things change. People change."

"Not that much," Delphine said.

A soft knock came at the door before it was opened, revealing a young maid. "Mr. Vincent Paterson has come to call for you, my lady," she revealed.

Delphine felt dread wash over her at that news. She wondered what Vincent wanted now. "Inform him that I do not wish to see him."

The maid's eyes grew wide. "But he was rather adamant that he wished to speak to you. I do not think he will leave without seeing you."

The last thing she wanted to do was speak to Vincent, but she didn't wish to cause a commotion by having him removed from the manor.

"Very well," Delphine conceded. "I shall be right down."

After the maid departed, Delphine rose from her seat. "What fresh torment do you think Vincent wishes to speak about?"

Charlotte grinned. "Perhaps he might surprise you and speak of bunnies or whatnot."

"I doubt that," Delphine said.

"Would you care for me to accompany you?" Charlotte asked.

Delphine expressed her gratitude to her friend with a heartfelt glance. "That is kind of you, but Vincent is my cousin. No matter how annoying or obnoxious he is."

Rising, Charlotte said, "Then I shall see you at breakfast, where I expect to hear all about your meeting."

After they departed from her bedchamber, they walked towards the main level as they both seemed to retreat to their own thoughts.

Delphine stepped down onto the marble floor of the entry hall and turned towards Charlotte. "With any luck, this conversation will not go on for very long."

Charlotte tipped her head. "For your sake, I hope so. But when in doubt, speak about bunnies."

A laugh escaped Delphine's lips. "What is it with you and bunnies this morning?"

"Bunnies are a safe topic and who doesn't love those fluffy animals?" she asked. "They are so unpretentious."

Delphine was grateful that her friend seemed to break some of the tension that she felt. "I am ready to face my cousin now."

She spun on her heel and approached the drawing room. Once she stepped inside the small room, she saw Vincent sitting on the settee, sipping a cup of tea as if he had no care in the world.

He rose when he saw her. "Cousin," he said as he kept hold of his teacup. "You certainly took your time coming down."

"What is it that you want, Vincent?" she asked, forgoing pleasantries.

Vincent smiled at her, as if he found her directness to be amusing. "I have come to say goodbye."

Now what game was her cousin playing? "You are?" she asked.

"Yes, I have confirmed that you are alive and well, and that the title remains with you," Vincent said, placing the teacup down onto the tray.

Delphine stared at her cousin, questioning why he was being so agreeable. He was never agreeable. In fact, that was one thing she could always count on.

Vincent bowed. "I hope you have a most pleasant soiree this evening. I have heard it is in your honor."

"It is," she replied. If he was attempting to secure an invitation, he would be sorely mistaken. She had no desire to have him there.

"Well, I must not dally," Vincent said with a bow. "I will be seeing you, Cousin."

Delphine remained rooted in her spot as Vincent walked past her and out the main door. She had never had a conversation with her cousin that hadn't ended in one of them insulting the other. It was almost unnerving.

Perhaps her cousin had finally come to accept that she was worthy of her title. But that seemed unlikely.

So what was he up to?

Chapter Eighteen

As Bennett descended the grand stairs, he saw Delphine emerging from the drawing room with a perplexed look on her face. It was evident that something was troubling her deeply.

He came to a stop on the last step and asked, "What is wrong?"

Delphine's eyes widened as she turned to face him, appearing startled by his sudden appearance. "Bennett, where did you come from?"

"I just came from my bedchamber," he replied.

"Yes, quite right," Delphine muttered distractedly, her hand absently smoothing down the folds of her dress. "Shall we adjourn to the dining room for some breakfast?"

Bennett's curiosity was piqued, and he wasn't about to let Delphine walk away without an explanation of what was troubling her. "Did something- or someone- upset you?"

Delphine sighed. "It is Vincent," she replied. "He came to tell me that he was leaving."

"And this upset you?"

A line between her brow appeared. "Vincent is not

thoughtful. Never has been. So why come and talk to me at all?"

Taking a step towards her, Bennett replied, "People can change."

"Not Vincent. He is incapable of change," Delphine asserted.

Grady cleared his throat from his position in the entry hall. "If I may, my lord, I would be happy to ensure Mr. Paterson has truly left the village."

With a glance at Delphine, Bennett asked, "Would this please you?"

"It would," Delphine replied.

"Very well," Bennett said before meeting Grady's gaze. "Will you inform us when Mr. Paterson departs from the village?"

Grady tipped his head. "Yes, my lord," he responded.

After Grady departed from the entry hall, Bennett offered his arm. "May I escort you to the dining room?"

Delphine stared at his arm, not making a move to accept it. "Do you think I am being foolish?"

"No, I do not," he answered.

"I didn't always have an immense distrust of Vincent," she shared. "When we were younger, we used to be playmates. But that all changed when my father started to grow ill."

Bennett smiled. "You don't need to explain yourself to me, Delphie."

"But I feel as if I do," she said. "I am generally a very trusting person, but I can't be that person around Vincent. Frankly, he just irritates me to no end."

"Your cousin is gone, and our breakfast is going to grow cold soon," Bennett remarked.

"Yes, of course," Delphine said as she placed her hand on his sleeve. "Why do you suppose Vincent didn't ask for an invitation to the soiree this evening?"

While Bennett started to lead Delphine down the corridor, he shrugged. "He might not enjoy social events."

"No, he thrives on them," Delphine said.

Bennett patted her hand. "You might be reading too much into this," he said. "Do not let Mr. Paterson occupy any more of your thoughts than he already has."

"You are right. I shall not give my cousin any more heed," Delphine remarked with a dramatic wave of her hand.

With a knowing look, he asked, "You are thinking of him right now, aren't you?"

"Yes, I am," she admitted. "But I will stop. I promise."

He chuckled. "What if I distracted you by telling you that our butler was a rag-picker when he was young."

Delphine gave him an odd look. "How did he come to work at such a grand estate then?"

"White attempted to sell some scraps of bones to my father and he took pity on him, especially when he learned that he was an orphan," Bennett said. "He started out washing dishes and assisting with the cook."

"It is impressive that he worked his way up to being a butler," Delphine remarked.

Bennett dropped his arm as they arrived at the dining room. "It is," he agreed.

They stepped into the dining room and he saw Miss Eden was sitting at the long, rectangular table.

"Miss Eden," Bennett greeted as he pulled out Delphine's chair.

She acknowledged him with a tip of her head before shifting her gaze towards Delphine. "What did Vincent want?" she asked. "Did he come to grovel for your forgiveness?"

Delphine shook her head. "No, he came to tell me that he was leaving."

"For what purpose?" Miss Eden asked.

"I'm not rightly sure," Delphine said, reaching for a napkin to place on her lap. "But I am glad that he is gone."

Miss Eden tilted her chin. "As am I."

A footman placed plates of food in front of them and took a step back.

Bennett reached for a fork and knife. "I do hope everyone is excited for the soiree this evening."

"Yes, but I will admit that I am looking forward to leaving Brockhall Manor tomorrow morning," Miss Eden shared. "I have not slept well since we arrived and I miss my bed."

"About that…" Delphine started. "I do not think I am going to be returning home at this time."

Miss Eden furrowed her brow. "Whyever not?"

With a glance at Bennett, Delphine replied, "I think it would be best if I do not spend additional time with Mr. Simpkin since I plan to void our marriage."

"Not this again," Miss Eden huffed. "Just think of your future. People will talk and your reputation will be tarnished indefinitely. Is that what you want? To become a laughingstock amongst high Society?"

"I have weighed the consequences and I think it is in my best interest," Delphine said.

In a voice that clearly displayed her disapproval, Miss Eden asked, "What of George's best interest? After all, you married him in good faith."

Bennett did not like the way that Miss Eden was speaking to Delphine, but he didn't think it was his place to intercede. He had learned never to get between two women arguing… for any reason.

In a calm voice, Delphine replied, "I do not remember marrying Mr. Simpkin—"

Miss Eden spoke over her. "Perhaps you do remember, but you reneged once you found a rich lord to court you."

Delphine's mouth dropped. "That is entirely unfair of you

to say, and not the least bit true. My memories have yet to return."

Shoving back her chair, Miss Eden said, "It is awfully convenient if you ask me. But I do think you are treating George most unfairly."

"Why do you keep referring to Mr. Simpkin by his given name?" Delphine asked, clearly finding it as disconcerting as Bennett did. "Did he give you leave to?"

"We are friends, which is something else you have conveniently forgotten," Miss Eden snapped back.

"Charlotte..."

Miss Eden tossed her napkin onto the table. "You can stop, Delphine. I knew it was a mistake to come here," she declared before she stormed off.

Delphine watched her friend leave the dining room with a look of astonishment on her face. In a soft voice, she asked, "Am I being selfish?"

"So what if you are? You must think of yourself and your future," Bennett encouraged. "Do you truly want to stay married to Mr. Simpkin?"

"No, but am I the villain in this story?"

Bennett shifted in his seat to face her. "Absolutely not!" he exclaimed. "You are doing what is best for you."

"And what of Mr. Simpkin?" Delphine asked. "No doubt that his reputation will suffer as a result of voiding our marriage."

"You are overthinking this," Bennett said.

Delphine's eyes grew sad. "I have been so focused on what I have wanted that I haven't even considered the consequences for Mr. Simpkin," she said. "Does that make me a terrible person?"

Bennett couldn't help but find the question laughable. Delphine was one of the most kindhearted individuals he had ever encountered. "No, it does not," he rushed to assure her.

"I have never seen Charlotte so angry before," Delphine said. "In all my years, she has never spoken so harshly to me."

"It is all right if friends have disagreements," Bennett attempted. He wasn't quite sure what he could say to provide her comfort.

Delphine pushed back her chair and rose. "I need to go speak to her at once."

Rising, Bennett asked, "And say what?"

"I don't know," Delphine sighed. "I just do not like the thought of her being so angry with me."

Bennett waited until Delphine met his gaze before saying, "Sometimes your friends think they know what's best for you, but you must follow what your heart dictates."

"What if my heart is wrong?"

"Only you can decide that," Bennett replied. "But I will support you in whatever decision you make."

Delphine's face softened. "Thank you. That means a great deal to me."

Bennett wanted to add that *she* meant a great deal to him, but he didn't dare say something so bold.

Winston's booming voice came from the doorway. "I have heard from the judge that will hear your case," he announced, holding up a piece of paper.

"You have?" Delphine asked.

With a purposeful stride, Winston approached them and smiled. "The judge has agreed that your case has merit and will hear arguments from both sides before making a ruling."

Delphine bit her lower lip, looking unsure. "Is that good news?"

Winston's smile grew even broader. "Yes, this is wonderful news. Judge Ross is known to be rather progressive in his views on marriage and is a good friend of the barrister I trained under. I know precisely the argument I need to present to persuade him," he explained. "If all goes according to plan, it should only be a short time before Delphine is husband-*less* once more."

Delphine's entire face seemed to light up. "Thank you, Winston," she gushed.

"That is what I do," Winston remarked smugly. "I make dreams come true."

Bennett looked heavenward. "Dear heavens, you are far too cocky for your own good."

"Trust me, you want a barrister that is a little full of himself," Winston stated good-naturedly.

Taking a step back, Delphine said, "I should go talk to Charlotte. Although, she might become more upset with me than she already is."

After Delphine departed from the dining room, Winston gave him an inquisitive look. "The real question is how soon after her marriage is void are you going to offer for her?"

"I am not quite sure," Bennett said.

Winston reached down to Bennett's plate and stole a piece of toast. "A word of advice- I wouldn't wait too long."

Bennett would marry Delphine anytime or anywhere, but he didn't want to do anything that would cause a greater scandal.

Delphine headed up the grand staircase as she went in search of Charlotte. She knew her friend was angry with her, but she didn't entirely understand the reasons behind it. This wasn't the first time she had told Charlotte of her intentions to void her marriage. So why did she react so harshly? And why was she so concerned for Mr. Simpkin's reputation?

As she passed by the library, she saw Charlotte pacing in front of Mr. Simpkin, who was sitting on the settee.

But rather than make her presence known, Delphine remained just outside of the door as she watched them.

Mr. Simpkin's voice drifted out into the corridor. "You are making a big ado out of nothing."

"She wants to void the marriage," Charlotte said, tossing her hands up in the air.

"Yes, and we planned for that," Mr. Simpkin responded, leaning back against the settee.

We?

Since when were Mr. Simpkin and Charlotte a team? And what had they been planning?

Charlotte stopped pacing and turned to face Mr. Simpkin. "How can you be so calm about this?" she asked. "Just think of your reputation."

"That is the least of my concerns," Mr. Simpkin stated.

"What of *my* reputation?" Charlotte demanded. "I will be ruined, right alongside you."

Mr. Simpkin smiled. "You are working yourself into a frenzy for no reason. Just trust me and it will all work out."

Charlotte frowned. "I do trust you, but nothing is working out as simply as you claimed it would."

"Yes, there were some unforeseen complications, but that is neither here nor there," Mr. Simpkin said. "We must look forward to our future."

Delphine couldn't quite believe what she was overhearing. It was evident that Mr. Simpkin and Charlotte had formed an attachment, but what had they been planning? None of this made any sense.

Elodie's voice came from next to her, causing her to jump. "May I join you in your eavesdropping endeavor?" she asked in a hushed voice.

With a slight nod, Delphine turned back towards the library and watched Mr. Simpkin rise. He placed his hand on Charlotte's shoulders and leaned in. "Be patient, my dear, and everything you seek will be yours."

Charlotte seemed to consider his words before saying, "I just wish it hadn't come to this."

"She left us with little choice," Mr. Simpkin responded, dropping his hands to his sides. "Now run along before anyone notices your absence."

Elodie placed a hand on Delphine's arm and pointed towards the parlor, indicating they should hide, and quickly.

Delphine followed Elodie into the parlor and closed the door behind her. What had she just overheard? And who was the "she" that left them with little choice? Was it her?

Elodie's voice broke through her thoughts. "Are you all right?"

"How much did you overhear?" Delphine asked.

"Most of it," Elodie replied with a look of sympathy. "But you should know that Mr. Simpkin and Charlotte often speak to one another in private."

Delphine pursed her lips together. "How have I been so blind?" she asked.

"Does it matter if they have formed an attachment?" Elodie asked. "After all, you intend to void the marriage."

"That is true. I hold no affection for Mr. Simpkin but why didn't Charlotte tell me that she held him in high regard?"

Elodie shrugged. "You are married to Mr. Simpkin."

"Which is more perplexing," Delphine remarked. "I would never have agreed to the marriage had I known Mr. Simpkin and Charlotte cared for one another."

"What if you didn't agree to it?" Elodie suggested.

Delphine shook her head. "No, Charlotte would never do such a thing to me. We have been friends for as long as I can remember."

"People change."

"Your brother said as much, but I do not believe Charlotte would go along with something so nefarious," Delphine insisted.

Elodie didn't look convinced. "Do you not find it odd that

Miss Eden accompanied you to Gretna Green?" she asked. "People usually do not bring friends along when they are eloping."

Delphine had to recognize that Elodie did have a point, albeit reluctantly. "She said that I invited her along."

"And you believe that?"

"I had no reason to question her," Delphine replied. "She has never lied to me before."

"Or at least you haven't caught her in a lie," Elodie said.

Delphine brought a hand up to her head as she tried to decide what she should do. Should she confront Charlotte with what she knew at once or wait until she returned home?

Elodie opened the door and peeked out into the corridor. "It is empty," she revealed.

"You can go," Delphine encouraged. "I am going to stay here for a while."

With a knowing look, Elodie asked, "Are you hiding from Miss Eden?"

Delphine grimaced, wondering how Elodie had seen through her so easily. "Perhaps," she admitted.

"I do not blame you," Elodie said. "This is why I do not have very many friends. They will betray you at the drop of a hat."

"Charlotte wouldn't betray me," Delphine said.

Elodie lifted her brow. "Did we not hear the same conversation?" she asked.

Delphine walked over to the settee and dropped down in the most unladylike fashion. None of this was making any sense. "Why did Mr. Simpkin want to marry me if he cares for Charlotte?"

"Greed. Power." Elodie paused. "Do I need to go on?"

"But Mr. Simpkin claimed he wanted to win my affection," Delphine replied. "Why would he say such a thing if he was having an affair with Charlotte?"

Elodie came to sit down next to her. "I cannot answer that, but I have never liked Mr. Simpkin."

Delphine huffed. "You sound just like your brother."

"Good, at least I am making some sense then," Elodie said. "If you void the marriage to Mr. Simpkin, then he gets nothing. That is quite the incentive to ensure the marriage stays intact."

"But Winston is confident that we will be able to void the marriage," Delphine said. "It will just take some time."

Elodie bobbed her head. "I do hope you will be more careful when selecting your next husband," she teased.

An image of Bennett came to Delphine's mind and she felt a smile come to her lips. "I will be," she said.

"Since that is now resolved, we should start preparing for the soiree," Elodie remarked.

"But we just had breakfast."

Elodie laughed. "I am surprised that my mother hasn't found us yet…"

Her words had just left her mouth when Lady Dallington stepped into the room. "There you two are," she stated. "It is time to prepare for the soiree."

With an "I told you so" look, Elodie rose from her seat. "I do so enjoy preparing for a social event that is hours and hours away," she joked.

Lady Dallington didn't comment on her daughter's attempt at humor. Instead, she turned to Delphine and said, "We have much to do and very little time to do it."

Rising, Delphine asked, "What would you like me to do?"

"First, we must ensure the ballgown that my lady's maid altered for you is a perfect fit," Lady Dallington replied. "Then we shall move on to selecting jewelry for you to wear tonight."

"That won't be necessary," Delphine said, "I do have a coral necklace that I was wearing when I was brought here."

"I think it would be best if you wear some of my pieces,"

Lady Dallington said. "I do believe you will find many of them to your liking."

Delphine found Lady Dallington's generosity to be rather touching. "Thank you, my lady," she said.

Lady Dallington waved her hand dismissively in front of her. "Think nothing of it, Dear," she said. "Come along. No lollygagging."

Elodie spoke up. "Do I have time for a nap?"

"I suppose we can schedule that in, assuming it is a quick rest," Lady Dallington responded.

"What about a break for biscuits?" Elodie pressed.

Lady Dallington gave her daughter an exasperated look. "You can eat biscuits while you are having your hair styled."

That seemed to satisfy Elodie and she followed her mother out of the room. Delphine knew that she should follow after them, but her heart was heavy. Charlotte was keeping her affection for Mr. Simpkin a secret and that greatly bothered her. What else was she keeping from her?

Elodie stuck her head back into the room. "Are you coming, Delphine?"

"I am," she confirmed.

As they headed down the corridor towards their bedchambers, Lady Dallington glanced over at Delphine and said, "Considering the state of your marriage, I would recommend you not dancing a set with Mr. Simpkin."

"I have no objections to that," Delphine said. The thought of Mr. Simpkin holding her in his arms did not sound the least bit appealing. His touch had no warmth behind it. Not like Bennett's. She would never tire of being in his arms. His strong, comforting arms. They had always made her feel safe. And cherished.

Charlotte's voice came from behind them. "Delphine, may I speak to you?" she asked, her words sounding cordial enough.

Elodie leaned closer to Delphine and asked in a hushed voice, "Would you like me to engage in fisticuffs with her?"

"No, that is not necessary," Delphine replied before turning around with an expectant look to face her friend.

Lady Dallington touched her sleeve. "We will be waiting for you in my bedchamber."

Delphine tipped her head in response.

As they continued down the corridor, Charlotte approached Delphine and came to a stop in front of her. "I wanted to apologize for my harsh words earlier," she said.

"You do?" Delphine asked.

Charlotte gave her an apologetic smile. "I had no right to speak to you in such a manner and I feel awful. You have every right to void your marriage and I was wrong to suggest otherwise."

Delphine pressed her lips together, not knowing what she should say. It wasn't the time or the place to confront Charlotte about her feelings for Mr. Simpkin. But what had caused Charlotte to have such a change of heart?

Charlotte continued. "Please tell Lady Dallington that I am most grateful for the ballgown that she had delivered to my bedchamber."

"I will," Delphine replied. There. That was safe. And not at all confrontational.

Her friend smiled, or rather, beamed. "I am looking forward to this evening."

"As am I," Delphine replied, attempting to keep the confusion off her expression. "But I should be running along. I do not want to make Lady Dallington wait for me."

"Then you should run along, especially since this night is all about you," Charlotte encouraged.

Delphine hesitated for a moment before she walked away from her friend. Charlotte was acting odd, and she wasn't sure why that was. Perhaps it was as simple as Charlotte feeling guilty for deceiving her.

Chapter Nineteen

Dressed in his finery, Bennett stood in the parlor as he waited for his family's arrival so they could join the soiree. His thoughts wandered to Delphine. He hadn't seen her since breakfast.

As if his thoughts had conjured up Delphine, she stepped into the room wearing a green gown with an intricate net overlay. Her hair was piled atop her head and two long curls framed her face.

Her beauty never failed to captivate him, leaving him to wonder how she managed to grow more enchanting with each passing day.

Delphine smiled and held out the folds of her gown. "How do I look?" she asked.

How was he supposed to answer such a question? He didn't dare tell her the truth for fear that she would see right through him and know that he cared for her. He decided to tell a halfway truth. "You look lovely, as always," he said. That was safe and did not lay his heart bare.

"This is one of Melody's new gowns that your mother had altered for me," Delphine said, dropping her hands.

"It does you justice," Bennett said.

Delphine walked closer to him but stopped a short distance away. "Your family has been so kind to me. How do you suppose I can repay them?"

Marry me.

That is what Bennett wanted to say, but she was still a married woman… for now. He would have to wait and bide his time.

Bennett clasped his hands behind his back so he wouldn't risk reaching out to touch her. "There is no need to repay them. We are just glad that we were able to help you during a difficult time."

The smile on Delphine's lips faded. "You were right about Charlotte and Mr. Simpkin. There is something going on between them."

"I'm sorry," Bennett said, unsure of what else to say.

"There is no reason to apologize," Delphine responded. "It is not as if I hold any affection towards Mr. Simpkin."

Bennett nodded. "True, but you are still married to him and he has no right to be having an affair with Miss Eden."

Delphine sighed. "I had hoped you were wrong."

"As did I," Bennett admitted.

After he said his words, Mr. Simpkin stepped into the room with Miss Eden on his arm. He cast Bennett an annoyed glance before his eyes settled on Delphine. "You look beautiful," he praised.

Delphine seemed to muster up a smile. "Thank you."

Charlotte removed her arm from Mr. Simpkin and hurried over to Delphine. "You look radiant," she declared. "I have no doubt that I will pale in comparison to you."

"You do not give yourself enough credit, my de…" Mr. Simpkin's words came to an abrupt halt and he shifted uncomfortably in his stance.

Charlotte did not acknowledge Mr. Simpkin's words, but instead, turned back to Delphine. "Are you nervous?"

"What do I have to be nervous about?" Delphine asked.

"All eyes will be on you," Charlotte replied.

Mr. Simpkin stepped forward and said, "If Delphine has no objections, I hope to leave at first light tomorrow so we can return home at a reasonable hour."

Delphine exchanged a glance with Bennett before saying, "Actually, I intend to extend my visit at Brockhall Manor."

"Whatever for?" Mr. Simpkin asked. "You and I both have responsibilities back home."

"Yes, we do, but my responsibilities are my own, not yours," Delphine responded.

Mr. Simpkin furrowed his brow. "I don't understand what you are saying."

Delphine squared her shoulders before saying, "I do not think it is prudent to spend time with you since I am seeking to void our marriage."

"Do you now?" Mr. Simpkin demanded.

"I'm sorry, but I do not wish to remain married to you, assuming I have the choice," Delphine replied.

Mr. Simpkin clenched his jaw. "I had hoped that this was just a passing whim, but I do not think you have thought this decision through."

"I have, and Lord Winston has already heard from the judge who will preside over our case," Delphine said. "He feels confident that the judge will rule in my favor."

Scoffing, Mr. Simpkin asked, "So that is it? You made the decision for us."

"There is no 'us,'" Delphine stated. "There was never an 'us.'"

Mr. Simpkin took a commanding step towards Delphine and Bennett moved to step in front of her. "Get out of my way, my lord," he demanded. "I need to speak to my wife."

Bennett stood his ground. "Not like this," he said. "You are angry."

"Now you are offering up advice on my marriage?" Mr.

Simpkin asked. "You just want Delphine for yourself. How do I know this isn't your doing?"

Delphine stepped out from behind Bennett. "Lord Dunsby has been nothing but a friend to me. I came to the decision on my own."

Mr. Simpkin's eyes narrowed. "Do you truly think I will just walk away and let you void our marriage?"

"It is the right thing to do since I do not remember anything about it," Delphine replied.

"I care for you, Delphine!" Mr. Simpkin exclaimed.

Bennett clenched his hands into balls at his side, knowing Mr. Simpkin was just grasping at straws now. But it was not his place to say so.

Delphine lifted her brow. "You have a funny way of showing that, considering I know about you and Charlotte."

Miss Eden's mouth dropped. "Whatever do you mean?"

"I know you two care for one another," Delphine replied.

"No, no, no, you have it all wrong," Miss Eden rushed out. "I have been trying to help George… er… Mr. Simpkin…"

Delphine put her hand up. "You can stop with the lies. I overheard you two in the library earlier today."

Miss Eden's shoulders slumped. "We didn't want this to happen, but it just did," she revealed. "I'm sorry."

Mr. Simpkin waved his hand in front of him. "We do not owe Delphine an explanation."

Bennett spoke up. "You might be interested to know that a woman can petition for divorce from a husband in cases of adultery in Scotland."

"This was your plan all along!" Mr. Simpkin shouted. "You tricked us."

"You will have to be a little more convincing when you appear before the judge," Bennett mocked.

Miss Eden's eyes grew panicked. "Delphine, you must believe me that I didn't plan this," she insisted.

"Why didn't you tell me the truth?" Delphine asked.

"I don't know, but I was wrong not to do so," Miss Eden said.

Mr. Simpkin came to stand by Miss Eden. "Enough talking, Charlotte!" he ordered as he reached for her arm. "Come along. There is no point in staying here a moment longer since we are no longer welcome."

Miss Eden yanked her arm back. "I am not going anywhere yet. I want to explain myself to Delphine."

In a low growl, Mr. Simpkin said, "You are making a fool of yourself."

Turning back towards Delphine, Miss Eden clasped her hands in front of her and winced. "I do not want to lose you over this," she stated dejectedly.

Delphine regarded Miss Eden with wariness in her eyes. "I just do not understand why you didn't tell me the truth when you first arrived."

"I wanted to, but I was scared," Miss Eden admitted. "I hadn't planned on falling in love with Mr. Simpkin."

"Charlotte! You must stop talking!" Mr. Simpkin shouted.

Lady Dallington's concerned voice came from the doorway. "Dear heavens, what is all the shouting about?"

Mr. Simpkin reached for Miss Eden's arm as he addressed Lady Dallington. "Thank you for your hospitality, but I am afraid Miss Eden and I will take our leave now."

"Now?" his mother asked. "It is dark outside and our guests have already started to arrive."

"Then we shall stay at the boarding house in the village," Mr. Simpkin stated before he led Miss Eden out of the room.

His mother turned her questioning glance towards Bennett. "Do you care to explain what just happened?"

No.

But did he have a choice?

Bennett opened his mouth to explain but Delphine spoke first. "I'm afraid Mr. Simpkin and Charlotte were displeased that I would not be traveling home with them."

Elodie entered the room and muttered, "Good riddance."

"Precisely," Delphine responded. "Let's not have their outburst take away from our fun this evening."

His mother looked conflicted. "Very well, but I will expect to hear all about what truly happened tomorrow."

Bennett walked over to Delphine and asked in a hushed voice, "Are you all right?"

"I am," she replied.

"There is no shame in not being all right with all of this," he assured her.

She met his gaze. "For what purpose?" she asked. "I wish things had been different but I do not harbor any ill-will towards Charlotte. I am glad that she found love, and I hope she finds happiness with Mr. Simpkin."

"You are truly extraordinary," Bennett said, knowing he had spoken no truer words.

Delphine's lips twitched. "You are being far too complimentary of me this evening."

"I'm afraid I merely speak the truth."

His mother cleared her throat. "Are you two quite done?" she asked. "I merely ask because we have a house full of guests and they are all waiting to meet Delphine."

Knowing his mother made a valid point, he offered his arm to Delphine and said, "I hope you are ready for this."

"It will be much easier now that Mr. Simpkin is not present," Delphine stated. "He truly vexed me."

Bennett chuckled. "You said it, not me."

Stepping into the room, Melody announced, "I am here."

"Good, and just in time to go to the ballroom," Lady Dallington said.

Melody's eyes roamed the room. "Should we not wait for everyone else?"

Elodie leaned closer to her sister and whispered something into her ear.

Melody seemed to nod her understanding before saying, "I agree. I never did particularly like Mr. Simpkin."

"No one did, but he was a guest in our home," his mother expressed, turning her head towards the corridor. "Ah, your father has just arrived. Let us go now."

While Bennett led Delphine out of the room, he said, "I am glad that you are here… with me."

"As am I," she responded.

Delphine was tired of smiling. She had been standing in the receiving line for what felt like hours as Lady Dallington introduced her to her guests. If this was what the Season would be like, she wanted nothing to do with it.

Perhaps the reason why she felt such discomfort was because of how she had left things with Charlotte. She truly wasn't angry at her friend, but why had she kept her feelings for Mr. Simpkin from her? And why had Charlotte pushed her to remain married to him, despite being in love with him? None of that made any sense.

But she truly didn't wish to ruin Charlotte by petitioning for divorce on the grounds of adultery. She hoped that Mr. Simpkin wouldn't fight the marriage being voided, knowing the dire consequences for Charlotte.

Delphine glanced down the line and saw Bennett. He was speaking to an older woman and a smile was on his face. She didn't think she would ever tire of being in his presence. The way he made her feel was something she would never take for granted. She felt safe. Loved. But she didn't presume that he loved her. Cared for her, maybe, but not loved.

But she loved him.

Before she had arrived, she had an unfavorable view on

marriage, but everything changed when Bennett had saved her.

He had saved her in more ways than one.

And now she wasn't afraid of marriage, at least not to him.

She was rather saddened that she wouldn't be dancing the first set with Bennett. But it would be entirely inappropriate for them to do so since she was still married to Mr. Simpkin.

Lady Dallington turned towards her and asked, "Shall we adjourn to the ballroom for the dancing?"

Delphine let out a sigh of relief that this was finally over. "Yes, I think that is a brilliant idea."

"You did well, Dear," Lady Dallington praised.

"All I did was smile and curtsy when directed. It was hardly praiseworthy," Delphine responded.

Lady Dallington gave her an understanding look. "That is what one does in your position. You are to ensure that your guests feel welcome."

Elodie spoke up from next to them. "Whoever came up with the idea of having a receiving line should be drawn and quartered."

"It isn't that bad," Lady Dallington argued.

"It is exhausting, considering no one cares if I am here to greet them," Elodie said.

Lady Dallington placed a hand on her daughter's shoulder. "I care," she assured her.

Elodie huffed. "Then you are the only one." She turned her head towards the crowd. "Where did Melody wander off to?"

"I don't know, but she has seemed rather preoccupied as of late," Lady Dallington responded.

"That is just Melody," Elodie said. "She has always preferred to be alone, but it has only gotten worse since we returned from boarding school."

"Well, that won't do when we go to London for the

Season," Lady Dallington stated. "She needs to be seen by the *ton*, as do you."

Elodie clapped her hands together. "Oh, hooray!" she exclaimed. "I love nothing more than being on display for strangers."

Lady Dallington shook her head. "You are impossible, Child."

Winston came to a stop next to them and asked, "Why is Melody speaking to Lord Emberly?"

"She is?" Elodie asked as her eyes roamed over the room. "That man is far too serious for my liking. He once told me that I was being utterly ridiculous."

"That was not very nice of him," Delphine said.

Elodie shrugged. "I was speaking of the war and expressed my opinion that if Wellington was a woman then we would have already declared victory."

Winston chuckled. "I agree with Lord Emberly. That is a ridiculous notion."

"Is it?" Elodie asked. "Why can't women serve in the military? We would bring unique perspectives to the war."

"War is a serious endeavor, and you are hardly serious," Winston said, giving her a knowing look.

Delphine had to admit that Winston did have a point, but she refrained from mentioning it to Elodie.

"Regardless, Lord Emberly would make a fine husband for Melody," Lady Dallington stated. "He is wealthy and lives in the next county over."

Elodie made a face. "Surely she could marry someone else. Anyone else, really. He is far too dull for my tastes."

The sound of the half-orchestra warming up could be heard in the ballroom, drawing everyone's attention.

"It is time," Lady Dallington said as she gestured towards the ballroom.

As Delphine turned to follow Lady Dallington, a tap came at her shoulder and it was followed by, "My lady."

Delphine shifted her gaze and saw a young maid was holding a note up to her. "Miss Eden asked for me to deliver this note at once," the maid informed her.

"Thank you," Delphine acknowledged as she accepted the note.

She opened the note and read:

I am truly sorry for what transpired between us and I don't wish to leave until I have a chance to apologize… again. Please meet me in the gardens.

Bennett's voice came from next to her. "What is wrong?"

Delphine handed him the note. "Charlotte wants to make amends before she returns home."

"Now?" Bennett asked as his eyes perused the note.

"Apparently so," Delphine replied. "I should go and speak to her."

Bennett gave her a look of disbelief. "What of the soiree? After all, it is being held in your honor."

"I shouldn't be long," Delphine said. "But Charlotte is right. I am not quite ready to say goodbye to her, or our friendship."

Bennett looked conflicted but thankfully he didn't press her. "Very well. I shall make excuses for you, but you must strive to hurry."

"Thank you," Delphine responded. "You are a true friend."

Friend.

That is not what she wanted him to be.

Bennett brought a smile to his face, but it appeared forced. "Yes, I am a good friend," he said, his voice tripping on the last word.

Why had she gone and said something that had made it

awkward between them? She wished she could take back her words, but it was too late.

In an encouraging voice, Bennett said, "You should go and speak to Charlotte before anyone notices your absence."

"I will, and I appreciate your understanding that this is something I need to do," Delphine remarked.

Bennett's smile no longer seemed forced. It appeared to be genuine. "I will do anything to ensure your happiness," he declared.

The way he said his words, she believed him.

Delphine returned his smile before she headed down the corridor that led to the gardens. She wasn't quite sure where she was to meet Charlotte, but she doubted her friend was hiding from her. Most likely, she would be out in the open.

Stepping onto the veranda, she saw Charlotte standing by the tall hedges that led into a garden maze.

Charlotte's face held a look of relief when her eyes landed on Delphine.

Delphine approached her friend and said, "I received your note."

"Thank you for coming," Charlotte said as she started fidgeting with her hands in front of her. "I felt awful for how we left things and I wanted to apologize before we departed for the boarding house."

"Does Mr. Simpkin know you came here to apologize?" Delphine asked.

Charlotte winced. "I told him that I was saying goodbye, but I left out the other part," she admitted. "I just…" Her voice trailed off as she glanced at the veranda. "I would prefer if we had this conversation in private."

"No one can overhear us," Delphine assured her.

"Perhaps. But I would feel better if we moved to the maze," Charlotte said.

Delphine didn't think that was necessary, but she saw no reason to argue with Charlotte on this. "All right, but we must make this conversation quick. I do not think my absence will go unnoticed for long."

Charlotte nodded her understanding as she turned to enter the maze. Delphine followed her and it wasn't long before they reached the center. But when they arrived, she saw that they weren't alone.

Mr. Simpkin.

Why was Mr. Simpkin here? And why had Charlotte kept that detail from her?

Delphine turned her questioning gaze towards Charlotte. "What is this?"

Charlotte approached Mr. Simpkin and he slipped his arm around her waist. "Mr. Simpkin also wanted to say goodbye," she said.

"But you said…" Delphine started.

Her friend spoke over her. "I know what I said, but that was to ensure you would leave the soiree to meet me."

"Well, here I am. What do you truly want?" Delphine asked.

A smirk crept onto Charlotte's face, her expression turning steely. "It is not about what I want, but what Mr. Simpkin desires."

With trepidation in her voice, Delphine inquired, "Which is?"

In a swift movement, Mr. Simpkin retrieved a pistol from the waistband of his trousers and pointed it at Delphine. "I want you to die," he sneered.

Chapter Twenty

As Delphine walked away, Bennett had the strangest urge to go after her but he needed to give her time to speak to Charlotte.

White approached Bennett with an air of urgency and said in a hushed voice, "The rider has returned from Gretna Green and he wishes to speak to you."

Bennett's eyes roamed over the crowded hall. "Can it not wait?"

The butler's demeanor grew unusually stern. "I believe you will want to hear this at once, my lord."

Recognizing the gravity of the situation, Bennett relented. "Very well. Where is he?"

"In your study," White informed him.

With any luck, his departure would go unnoticed amongst the guests and his family. He did not wish to upset his mother by disappearing during the middle of her soiree.

Bennett headed towards the rear of the manor, acknowledging the guests that he passed by with a slight nod. He arrived at the study and saw the short, stout footman standing in the center of the room.

"This had better be important," Bennett said in a firm voice.

"It is, my lord," the footman replied.

White had followed him into the room and closed the door. "Hugh is not one who is prone to exaggeration."

Bennett turned his expectant gaze to Hugh. "What did you discover?"

Hugh took a deep breath before saying, "Per your order, I found the anvil priest that married Mr. Simpkin and Lady Dunrobin, but he didn't truly marry them."

"I beg your pardon?" Bennett asked, his voice rising. "What are you saying?"

The footman's eyes grew determined. "When I spoke to the anvil priest, he told me that he clearly remembered the wedding since they had brought along a witness. Which is not very common when you are eloping."

Drats. This was a waste of his time. "I know all about how Miss Eden accompanied them…" Bennett started.

"Miss Eden?" Hugh asked. "No, the witness was Mr. Paterson, who was supposedly the bride's cousin."

Furrowing his brow, Bennett pressed, "I don't understand. Mr. Paterson is, in fact, Lady Dunrobin's cousin."

"Yes, but upon further questioning, the anvil priest shared that the bride's blonde hair had been neatly coiffed, despite a long carriage ride," Hugh shared. "He had found that odd since most couples who travel appear somewhat disheveled when standing in front of him."

Bennett reared back at that startling revelation. "Are you sure? I need you to be sure."

Hugh nodded. "Yes, my lord, and the anvil priest is willing to testify under oath to those facts," he asserted.

Running a hand through his hair, Bennett couldn't believe it. Mr. Simpkin hadn't married Delphine since she had dark hair. So who had he married? Had it been Miss Eden? That would certainly make sense, but why the deceit?

With the anvil priest's testimony, the judge would have no choice but to void the marriage since it was done through deception.

Hugh spoke up. "I asked around and no one saw a young woman that fit Lady Dunrobin's description. I do not think she ever made it to Gretna Green to begin with. I suspect she jumped out of the coach on the way to Gretna Green."

Bennett had so many questions but he needed to inform Delphine of what Hugh had discovered. But she was with Miss Eden.

His heart dropped.

Her friend had been in on the whole thing and she was meeting with the woman in the gardens… alone. He needed to find Delphine and ensure no harm had befallen her.

Turning towards White, Bennett ordered, "I want every available footman to meet me in the gardens at once."

White looked unsure. "Will that not cause a commotion amongst the guests?"

"I do not care about that," Bennett said. "Lady Dunrobin went to the gardens to meet with Miss Eden, and I want her found."

Understanding dawned on White's expression. "I will go round them up now, my lord."

Bennett refused to wait another moment longer. He needed to go find Delphine, and quickly. As he raced out the back door, his eyes roamed over the vast gardens. Where was Delphine?

His eyes landed on the garden maze, knowing that high hedges provided privacy to anyone who entered it. That is where they had to be. In a few purposeful strides, he arrived at the entrance of the maze and stopped to listen.

He heard nothing.

What if he was wrong? Time was of the essence and he didn't have the luxury of making a mistake. He didn't know what Miss Eden was capable of, which is what scared him the most.

Bennett continued down the maze as he tried to make out any sounds that would indicate Delphine was in here.

Finally, he came to a stop when he heard hushed voices from the next path over. He kept his steps light as he turned the corner.

To his horror, he saw that Mr. Simpkin was pointing a pistol at Delphine, his finger twitching on the trigger. Miss Eden was standing next to him and she didn't appear the least bit concerned about her friend's well-being.

Knowing he needed to do something or risk Delphine being shot, he shouted the first thing that came to his mind, "Wait!"

Mr. Simpkin shifted the pistol towards him. "What are you doing here?" he demanded. "You shouldn't be here."

Taking a step towards Delphine, he replied, "I could say the same about you. I thought you two were staying at the boarding house in the village."

"We are, but we had some unfinished business that we had to see to before we left," Miss Eden said.

Delphine kept her gaze on the pistol as she shared, "I am the unfinished business."

"I figured as much, considering they need you dead to conceal their deceit," Bennett said, wishing that he had taken the time to retrieve his father's dueling pistols.

Turning his attention towards Mr. Simpkin, Bennett continued by asking a simple question. "Isn't that right, Mr. Simpkin?"

Mr. Simpkin scoffed. "And what do you know of our deceit, my lord?" he jeered.

Bennett moved over to stand next to Delphine and hoped he was correct in his assumptions. "I know that you married Miss Eden, who pretended to be Delphine, because she escaped from the coach on the way to Gretna Green."

Delphine gasped. "How could you betray me like this?" she asked, her voice betraying her emotions.

Charlotte's expression shifted to one of amusement at the accusation. "You always thought you were better than me, but who has the upper hand now?" she taunted, a hint of triumph in her voice.

"I have never thought I was better than you," Delphine asserted.

"I wish you had stayed dead when you jumped out of the coach," Charlotte declared.

Delphine's eyes grew wide in disbelief. "Is that how I ended up in the woodlands, running from you and Mr. Simpkin?"

"And me," Mr. Paterson said from behind Bennett. "How could you have forgotten your own cousin so easily?"

Turning to face her cousin, Delphine asked, "What are you doing here?"

"I couldn't miss out on all the fun," Mr. Paterson sneered, his tone dripping with malice.

Delphine's voice quivered with a mix of confusion and trepidation. "Why are you doing this?"

Mr. Paterson joined Mr. Simpkin, brandishing his pistol as he spoke. "The reasons are quite simple," he replied. "I want your title, and Mr. Simpkin wants your business. And in order for us to both get what we want, you have to be dead."

Mr. Simpkin cocked his pistol. "It is a shame that you brought Lord Dunsby into all of this," he said. "Now he has to die, too."

Delphine moved to stand in front of him, much to his chagrin. "Do not shoot him!" she exclaimed. "He has nothing to do with this."

"I'm afraid he knows too much," Mr. Simpkin responded.

Bennett needed to buy some time. If he did, perhaps the assembled footmen would come looking for him. "But I am not the only one who knows what you did," he said, coming out from behind Delphine.

Mr. Simpkin's mask slipped slightly and he looked unsure for the first time. "Who else knows the truth about my marriage?"

"I am sure my whole household staff knows by now," Bennett said. "And if we turn up dead, I have no doubt they will tell the constable what they know. It will only be a matter of time before you hang for our murders."

Miss Eden narrowed her eyes. "He is bluffing," she said.

Bennett shrugged. "How else could I have discovered the truth about the farce of your marriage?"

Mr. Simpkin's pistol wavered in his hand. "He is right. If we kill them, then the truth will come out."

"But we can't just leave them," Miss Eden said. "They know too much. We will be ruined and we will have nothing to show for it."

"We will make do," Mr. Simpkin responded.

Miss Eden tossed her hands up in the air. "How?" she asked. "The creditors are knocking at your door. The only way for you to keep your lands is for you to inherit Delphine's business and I refuse to be poor."

Delphine interjected, "If you let us walk away, I can speak to your creditors and perhaps we can come to a fair price on your lands."

"No, you do not get to swoop in and save the day!" Miss Eden shouted. "We planned this out meticulously and you ruined it. You were supposed to die on the way back to Skidbrooke, but you refused to leave your precious Lord Dunsby."

Bennett noticed that Mr. Paterson hadn't said anything in a while and the intensity of his glare was directed at Delphine. Instinctively, he positioned himself in front of her, shielding her from any potential harm.

"Move aside, my lord," Mr. Paterson ordered.

"I will not," Bennett said firmly.

Mr. Paterson shoved the pistol towards him, his threat chillingly clear. "Do not think I will hesitate to kill you," he warned. "But it is not you that must die. It is Delphine. I want that title. It should have been mine in the first place."

Bennett stood his ground, refusing to yield. "If you want Delphine, you are going to have to kill me first."

"Gladly!" Mr. Paterson said as he cocked the pistol.

As Bennett braced himself for the worst, he heard another voice, authoritative and commanding, pierce through the tense air.

"Put the pistols down or suffer the consequences!" the voice demanded, its tone brooking no argument. "I will only ask once."

Turning slightly, Bennett caught sight of Grady standing resolutely with two other men by his side, each armed with pistols aimed squarely at Mr. Paterson and Mr. Simpkin.

Being the coward that he was, Mr. Simpkin dropped the pistol to the ground and took a step back.

"What are you doing?" Miss Eden demanded. "You can't give up so easily."

"It is over, Charlotte," Mr. Simpkin responded with a look of regret in his eyes.

"No, no, no…" Miss Eden rushed out. "I refuse to give up. We have worked too hard to throw it all away now."

Bennett could see the panic in Miss Eden's eyes and he suspected she might do something foolish. In a swift motion, he retrieved Mr. Simpkin's pistol and handed it to one of the constables.

Grady turned his attention towards Mr. Paterson. "Lower your pistol, and I will put in a good word for you with the judge."

Hatred flashed in Mr. Paterson's eyes as he stared at Delphine. "This isn't over. You have no right to that title. It should be mine!"

"The pistol?" Grady asked, holding out his hand.

Mr. Paterson remained defiant, despite the overwhelming odds against him. "No," he said. "No judge will take the word of a mere servant over that of an earl. All I need to do is kill Delphine and everything I desire will finally be mine!"

As Mr. Paterson's finger twitched on the trigger, Bennett knew he had to act quickly or Delphine could lose her life. Without hesitation, he lunged forward and tackled Mr. Paterson to the ground, fiercely wrestling the pistol away from him.

Rising to his feet, Bennett handed the pistol to Grady with a sense of satisfaction, knowing Delphine was safe. "Get this man out of my sight."

Grady's tone was stern as he addressed Mr. Paterson, who was struggling to regain his composure. "Just so you know, I am a Bow Street Runner and my two companions are constables. We heard every single word of your despicable plans. And if it were up to me, all three of you would be transported for your crimes."

One of the constables stepped forward and grabbed Mr. Paterson's arm. "We will take it from here," he said. "If you aren't good, we will parade you through the ballroom so everyone can see you being arrested."

Delphine watched Miss Eden's retreating figure before shouting, "Wait!"

"What is it?" Bennett asked.

With purposeful strides, Delphine went to stand in front of Miss Eden. "I thought we were friends."

Miss Eden scoffed. "You thought wrong, my lady," she mocked. "You lived your perfect life and you had no idea how much I despised you for that. At least now I don't have to pretend anymore."

Bennett slipped his arm around Delphine's shoulder and said, "Let her go, Delphie."

"You are right," Delphine said, leaning into him. "Goodbye, Charlotte."

Miss Eden's face contorted with pure hatred as she glared at Delphine. "No, you don't get to win... not like this."

A constable yanked on Miss Eden's arm. "Let's go, Miss."

As the constables forcefully led the prisoners away, Grady approached Bennett and said, "I'm sorry that I didn't make my presence known sooner but I wanted to ensure we got a confession that was admissible in court."

"I am just grateful that you were here to stop them from shooting us," Bennett said.

"As am I," Grady responded. "I followed Mr. Paterson out of the village, only to see him circle back towards the manor. It was evident that he was up to no good so I quickly enlisted the help of the constables."

"Thank you," Bennett said, hoping his gratitude was adequately expressed. He owed their lives to this man. "How can I repay you?"

Grady tipped his head. "I will send you my bill, my lord," he responded before he walked off, leaving him alone with Delphine.

Sensing the weight of unspoken words between them, Bennett turned to face Delphine, only to find himself utterly speechless.

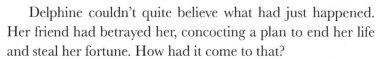

Delphine couldn't quite believe what had just happened. Her friend had betrayed her, concocting a plan to end her life and steal her fortune. How had it come to that?

Bennett watched her with concern in his eyes as he asked, "Dare I ask if you are all right?"

"Yes... no... I don't know," Delphine admitted. "Everything I thought I knew was a lie."

"Not everything," Bennett responded.

Delphine wrapped her arms around her waist as she

attempted to make sense of what she knew. "I can't believe Charlotte would do something so nefarious. I thought I knew everything about her."

"Greed can be a powerful motivator," Bennett said.

She heard what he said, and she knew he was attempting to comfort her, but his words fell flat. Charlotte hated her so much that she wanted her dead. How had she not seen through her friend's façade?

The worst part was that she wasn't entirely surprised by Vincent's actions. She had long suspected his desire for her demise, but never imagined he would be so brazen as to attempt it outright.

Bennett took a step closer to her, but still maintained a proper distance. "You did nothing wrong."

"I must have," she replied. "My dearest friend turned out to be my greatest enemy. How can I reconcile that fact?"

"Miss Eden deceived everyone, not just you."

"But I should have known," Delphine asserted.

Bennett reached out and touched her sleeve. "You must not blame yourself. It will do no good and only bring you misery."

Delphine shifted her gaze over his shoulder, knowing what he was asking was easier said than done.

"Delphie…" Bennett sighed. "I know this might not be the ideal time to speak of such things but I'm afraid I cannot wait any longer."

"What is it?" Delphine asked, bringing her gaze back to meet his.

Bennett's usual composed demeanor wavered, replaced by a rare glimpse of uncertainty in his eyes. "Now that we know you were never truly married to Mr. Simpkin, I was hoping that we might come to an understanding."

Delphine had longed to hear those words from Bennett, but she couldn't tie herself to him. Not now. With a heavy heart, she said, "You must know that my reputation will be shrouded in scandal once the truth comes out about what Mr. Simpkin did."

"I do not care about the scandal," Bennett said.

"You should," Delphine insisted. "You must think of what a scandal would do to your family. It could even jeopardize your sisters' prospects this Season."

Bennett closed the distance between them, their faces mere inches apart. "Do you want to know what I think?" he asked, his eyes searching hers.

With him so near, Delphine felt her heart quicken, its erratic beats betraying her composure. Try as she might, words eluded her in his presence. How was it that he held such power over her? Though he awaited her reply, all she could manage was a nod.

"I believe it is perfectly acceptable to be a bit selfish, especially at a time such as this," he said, his voice soft yet resolute. "Because, my dear, I do not think I could bear to ever let you go, especially now. You must know that I love you with everything that I am."

Fearing she may have misunderstood, Delphine's voice was tinged with hesitation. "You love me?"

"I think a part of me started falling in love with you the moment I found you in the woodlands," he replied. "Since then, you have consumed my every waking thought, and when I dream, it's of you."

Tears welled up in the corners of her eyes at his heartfelt declarations, but she made no effort to halt them. These tears were born of happiness, a testament to the overwhelming emotion coursing through her.

Bennett grew solemn. "Was I wrong to assume you held some affection for me?"

Delphine shook her head. "No, you weren't wrong," she replied.

"Then why are you crying?"

She knew there was only one thing left to say, and she

drew in a deep breath to steady herself. With a voice quivering with emotion, she uttered, "I love you, Bennett."

A wide grin spread across his face. "Do you love me enough to marry me? Because, quite frankly, I won't accept no for an answer," he said, his tone laced with determination. "And before you decide, I promise that I will let you manage your own estate and goat cheese business, and we will be equals, in every sense of the word."

Feeling a mischievous impulse, Delphine asked, "Was that an offer?"

"It was, but I can do better," Bennett replied with a chuckle, dropping to one knee before her. "Delphine, my love, will you do me the great honor of marrying me?"

She returned his smile. "Yes, yes, I will marry you!" she exclaimed, her heart overflowing with joy.

As Bennett rose to his feet, he reached out to cup her right cheek tenderly. "I have loved no other as I love you," he whispered. "You have my whole heart." With gentle fingers, he brushed away a tear that trailed down her cheek.

"I never thought I could be this happy," Delphine admitted.

Bennett's eyes were fixed on her as if nothing else in the world mattered. "I have learned what love truly is because of you," he said. "I promise to be the type of man who will never let you down."

Delphine could feel his warm breath on her lips and she found that she desperately wanted to kiss him. "May I kiss you?" she asked, her voice barely above a whisper.

He grinned. "You do not need to ask permission."

With hesitant anticipation, she lifted herself onto her tiptoes, her heart fluttering as she pressed her lips against his, not knowing if she was terribly bad at it.

She broke the kiss and leaned slightly back. "Did I do that right?"

"I'm not entirely certain," he replied, his voice soft and playful. "Perhaps we need another kiss to confirm."

Embracing her tenderly, he drew her closer, his arms enveloping her in warmth as their lips met once more. This time, the kiss was deeper, making her feel cherished. It was the way every woman wanted to be kissed by the man she loves. She had never looked forward to forever as much as she did with Bennett by her side.

Bennett moved to rest his forehead against hers. "You do that spectacularly well, my love," he praised. "I do not think I will ever tire of kissing you."

Delphine could faintly hear the strains of music drifting from the ballroom. As much as she wished for this moment to stretch into eternity, she knew their absence would not go unnoticed for long.

"Shall we return to the ballroom?" she suggested reluctantly, acknowledging the inevitable.

"Yes," Bennett agreed, but not before capturing her lips in a tender kiss.

She laughed softly against his lips. "Your words and actions seem to be at odds," she teased.

"We should go back," Bennett conceded, holding her close, "but I'm not quite ready to let you go."

"Well, I suppose a few more moments won't make a difference," Delphine relented, content to linger in his embrace a while longer.

Epilogue

Three weeks later…

Today was the best of days. It was to be his wedding day! Bennett couldn't quite seem to quell the excitement that was growing inside of him at that thought. Since the moment he had first offered for Delphine, he had been eagerly counting down the days, hours, and minutes until this very moment.

It had taken them some effort to get to this point. The morning after the soiree, Winston had traveled to Scotland to meet with the judge to discuss voiding Delphine's marriage. When he presented the facts of the case, the judge promptly agreed to nullify the marriage, citing deception as the main reason. Furthermore, the judge agreed to transport the conspirators of the deception to Australia, ensuring Delphine would never have to see them again.

Once Winston returned, Bennett promptly posted the banns and waited impatiently as Delphine returned to her country estate to ensure her affairs were in order. He did not like being away from his betrothed- even for a moment. But he understood her reasoning and had no desire to curtail her independent streak. That was just one of the many things he loved about her.

But Delphine was back at Brockhall Manor. Where she belonged… with him.

As he descended the stairs, he saw Elodie pacing in the entry hall. "Whatever is wrong?" he asked, stepping onto the marble floor.

Elodie came to a stop and turned to face him. "I am trying my best to not soil this gown for your wedding service."

Finding the situation amusing, Bennett teased, "I thank you for your efforts. I wouldn't be able to marry Delphie, knowing your gown was soiled."

"You joke, but Mother was adamant that I stay away from toast," Elodie shared.

"What is wrong with toast?"

Elodie held up her hands. "She is concerned with the butter on my fingers leaving a stain on my gown."

"Then do not butter your toast," he suggested.

She huffed. "What is the point of eating bread at all?"

Bennett placed his hand on his sister's sleeve. "This conversation is pointless, and I have much more important things to worry about right now."

Melody gracefully stepped into the entry hall with a piece of bread in her hand. "Yes, you are to be married."

Elodie's mouth dropped. "Are you eating bread with butter on it?"

"I am," Melody confirmed.

"Are you not worried about soiling your gown?" Elodie asked.

Melody grinned. "I am not. I am perfectly capable of keeping my gown unsoiled."

Bennett dropped his hand and shook his head. "I do not care who eats bread but do not bring it to the chapel."

Elodie nodded in agreement. "I agree," she replied. "But, out of curiosity, do you have a rule against biscuits?"

"I would prefer it if no one ate during the service," Bennett said.

"Fine," Elodie muttered, looking put out.

Winston's amused voice came from behind them. "You truly have high expectations for the day, Brother."

Bennett chuckled. "We are having a luncheon before Delphine and I depart for Scotland. I promise that there will be bread and butter there."

Melody's eyes lit up. "I am envious that you will be staying in Delphine's castle. I hope to see it one day."

"And you will," Delphine said as she approached them. "I promise I will throw a house party once our wedding tour is over."

Bennett moved to Delphine's side and kissed her cheek. "Are you ready to get married?"

Delphine shrugged one shoulder. "I suppose so," she sighed. "I had nothing else to do so I thought it was as good of a day as any."

Elodie laughed. "Delphine is going to fit quite nicely into our family."

"It is a good thing that I saved her from certain death… twice," Bennett declared. "I almost can't help but do heroic things."

"Good gads, do you hear yourself speak?" Winston retorted before shifting his gaze to Delphine. "Do you truly wish to marry my brother?"

Delphine's eyes lit up. "With all my heart."

Lady Dallington entered the entry hall and announced, "It is time for us to depart for the service. Your father sent word that he will meet us at the chapel."

Bennett offered his arm to Delphine. "May I escort you to the coach?"

"Thank you," Delphine murmured.

As they walked out the main door, Bennett asked, "Any regrets?"

"My only regret is that I did not find you sooner," Delphine replied.

Bennett brought her hand up to his lips and kissed it. "I love you, Delphie," he said. "And I feel the same as you."

They came to a stop in front of the coach and Bennett assisted Delphine into the conveyance. Once she was situated, he climbed in and sat next to her.

Bennett closed the door and turned to face her. "We are alone," he said with a mischievous grin.

"That we are," Delphine murmured as she leaned forward and pressed her lips against his.

As Bennett wrapped his arms around her, pulling her in close, the door opened and Elodie exclaimed, "They are kissing... again!"

Not feeling the least bit repentant, Bennett asked, "What is it that you want, Sister?"

"Mother told me that I had to ride in the coach with you," Elodie shared as she sat across from them. "But it is in protest."

Bennett dropped his arms and leaned back. "I am not sure why Mother was so adamant since we are practically married in the eyes of the *ton*."

"Trust me, I would rather be anywhere but in a coach with two love birds who can't seem to keep their hands off one another," Elodie insisted.

Delphine reached up and smoothed back her dark hair. "Fortunately, we do not have to travel far since the chapel is near your manor."

Bennett reached for Delphine's hand and intertwined their fingers. "Do you take issue with us holding hands?" he asked, addressing his sister.

Elodie considered them for a moment before saying, "I will allow it."

"You are most generous," Bennett teased.

As the coach made its way to the chapel, Bennett couldn't

help but turn his gaze towards Delphine. A smile tugged at his lips as he reflected on how she was everything he had ever wanted and more.

"You are smiling, Brother," Elodie remarked.

"Indeed, I am," Bennett replied as he met Delphine's gaze. "I am looking forward to my future because I know each day will be better than the last."

Delphine nudged his shoulder. "I love you, too."

Bennett leaned in and kissed her on her cheek, his lips lingering. He had never known such happiness before, and it was all because of Delphine. For the day he met her, he found the missing piece of his heart.

The End

Next in series...

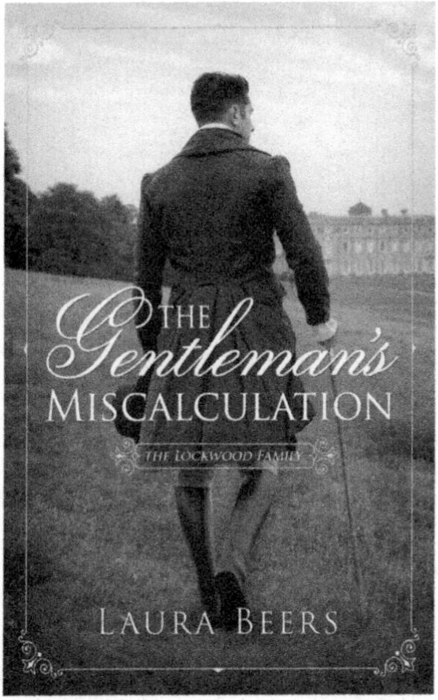

Lord Winston Lockwood is haunted by his past and bound by social expectations. He remains at Brockhall Manor to ensure his aunt and her son remain safe from her abusive husband. Adding to his frustration, Miss Bawden's constant presence threatens to drive him mad.

Amid the upheaval of her father's newfound title, Miss Mattie Bawden is struggling to help her cousin cope with the tragic loss of her parents. Desperate for assistance, she turns to the last person she would ever expect: the insufferable Lord Winston.

As they call a truce, they soon realize how indubitably well-suited they are as friends. But when a dire threat looms, bringing danger to their very doorsteps, Winston understands he must confront his own feelings and risk revealing his true emotions, or he could lose the woman he has come to realize he cannot live without.

Other series by Laura Beers

The Beckett Files

Regency Brides: A Promise of Love

Proper Regency Matchmakers

Regency Spies & Secrets

Gentlemen of London

Lords & Ladies of Mayfair

About the Author

Laura Beers is an award-winning author. She attended Brigham Young University, earning a Bachelor of Science degree in Construction Management. She can't sing, doesn't dance and loves naps.

Laura lives in Utah with her husband, three kids, and her dysfunctional dog. When not writing regency romance, she loves skiing, hiking, and drinking Dr Pepper.

You can connect with Laura on Facebook, Instagram, or on her site at www.authorlaurabeers.com.

Made in the USA
Coppell, TX
01 October 2024

37954261R00174